THE HARLOT'S GARDEN

by

NIKKI DEE

Book one of the Sansome Springs Trilogy

The Harlot's Garden

ISBN 13: 978-1505340402

ISBN 10: 1505340403

This work is a work of fiction. Name, places and incidents are either products of the author's imaginations or are used fictitiously. Any resemblance to any event, incident, location or person (living or dead) is entirely coincidental.

Published with the assistance of WordPlay Publishing Ltd

www.wordplay-publishing.com

A note from the author

I had a clear of idea of how my story would unfold. It's set in my home town...

On roads I have walked, waterways I have crossed, factories I worked in and bars I have drunk in.

This was to be my story, but Ruby took over and made it hers. I hope you like it.

At the end of each chapter is an historic clipping from a local newspaper - 'Berrow's Worcester Journal, the World's oldest newspaper'. For many years I've enjoyed their archive page and the fascinating hours spent researching times past that it has inspired.

I reproduce them here courtesy of the Worcester News.

To learn more about Nikki Dee and her writing visit
www.nikkidee.net

WORCESTER 1760

Matthew Morgan's cooling body swung from the gallows on Red Hill as a church bell tolled the hour. Across the river Matthew's bride of just a few months howled in agony as she heard a bell toll. She howled once more and then shuddered as a tiny bundle of unwanted life entered the world.

Before she could give herself over to her grief the devastating pains began again and Susan turned pleading eyes to her friend Ann. “Oh dear God no, not two of 'em?” Susan gripped Ann's hand and begged. “If you love me Ann, take one and drown it. I swear I'll never ask you for anything else but drown one today. Please.”

Before Ann could reply the second twin made her way silently into the world. She was smaller than the first but looked well enough to Ann who bound the two tiny girls together and placed them at Susan's breast. “I won't drown them and I won't hear you ask me again. I'll love 'em if you can't.”

The two women instinctively held hands then as they heard the sound of approaching hoof-beats. The sacking that was pinned across the doorway was thrust aside and Chambers, Henry Daventor's land agent walked in to the little hut.

They were hiding on Daventor's land and by rights Chambers should be turning them off but he'd known and liked Matthew and had felt heartsick for the plight Susan found herself in. He had let her use this space to get through the birth in safety.

Now he spoke urgently. “You'll be safe enough here tonight but you must be gone at first light. Mr Daventor is coming home with his bride tomorrow, he can't find you here or I'll lose my place. You must go, I can't help you anymore. He'll have me deported, or worse. I'm sorry.” Susan Morgan, seventeen, widowed and now the reluctant mother of two brats, longed for death as she'd once longed for Matthew.

Last Thursday night, between 11 and midnight, a live male child, supposed to be about six weeks old, was found at a door in the parish of St Clement, Worcester. It had on a dirty white whittle and ruffled shirt and near it lay a small bundle containing two or three caps. The officers of the parish, having notice of the matter, caused the child to be immediately taken into the care of the parish, and all proper methods are being used to find out the unnatural mother.

(Copyright and courtesy of the Worcester News)

CHAPTER ONE 1774

Fourteen year old Ruby Morgan wallowed and slid through the stinking mud as she struggled to keep her eyes on the flickering light being held by Chambers, whilst keeping the box that contained her few treasures out of the filthy mire. Apart from the light she was miserably trudging behind the night was black and she had only her own local knowledge to guess what she was walking through and what pitfalls were ahead of her. She kept the light in sight and prayed she'd be safe soon.

They had left home, in St John's, and headed downhill, so she knew they'd be crossing the river soon. She could smell the tang of the Severn and feel the icy wind rip through her soaking clothes then at last felt wood and not mud under her feet. "Put your box down for a moment girl, you need to save your strength." Chambers advised her gruffly, as he moved a step forward and reached for the bell that would hail the ferryman. The familiar bell rang out in reply soon enough and they knew the ferry was on its way.

All too soon it was there and they clambered aboard. She turned back the way she had come, not seeing anything but knowing her home and her sister lay behind her. She tried to be brave and strong but the thought of not seeing her sister again reduced her to desperate tears. Small and scared as she was she vowed Daventor would pay one day for this.

The noise of the river changed and as she heard the water slapping the land at the other side she braced herself for the jolt that she knew could knock the unwary off their feet. The mud was deeper and the stink worse on the other side and she clenched her teeth as she battled to keep upright and protect her precious cargo.

She was tired and scared, but she was also brave and determined and she would not ask Chambers to help. If she was to cope alone she'd better start getting used to it, she told herself bravely.

They passed through the area where the boats loaded and unloaded and here was some activity even though it was night time. She saw lights moving around and heard curses mingle with sounds of splashing and the occasional thud as something hard smacked into something soft.

The houses here were poor wooden shacks that leaned into each other as though listening to each other's secrets. As they made their way uphill the noises coming from some of these dens put speed into Ruby's feet. Once at the brow of the hill though the space opened out again and the air was sweeter. Occasionally she glimpsed a grand house as they hurried on and then at last they were on the firm level ground and walking through Worcester.

She saw the shops and workshops that kept the city going, but that she knew nothing of and then on out through the town passing the fancy houses that had been built by the rich men who needed to be near to the heart of the city and it's business but far enough away to give their wives and daughters pretty views to occupy them. Once these houses were behind them there was nothing but wild, open space all around them and the ground once again became treacherous underfoot. Ruby shivered as the howling wind buffeted at her clothes and she began to fear the night would never end but the light stopped moving at last. They stood alongside a row of cottages that looked as though they would fall at any moment though there were dim lights apparent inside them. She stood still; breathless, cold, hungry and above all else terrified.

Chambers held the lantern up high and pointed to the left where she saw an alley between two of the cottages. He said "See that light down there? That's where you must go now."

"But I don't know what's down there, are you leaving me here alone?"

"Just go now, they're waiting for you." His voice was distant, she was on her own from now on.

She clutched her precious wooden box and moved closer to the doorway of a small building, she hesitated outside momentarily and was slightly reassured when she heard laughter coming from inside. She'd not had a lot of laughter in her life and was encouraged by it. She raised her chin and bravely stepped in.

A huge fire in the corner of the room was the source of the light and also the smell of good roasting meat that made her mouth water. Ruby stood, rooted to the spot as she surveyed the scene before her.

There were men here, more men than she'd ever seen in one place, all drinking, some of them were laughing and many of them were playing what seemed to be some kind of game. There was much banging down of coin and picking up of cards along with good natured cursing.

Other groups of men were eating from great platters of food set in the middle of the table, each man held a hunk of bread as he fished into the bowl with his fingers for the chunks of meat or potato and then mopped up juices with the bread, making Ruby's belly growl with hunger.

A pretty girl about her own age approached her. Her red curls danced around a sweet little rosy face, and green eyes sparkled down at Ruby. She seemed to dance as she walked and one or two of the drinking men called out to her or tried to grab her as she passed by but she laughed and poked her tongue at them.

“You must be Ruby.” She said cheerfully. ”I'm Mary. Don't look so scared, this lot makes a lot of noise but there's no harm in 'em. Come and sit in the warm with me and have a bite to eat. John will be here to get you as soon as he can.”

Ruby followed her gratefully, she didn't know who John was and had no idea what she was scared of but she was grateful for the warmth and light and was soothed by the kindness of Mary.

Everything in her life had changed in a few short weeks, but the worst thing was being without her twin sister Ellie.

They'd not been separated before and Ruby was missing her dearly. She could cope with anything if Ellie was beside her, but without her she didn't know how she'd manage.

She'd almost given up trying to control anything in her life in the past few days and now found it easier to just do as she was told. When Mary put a steaming plate of food in front of her and said "eat," Ruby devoured the fragrant dish of rich stew in silence as the other girl chattered away. She hungrily mopped up the juices with hunks of fresh bread as she'd seen the men doing.

After she'd cleared the platter Mary handed her a cup of something hot that smelled rich and wonderful, but like nothing she'd smelled before, Ruby looked at Mary questioningly. “Drink it quick afore he sees I gave it you. It's his chocolate and it'll keep you warm for hours.” Ruby drank the delicious brew down greedily and hoped that she'd have much more chocolate in her life in the future.

Wherever it was she had ended up, the food and drink were better than any she'd tasted before, she looked about her again, this time feeling a little less afraid and even smiling as Mary told her who each man was and her opinion of him.

The door swung open and a man entered the inn, Ruby could see he was tall and broad but his hat and cloak kept his features hidden. He looked up and his eyes scanned the room lighting at last on Mary who nudged Ruby and told her this was John and she must go with him. As Ruby reluctantly stood up Mary saw the fear in her eyes and took pity on her, she held both her hands in hers and smiled at her. “I know you're scared now but you'll be safe where you're going. I used to live there afore I came here. I'll come to see you in a few days if you like, we can be friends.” Ruby smiled gratefully, maybe she had lost her sister for the time being, but at least she'd made a new friend.

John had a pony and trap waiting for them outside and

he held the horse steady as she clambered up, then he passed up her box and smiled as she clutched it firmly to her chest as they sat side by side on the battered wooden seat while the pony trotted on home. John glanced at her once or twice as they made their way through the darkness, she sat in silence, all huddled up into herself and trying not to touch him. Her hair lay heavy and lank on her shoulders, she was far too thin and terribly white faced. She could only be half the size of Mary he thought. His heart went out to the poor child.

"No harm will come to you where you're going. You'll work harder than you have in your life before I dare say, but Ma 'ent one to make a body do what they don't want to do. She's only there to help folk out."

Ruby looked directly at him for the first time. The lantern was dim but it gave enough light for her to see that his face was creased and lined in what looked like a constant smile, and his voice sounded gentle.

She smiled grimly. "I didn't want to leave my sister and I don't want to have a baby, so how can Ma help me, whoever she is?"

John chuckled and nodded to himself. He'd thought at first she might be a bit daft, which was often a problem for Ma, because nobody wanted a baby born to an idiot did they? But this one was no fool, she was sharp. Scared maybe, but sharp. She'd do.

Ma Jebb was rough and tough and did what she did for money. John had worked for her for thirty five years and wouldn't say he was close to her, no one was. He watched all sorts come and go and Ma'd kept them all at a distance, but somehow he sensed Ruby might be different and provided the girl didn't disappoint he thought she'd do just fine with Ma.

The pony pricked up it's ears, knowing it was near to home and John sighed with pleasure knowing his nights work was almost done. He'd deliver this child to Ma and she'd be out of his hands. They turned slowly off the old track and the pony took them through an old stone archway and stopped dead, clearly this was the end of the journey. John helped Ruby down and led her towards a doorway.

As they stepped in through the doorway he lit the stub of a candle from his own lamp and gestured toward an alcove in the corner of a tiny room. "Get some sleep, quick as you can. You'll be safe enough tucked up in there, be up and ready at first light though, Ma'll be along to see you then." With that he was gone.

Her candle stub sputtered and she realised she only had a moment or so of light left and decided the only thing to do now was rest. She lay down in the alcove and waited for the candle to burn out. She was so weary yet lay sleepless, holding her little wooden box and listening to the confusing sounds she heard all around her. Clinking and banging, a laugh, a cry. Footsteps and crashes. She must have dozed because she woke up with a start at one point and reached for Ellie's hand. She cried herself back to sleep.

Mr Joseph Jones, the Worcester Cathedral ferryman, effected a rescue from the Severn near the Cathedral this week. While on the St Johns side of the river, he noticed that one of two little boys who were bathing was in difficulties. He promptly pulled his boat out to the boy and rescued him in the nick of time.

CHAPTER TWO

When Ma walked in at dawn it was almost a relief, Ruby had spent the night tossing and turning and imagining all manner of horrors, at least now she might learn what was to happen to her. Ma was a thin woman with sharp eyes and a sharper voice. She ordered Ruby to follow her and moved across the room quickly, expecting to be obeyed. She was definitely a sink or swim kind of teacher. She drew aside a faded red curtain and they entered a damp, dim passage. They were only halfway along this passage when the stench of urine and unwashed bodies hit Ruby as Ma spoke again.

"This here's the nursery." Ma declared as they walked into a long dim room. The noise of screaming was quite shocking. "We've been short of help so you'll find plenty to do, all my girls start off here. I always hope it'll put em off making the same mistake twice, but some of em just won't learn."

Ruby looked about the filthy room in horror, she was almost completely overwhelmed but Ma carried on talking regardless.

"You'll be working here with Sal." She kicked what looked like a pile of discarded sacks on the floor. The pile grunted and moved as Ruby saw it was a massively fat woman, fast asleep.

"She's deaf and dumb and lazy to boot, but she does have a way with the little ones and let's face it, she's fit for nothing else." Ma turned and glanced at Ruby who was standing stock still and speechless. "If I was you I'd put that little box of yours down get stuck in, you'll be living in here now and if you can't shut em up you'll get no peace cos you don't have all the advantages Sal has in here." Ma cackled and, almost as though she could hear what was said, Sal began snoring again.

Ruby clutched her box even tighter. "But where do...?"

"Don't ask me my lover." Ma shrugged. "Whoever used

to hold your hand has gone now and you're on your own. I've given you a place to stay and you'll get enough food to eat, sorting out these little bleeders is how you'll pay me back. They cry for a reason and it's your job to fix it." Noticing the look of horror and Ruby's face she nodded in some sympathy.

"I never liked taking care of em myself but in my line of business it has to be done. Over the years I've lost any patience I did have for em. Now then, you get on with it, if you need help kick Sal and she'll put you right. The only rule here is don't go nosing and poking around the place, if you want to know summat ask me, when I want you to know what's what I'll tell you. I can't abide a sneak, understand?"

Ma glared at her with clear threat in her eyes and it was all Ruby could do to nod and stammer out, "Yes Ma, I understand." With a grunt of satisfaction Ma was gone so Ruby put her box on the floor and went to wake Sal.

A series of nods, prods and head shakes soon established that Ruby was now in charge here and Sal would do whatever she was directed to do. That system would do as well as conversation and the two duly turned to the babies. It was some hours later that Ruby realised that the noise rarely stopped, it just eased from time to time. There were seven babies in the room and at any one time at least two were crying. Ruby had ceased to notice the smell but the unrelenting noise was driving her to screaming point.

By some miracle Sal seemed to understand her desperation and, picking up a couple of buckets from a small pile that were tucked away under a disused fireplace she gestured to Ruby to take one and follow her. She then led Ruby out through a doorway and down another narrow, dim passageway, the floor here was crooked and the walls leaned in towards each other, but there was a hint of daylight at the end. Then they were outside and into the biting cold, but blessedly quiet, fresh air.

Ruby shivered then stretched her back out and groaned in relief. Sal noticed and smiled. She mimed taking in deep breaths and then pulled Ruby over to the well. They sat, side by side, on an old stone wall for a few moments and Ruby looked up to the stars and knew it was up to her to make the most of this foul place at least until her own baby had come and was gone. She could see no other choice.

They filled their buckets with murky well water and made their way slowly back in, from then on when it all got too much Ruby would grab a bucket and steal a few precious moments of peace outside.

Yesterday in the forenoon, as a young woman was coming from Droitwich, she was stopped by two footpads near the Copcut Elm who robbed her of a bundle of clothes and her pocket in which were four shillings in money, a pair of scissors, a thimble and some other trifles.

She had a stout struggle with them in order to save her money but as they threw her down and beat her, they at last overpowered her and made their escape.

(Copyright and courtesy of the Worcester News)

CHAPTER THREE

As the days passed Ruby found she could differentiate between the natures of the babies. She knew which one would always greet her with a smile, and which one would scream as soon as she touched him. One poor little thing just never seemed to stop crying, so much so that he set the others off constantly, he didn't eat enough because he wouldn't stop screaming for long enough. She worried about him but she was also concerned for herself, she nearly picked him up and shook him once.

He wasn't hurt and he was dry, he wouldn't eat but he wouldn't stop screaming. She was at her wit's end trying to shut him up until she remembered her mother, years ago, carrying William about in her shawl when he was a baby and decided to try the same thing. She quickly wrapped the screaming bundle up tightly and bound him between her breasts and her belly and very soon he stopped screaming and just sobbed gently, then, after a few more moments he went to sleep.

She could see from the way Sal shook her head that the old woman didn't approve, but Ruby was beyond caring. She needed some quiet and it was this one that set all the others off. That night when she lay down to sleep he stayed strapped in and they both slept the whole night through.

As she watched over the babies that were growing bigger and stronger every day in the nursery she was ever more aware of her own baby growing in her belly and she wondered what would happen to them, all the babies that were born here, where did they go? There were no children running around so they must go somewhere. She wished she knew more about the things that would happen to her through the birth and then after but there was no one to ask.

She'd rarely seen Ma since that first night. The old woman might help girls in trouble but she had clearly been speaking the truth when she'd said she had no love for babies at all. John was always around but he wouldn't let her finish her questions, never mind answer them.

If she needed anything, food, drink or something moved he'd help but he wouldn't answer a question. Anyway she couldn't talk to him about having babies. She knew she'd be having this baby alone and learning as it happened. If only Ellie was with her, she missed her sister so much it was a constant pain in her chest.

They had slept in the same bed since the day they were born, falling asleep every night hand in hand. She thought she could hardly bear to live without her, yet somehow each day she woke and carried on. She shook her head refusing to allow tears to fall, there was no point in feeling sorry for herself.

She met a young girl called Lou who worked in the kitchen. She had a twisted leg and her left arm had only two fingers but her smile lit the room. She was the one who came to get Ruby when there was food ready and she was friendly enough but she didn't know anything except she'd been promised, by Ma, that when she was a bit older and stronger she could start to work with the babies.

She was well fed and seemed very happy with her life but wouldn't talk about anything Ruby wanted to talk about. What happens to the babies and where do the mothers go?

Ruby stepped outside one day on her way to the well and was surprised to find that the weather had begun to turn springlike. The ground was drying out into mud now, there were crusts forming over the oozing, stinking mess she'd been used to walking on.

The warmth actually made the smells worse but it was still quite wonderful to feel the hint of sun on her back and she could see more of her surroundings now the light was better and she was no longer huddling into her shawl for warmth.

All around her were walls of mud and stone with narrow

passageways between them, and here and there she could see windows that she'd never noticed before. At least half a dozen doors opened directly onto this enclosed area and the mud floor near the doors still oozed with the waste that had been thrown outside. A ditch that ran from one corner across the middle and out down one of the alleys. It was clear that as well as carrying running water, this ditch was the end result of all the slops and waste that were thrown in its general direction from these houses. It was at the side of this ditch that the well was placed.

As Ruby looked around enjoying the sun and the break she became aware that someone was watching her from one of the doorways. She looked up smiling, as a young woman stepped out from the shadows. "Hello, I'm Ruby."

"I'm Bella. I heard there was new girl in, you finding your way about then? How long have you been here?"

"A few weeks now." Ruby was delighted to find someone her own age who seemed to want to talk. "What about you, have you been here long?"

Bella nodded and grinned. "Feels like I've been here forever sometimes, couple of years though I reckon. Ma's tough but she's good underneath and it's better than being out there on your own with a baby." Bella stretched and faced the sun, almost purring.

"Do you look after babies as well?"Ruby asked her.

Bella laughed and Ruby's education into the ways of her world began. Bella explained that only the girls in trouble worked with the babies. Once their baby was born they could go back to their old life if they wanted or stay and work for Ma if they had nowhere to go. The two bigger houses that back onto this courtyard were brothels and Bella oversaw them both for Ma. She looked after all the girls and the couple of boys that worked there. They all lived together as a family, sharing the cooking and cleaning and they were open to the paying public providing pretty much anything that was requested.

Bella was a truly happy girl, she loved men and loved

sex and, having found Ma and discovering she could be paid and protected for doing what came naturally she thought her life was just about perfect.

Ruby's own opinion of men and sex was quite different, her faith in the goodness of people had been decimated when she'd been raped by someone she had loved and trusted, and then subsequently been banished by the only family she had ever known. She thought her life was as bad as it could get.

Meeting each other proved good for them both. Bella told Ruby things about her work that took her from a feeling of shuddering horror at the thought of sex to a state of helpless laughter at the ridiculous things some men will pay for. Bella would tell Ruby tales that could also make her cry with pity.

One of Bella's regulars was an old man who would only ever see Bella, all he ever wanted was to sit and drink tea whilst wearing her clothes and to be treated as a lady. She'd been seeing him for a long time and it was clear when she talked that she really liked him. "He's ever so clever Ruby and he tells me about books and music and stuff. I don't understand one half of it, but it don't half make me feel grand." He pretends to be grand lady and I'm his little maid, helping with his stockings and such.

Another one of Bella's stories made a lot of sense to Ruby and upon hearing it she ended up laughing more than she had ever laughed before in her life. Something she'd seen long ago and been very confused by was finally explained.

There had lived at Bransford, a small hamlet outside of St Johns, an old woman who was said to be a witch and most people gave her a very wide berth. She had a son, a large, awkward man who shuffled about with his head on the side grinning all the time. Everyone was wary of him but he only ever came into St Johns when the drovers were resting there and generally people forgot him until the drovers were due and then the children from the Great

House were warned to stay away from him.

One particular year though Ruby decided to disobey the rules, she needed to know what was so terrible about him and she convinced Ellie, along with Hugh and William, to follow him one night. The moonlight, along with knowing they were breaking the rules helped make the entire adventure seem deliciously eerie.

They skulked behind him as he headed to where the newborn calves were tethered. He stood upright and looked all about him furtively and then as quick as a flash he was down under the barriers and was in amongst the calves. In a matter of moments his trousers were down around his ankles and he was pressing himself urgently against the mouth of a calf. The children watched in bemused horror until he groaned loudly and pulled himself away from the still hungry, sucking mouth.

They ran away, confused and somehow shamed by what they had seen and never talked about it, or the questions it raised in their minds. Now at last Ruby understood what it was all about.

Bella listened to this story with her mouth agape then snorted. “He never did, with a baby cow, the dirty bastard.”

Both girls broke into peals of laughter and their friendship was sealed. From then on they met most days when they had a little time and Bella told Ruby all she knew about Ma and the houses that so far Ruby had seen but not entered.

In addition to the sex on offer, Ma Jebb's houses provided food and drink, along with playing cards and newspapers. A man could stay for an hour, or a day, if he could afford it. The prices were clear and the girls were the cleanest in town. The rooms were warm and comfortable places and it was not unusual for men to come and spent a few hours just for the chance to relax and be left alone.

No one was pressed to leave before they were ready. There were front doors and back doors and an alley way at the side. There were lit areas and darkened areas and plenty of trees and bushes for a man to hide behind if he felt the need. Whoever had taught Ma her business had done a very good job. It was possible to enter the house in broad daylight for all the world to see and it was also easy enough to come and go in total secrecy.

Ma had high standards, she wouldn't tolerate any of her girls helping themselves to a stray coin or bandying the names of the gentlemen about. Even talking about the business with anyone outside the house was strictly forbidden.

Three girls named Fanny Jones aged 18, Hannah Jones, 19 and Jane Harris, 16 were charged at Worcester Police Court with being disorderly in High Street at a late hour, early on Sunday morning. The conduct of the defendants was very disgraceful and they did not appear to be disposed to give any promise to behave better in future. They were each committed to gaol for seven days with hard labour.

(Copyright and courtesy of the Worcester News)

CHAPTER FOUR

Bella had given Ruby some stern advice when she first saw the baby Ruby had strapped to her chest. She explained in none too gentle terms that any sort of attachment was wickedly cruel to both of them. "When he's took away from you he's going to break his heart an' so are you. You can't keep him and you can't keep yours so stop living like a fool. Take him off now and let him get used to being on his own, it's got to happen so it's as well the poor little bastard learns now. You 'ent helping him or yourself. The old girl won't like it and it's best for you she don't find out."

Ruby sadly untied the bindings that night and handed the tiny baby boy to Sal who nodded her approval. She forced herself to stay away from him from then on and vowed not to make the same mistake again.

As her belly grew larger than she would have thought possible she began to find the lifting and carrying hard and she found she was forced to leave a lot of the heavier work to Sal as she took longer breaks. Eventually Ma came along with a new girl and told Ruby this was her replacement and she was to show her the ropes. This gave Ruby an excuse to move about a bit more without carrying a baby or a pail of slops and this gave her back enough of her old energy to seize the chance to find out about someone else and their problems, spending all day every day with Sal had driven her to distraction.

Jane told her she'd been in service at a big house in Droitwich and she been convinced the son of the house was in love with her. He'd given her a few tokens of his affection and they'd been sneaking out for walks in the grounds after dark.

Their special place was a fanciful summer house on the far side of the lake that had been built in years gone by and had been forgotten by recent generations. They would meet here when the house was asleep and swear eternal love. When Jane realised she was having his baby he swore he would marry her. He went straight to his Mama, told her the story and declared his intentions. Within two days he was packed off on a grand tour with his brother and a cousin, and Jane found herself at Ma's, vainly hoping he'd run away and rescue her.

Ruby barely had time to show Jane what was expected of her when her own birth pains started. Ma ushered her out of the nursery and into what appeared, from the outside, to be a separate building, but was in fact connected to the rest of the house by a cellar room.

Ruby felt all her old fear return, she was worried about the pain but she was more worried about what would happen to her and her baby afterwards, how would she live and who would help her? Ma at last decided to go some way towards making her feel better.

“I'm like a pedlar see, but what I sell is people. I provide whores for the gentlemen and I sell the babies what no one else wants. Different people want babies for different reasons and it's not my business to dig too deep. So long as they pay well, that's it for me."

Ruby gasped with pain and Ma tutted at the interruption. "Most of them are people with a bit of money who can't have one of their own. What a lot of folk don't realise is that all this business of society marrying society only breeds idiots and weaklings see, they need a bit of poor folks blood for strength and brains. That's where my work starts.”

She stopped talking then as Ruby's labour made her cry out. Ma moved to the foot of the bed and the serious business of giving birth began. Ruby was young, strong and healthy and within a very short space of time a healthy boy was delivered. Ruby was shocked that instead of easing, her pains got worse once the boy was born but Ma briskly told her to stop being so noisy, the worst was over so there was no need for the fuss to continue. Ruby groaned deeply and Ma turned back to her and smiled in delight.

“By god, I knew you were a good 'un the minute I saw you. You've got another one cooking in there 'ent you?”

Ruby was beyond caring, she just wanted it all to stop and fortunately, mother nature and Ma had enough experience between them to handle everything without Ruby's cooperation. She'd passed out.

Ma came back to see her a couple of hours later and told her what would happen next. “Twins you had my girl, must run in your family cos they don't in his, as far as I know. Now then, this 'ent no mother and baby home and I know you 'ent daft enough to have gone thinking it was."

Ruby was too emotional and uncomfortable to bother to reply but Ma waited in silence for the nod to show she was listening to every word before she would continue. "If you want to cry and get upset, cry it out now girl, then put it out of your mind. I know it hurts cos I've done it, we've all done it and we did it because we had to. Some does it easier than others, but you knew it had to be done.”

Ruby nodded again weakly.

“I 'ent stealing your babies and if you've changed your mind about giving em up then tell me now and we'll find a way of you paying me for all the food you've been eating. But ask yourself these questions first. If you walk out of here today with your babies where are you all planning to sleep and what do you suppose you'll all be eating? If one of em gets sick who's to pay for medicine? If you get sick who cares for them? Who's going to give you work? What future can you offer them?”

Ma stood back with her hands on her hips and waited for Ruby's nod before she continued speaking. As these were the very questions Ruby herself had been worried sick about, the nod was quick in coming. "I know I must give them up." She cried then and Ma broke a lifetime rule and patted her arm once in sympathy, then she passed her a damp cloth and told her to wipe her face.

“I do what I do because there's no other choice for girls

like you. Now, get your crying over with and then you'll be ready to make a fresh start. It's up to you, but it's done today, one way or the other. I like you well enough but this is a business and I won't waste time. Your little ones will be cared for properly. The first one, he's a good strong boy and I'll find a very nice family for him to go to. He'll have a future, an education and lord knows what else he'll have that wouldn't be getting from you."

Ruby nodded weakly. "I won't let you down Ma, I understand, really I do."

Ma put her head on one side as she considered Ruby, she was a tough little miss and no mistake but Ma had to make sure she was put in the picture fully now because she wouldn't put up with talking things over endlessly once a thing was done.

"The second boy, now he's got a twist in his leg and we'll need to see if it straightens a bit before I show him to anyone. He'll stay here and we'll feed him up and get him strong, then we'll find a place for him."

Ruby reached out to touch Ma's hand and the old woman saw her tears start again. "Don't you look at me with them cow eyes neither, he's perfectly happy and the last thing he needs is you crying over him. I'll leave you alone now, but think hard about what you want for yourself and for them. I can't give any more time to holding your hand. You got to make the choice today and that's the end of it."

Ruby didn't need more time and she told Ma so. She'd known the baby would have to go, the fact that she'd had two, not one, didn't change anything. She couldn't look after them and build the life she wanted for herself so they must go.

Ma nodded her approval and explained that Ruby would no longer be working with the newborns. Her first child would be handed over to a family today and it's twin would go as soon as he could be made strong. In future she'd be doing other work for Ma.

Yesterday, a man and two women were whipped at the cart's tail through the principal streets of Worcester, the man for stealing a handkerchief, one of the women for stealing some things, the property of her master, Mr Brace, a baker of this city, and the other woman for encouraging the former to rob her master, and afterwards receiving the goods stolen.

On the cart to which the women were tied, a label, in large characters, was pasted, specifying the crimes for which they were being punished.

(Copyright and courtesy of the Worcester News)

CHAPTER FIVE

Arthur Watkins was a very well set up gentleman, he had almost everything he needed in his life, he only lacked an heir and had been single minded since learning that his money could correct this one small flaw. He adored his wife who was a delicate, petite angel, she'd lost so many babies and damaged her own health before they both accepted that she'd never have one of her own. He wanted a strong newborn boy that he could pass off as his own and Ma had sent word that she had something she was certain would suit him.

Ruby wondered why her baby was deemed suitable and not the baby that had been born to Lily a week or so earlier and Ma explained that Mr Watkins was tormented about doing the right thing. He wanted a child from a decent, healthy girl and he wanted to meet the girl, what's more he was prepared to pay highly for this privilege.

Lily was healthy and pretty enough but she was stupid, and a gentleman might assume that a child of hers would also be stupid. Ruby on the other hand was quick and bright, a far better proposition. Ruby was still tired from the birth but she did trust Ma so she nodded as she agreed to do what Ma asked of her.

Ma went on to tell her a few more snippets about the gentleman. He was an important man, with a very good name. He was not from Worcester although one of his partners was. It was through this man that he'd heard about Ma Jebb and what she could do to help people in his situation.

"Your son could be rich and powerful one day, just so long as you don't spoil it by acting daft." Ma said. At that moment they were interrupted by John, to tell them the gentleman was here and waiting. Ma hurriedly reminded Ruby to follow her lead and offer nothing other than answers to the simplest questions

Ma entered the room with Ruby a step behind her, she

indicated with a nod that Ruby should sit opposite Mr Watkins. She did so and they sat in silence and watched each other carefully until

Mr Watkins nodded his approval. He asked if she could read and write, which of course she could. She demonstrated how quickly she could add a line of numbers and he appeared delighted with her. He smiled and patted her hand. “My dear, who is the father of your baby, can you tell me, was it your master?”

In an instant Ma stepped forward. “Say nothing Ruby.” Then she turned to Mr Watkins, “I'm sure you understand sir, we can't betray the confidence of anyone in these delicate situations. Your business will never be discussed here but neither will any other man's. Ruby is a strong, healthy girl as you can see. She's educated and nicely spoken which all that you asked for and more. We can't give you any information of the father though. Everyone's privacy must be respected here.”

He politely nodded his head to Ma then looked back at Ruby.

“Thank you for agreeing to let me see you Ruby. You won't see me again after today, so in view of that fact, is there anything you want to ask me before I go?”

Ruby ignored Ma's threatening stare and faced him directly. “Well Sir, I wonder where is your wife? I wonder why she didn't come with you to get your baby. Is she ill, or does she not want a baby that's not her own?”

Mr Watkins sighed and smiled sadly. “My wife wants a baby more than anything else in the world but she can't have one in the natural way and she's agreed with me that this is the only way left for us. She didn't want to come with me today because she is going to tell herself that your baby is her real baby. I'm to take him home and put him in his little bed and then she's going to wake up when he cries and attend to him as though he were her own baby boy.”

At that moment any doubt Ruby may have had vanished. She nodded her head and stood up ready to leave the room.

Mr Watkins however had a few more words to say. “Your baby is going to be very well loved and cared for. He's going to have a fine education and could become an important man one day if he comes with me but I won't take him unless you tell me you know it's for the best. I do believe a mother knows best and it's important to me that we have your blessing.”

Ruby looked him in the eyes for a full minute then said quietly. “You have my blessing, Sir.”

She left the room as Ma picked up the tiny bundle and handed it over to him.

On Sunday last, one Jane Lewis was committed to our county gaol at Worcester to await trial on suspicion of stealing and taking away a child, about two years of age, son of Catherine Yeates of Abberley.

It appears that she belongs to a gang of gypsies or kidnappers who make a practice of stealing children and afterwards ship them off from Liverpool or Chester for sale in Ireland.

(Copyright and courtesy of the Worcester News)

CHAPTER SIX

Ruby regained her strength quickly and found a multitude of tasks to keep herself both fully occupied and too tired to think over the following few weeks. Her mind was in disorder though, she slept badly and often woke up aware that she was missing something, her babies or her sister?

She resorted to using the drops Ma pressed on her and they helped. She worked at any task she was given and the friends that she'd made in her short time here left her to get on with it. They'd all been through the same kind of thing and, no matter how tough the girl thought she was or how dire the circumstance, it was a cruel thing to come to terms with.

She asked Ma once or twice about her other baby, the one with a twisted leg but Ma told her he was safe and well and that was all she needed to know. She must forget she'd ever had a child.

Eventually she stopped asking.

One of the jobs Ruby loved more than any other was taking the pony and trap to the spring and fetching the fresh water back for everyone in the house. The well water was often foul and the chance to have a couple of hours alone in the clean fresh air to get sweet spring water was something Ruby made sure to do as often as she could.

Bella and the girls warned her that it wasn't safe to be so far from the houses on her own but Ruby was already facing her greatest fear in living without Ellie. Being alone outdoors held no fear for her, besides which she wasn't always alone.

She'd take the trap to the inn where she had first met Mary and wait until her friend spotted her and could sneak out. As often as she could Mary would come to the spring with her and they'd have an hour or so to tell each other all their news. If Mary couldn't get away then they'd be content with a couple of snatched moments outside the inn. It was enough because it had to be.

Today was a day that Mary couldn't get away. “Sorry Rube, he's acting like a pig today. It's best I stay here. You all right girl, you're looking pale? What's wrong?”

Ruby confessed that Ma had talked to her about getting to work. She'd given her a month to get over the birth and wanted to know how Ruby planned to support herself now.

Mary laughed at her. “It's nothing to worry about you daft mare. It's all over in a matter of seconds and if you get lucky you might meet a fellow like my Bill. He's a miserable sod but he treats me well enough and I don't have to worry where me next meal is coming from. I flirt with him all night and keep him topped up with the drink and it's over before it starts."

Ruby smiled but it didn't reach her eyes. The idea of being with a man sickened her, and she didn't know what she could do to avoid it.

"Trust me Ruby, just lie down and shut your eyes and you'll be used to it in no time. I don't say you'll ever like it as Bella does mind, that girl 'ent natural.”

Their laughter this time was loud and sincere, Bella's enjoyment of sex was no secret. Their noise was cut short though as Bill had heard them and was now bellowing for Mary to get back into the house. The girls kissed each other quickly and parted. Ruby headed to the spring and resolved to face up to things tonight. Everyone else had to do it, why would she want to be any different to her friends?

When she got back she told Ma she was ready to go to work and Ma handed her over to Bella's tender mercies. “Don't worry Ruby, we've got a lovely young chap here whose been before and he's a gentle sort of man. I'll start you off easy but for my sake try to put a bloody smile on your face. The way you look right now is enough to soften the firmest of flesh, they want a bit of a welcome you know.”

Ruby bathed and dressed in some borrowed finery and then sat trembling in the little room and tried to smile as the young man came in. It was all over in a matter of seconds as they promised, but not in the way they'd have hoped.

He reached out for Ruby eagerly, a new face and a fresh body was always a thrill for him. He took her in his arms and bent his head hungrily to her breasts. As his mouth sank into her flesh the room seemed to spin and darken for her. She screamed and raked his face with her nails. He bellowed and, before Bella could get in and rescue him, Ruby had a handful of his hair in her grasp and he was clutching his head in pain.

Ma was furious at first but, seeing the panic in Ruby's eyes, and realizing that the young man had taken it as part of the fun, she relented. "I told you before you 'ent got to do nothing you don't want to. You should have told me you was afraid, for there's nothing worse for regular business than a whore that don't like it. I expect I can find enough work for you to do to keep you out of trouble and pay your way. There'd better be nothing else you'll turn your nose up at though."

On Monday, an Inquest was taken at Crowle on view of the body of a female bastard child who was strangled by her mother, Ann Pitt of Crowle, a single woman, and afterwards thrown into a pool with a large stone tied to its arm to sink the body, which was found on Saturday last by two little boys who were birds-nesting. The jury bought in a verdict of Wilful Murder against the said Ann Pitt whereupon she was committed to our County Gaol at Worcester to await trial.

(Copyright and courtesy of the Worcester News)

CHAPTER SEVEN

Ruby spent the next five years doing whatever Ma asked and loving every moment. She delivered babies, and held the mothers hand as she then gave the babies away. She patched up thieves who had come to grief either by a sword or knife and ended up at Ma's in need of rest and repairs. She bought, and sold, stolen goods under cover of darkness. She recruited girls and boys for the houses and made sure they kept themselves clean. She knew where the best laudanum could be purchased and she'd convinced Ma to let her set up her own still to produce Gin. She also taught Ma how to read and write. She turned her nose up at nothing.

In the early days she had travelled back to St John's several times in an attempt to make her peace with her mother and see her sister but had been turned away. Her mother wanted nothing to do with her and insisted that Ellie had left home the same week that Ruby had and gone into service with a family in Birmingham and had not been heard from since.

In time she accepted that her own past life was best left alone, she had a home and a family of sorts and if she ever had a second to herself in which to think about it she realised she was quite content.

Such heavy, long continued rains as we have lately had in these parts were scarce ever known before and by the excessive high and extensive floods which have been occasioned, it is feared great damages have ensued. The bridge over the Laugherne brook near this city has received great damage.

(Copyright and courtesy of the Worcester News)

CHAPTER EIGHT

Jess Jebb sat quietly in her private room, took a deep gulp of brandy and swirled it around her mouth, wincing as the spirit filled the raw hole that yet another rotten tooth had left behind. She sank back into her chair and sighed with pleasure. Darkness had fallen and this was her time to rest.

She worked hard all day and her boys and girls worked hard all night. She would sit here by the fire now until first light, dozing and listening to the sounds that made her life secure. Sometimes she sat alone, more often Ruby sat with her for a while. For now, she was alone.

As she listened to the familiar night sounds closing in around her she clearly identified hooves clattering into her courtyard, suggesting perhaps a young man escaping the vigilant eye of his Mama for a while. Next came the sound of a coach as it pulled up near the darkened side of the house, this perhaps warned of a nervous husband looking for an entertainment that only another man could provide. Now footsteps approached, a group of young men on an adventure, some nervous laughter, some confident leg pulling, testing themselves and each other. Only time would tell where their tastes lay.

Gradually layer upon layer of sound merged until the room was filled with a steady drone occasionally broken by a laugh, a cry, a muffled giggle or even a snatch of song. These sounds didn't disturb her, they reassured her. Her customers were happy and they were spending their money. Whatever a man wanted could be bought at Ma Jebb's house. No one in here would judge him, and no one out there would ever know about it.

Jess greedily drained the tankard, reached for the Worcester newspaper and started to read about the goings on of the rich and famous folk. Occasionally she liked to while away an hour this way, she wasn't quick with her reading, but thanks to Ruby and her lessons, it was gift that she now had and she cherished it.

Ruby had taught her to read, slowly and carefully, and now she could understand all that was written. Reading was a pleasure that had come to Jess late in life and she'd love Ruby forever for giving it to her. She'd always had a desire, almost an urgency, to know what was going on around her and now she could sit here and read all about it at her leisure. And pass judgement on the foolishness of folk.

She read about the fine foods the wealthy ate and the gowns the ladies wore. Who was marrying who, who had recently died and what the King was up to these days. On nights like tonight when she had taken more than enough liquor on board she could dream that she was one of the people she so envied.

She dreamed she was in the most beautiful ballroom she'd ever seen. It had walls of sparkling glass that were opened to let in fresh, rose scented air. She glided elegantly across a vast polished floor toward the luxurious velvet and gilt seating arrangements that were scattered around the edges. At one end of the room delicious drinks were being served in the finest crystal by staff lined up and ready help. A selection of delicate sweetmeats was arranged on silver platters for the dancers to enjoy. Tall green plants filled the corners of a lovely room and offered just enough privacy for a fleeting, stolen kiss.

Jess was dressed in a pale green silk gown and her silver slippers had matching green ribbons. She twirled around the dance floor on the arms of a tall handsome man dressed in dark blue and red finery all trimmed with gold. She laughed gaily and threw her head back carefully, knowing that her waterfall of gleaming red hair would look enchanting beneath the crystal chandelier that was twinkling with the light of a hundred candles above her head. Her partner smiled and lowered his face towards hers. She closed her eyes and waited for his kiss.

Ma was jerked awake quite brutally by Ruby, roughly raking the dying embers of the fire to get an hour more comfort from it. “Go to bed Ma, why don't you? A sleep is what you need. I'll keep an eye on things here.”

“I *was* asleep you noisy little cow but I'm wide awake now. Christ knows how you manage to make such a bloody noise all the time. No matter, I've got things on me mind and I wanted to talk to you sooner or later so sit yourself down.”

Ruby smiled to herself. These days she was a confident young woman and her fear of Ma had long gone. She and Ma worked well together, both being strong and hard working, and Ruby knew she was valued here. If Ma wanted her to listen as she talked, well, it was the least she could do. Half a dozen time this last month Ma had said she had something important to say and then changed her mind.

“Can't it wait until tomorrow Ma, I'm tired and you've had too much to drink?” Ruby picked up the discarded brandy bottle as she spoke and raised her eyebrows at Ma.

“Tired. Ha, at your age you shouldn't know the meaning of being tired. And it's none of your business how much drink it takes to keep me going. Now then, sit down and listen to me, this is important.”

Ma tutted impatiently as Ruby cleared a spot and made herself comfortable. She looked up at last fully prepared for Ma to fob her off again but it appeared that tonight was the night. Ma confessed that she felt she was getting to old to take care of all she had and she knew she'd begun to make mistakes. This last was something Ruby knew all too well and she hastily nodded in agreement. “Well that Vera's a mistake, true enough.”

All Ruby could see her doing was cost them money. She'd got an odd look about her, funny eyes and what sort of baby she'd deliver didn't bear thinking about. It wasn't anyone half decent that got her in the family way cos no one who weren't desperate would. They'd struggle to find the poor mite a home and as for Vera herself well, none of their gentlemen were likely to pay for an hour of her time, no matter how keen she was, and she was keen. Dirty mare.

"And talk about eat, she's a greedy cow, costing me a fortune she is." Ma grumbled on. "God only knows what I'm going to do with her."

Ruby had been thinking the same thing, she did the accounts, such as they were, and she knew better than most that things were going poorly. The truth was the bills were being managed, but they used to reckon on a certain amount of profit every month to put by but that amount was getting smaller every month, there was still plenty but it wasn't growing as it should and Ma had taught her that the column of numbers had to be bigger every month or there was something in the business not pulling its weight.

"We can't carry on this way, it needs a sharper brain than mine to take over and start bringing money in another way. I'm tired and I can't shake this cough off, to tell the truth I'm past my best. I want you to take over." Silence fell as Ma's words hung over them.

It was an overheated airless little corner and there was a very unpleasant smell mingling with the smoke from the fire and the candles. Ruby felt sick but whether that was from breathing in the foul air or the shock of hearing Ma say out loud what Ruby had day-dreamed about a hundred times she couldn't be sure. She knew she was special to Ma, there was no softness apparent in the woman but still Ruby knew she was favoured.

Her own son still lived here for one thing, his leg had stayed bent and Ma had never seemed to try to place him. He was healthy and his limp was barely noticed now, he raced about the place fetching and carrying and was generally agreed to be a delight. He called her Aunt, as he did all the girls. She was content to see him happy and well and had no need for him to know she was his mother. One day he'd ask questions and she'd always thought she'd let Ma decide how he should be answered.

"What exactly are you talking about Ma?"

“Everything. All the money, the houses and all the bloody worry that goes along of it. I'm not well and I've got to sort things out proper before it's too late. We've got two babies in and I've got no place for em to go and now there's another on the way. Not to mention what to do with that Vera. I'll tell you everything about how I do things and I want you to take it all over.”

Ma waited in vain for Ruby to reply.

“Ha. Ruby Morgan is struck dumb. My, oh my, I've finally got you to shut up and listen. You've usually got more than enough to say for yourself, took you by surprise have I?”

The old woman cackled in delight. Then she doubled over and coughed as though she couldn't stop and eventually spat into the fire. As the mess steamed and spit she looked at Ruby and tapped on the table impatiently. “Say summat then.”

Having been honoured with an invitation from the Rt. Hon the Earl of Coventry, the mayor, the sheriff, most of the aldermen and several other members of the Worcester Corporation dined with his Lordship on Tuesday at his seat at Croome where a most magnificent entertainment was provided on the occasion.

(Copyright and courtesy of the Worcester News)

CHAPTER NINE

Ruby wanted to know more about Ma's health but the old lady said she wasn't about to start talking about the ins and outs of her body with anyone but God. She wanted to hand over all the work to Ruby and then to be left alone to sit by the fire and dream her dreams.

This was something Ruby had dreamed of but never let herself believe it would really happen. Her five years here had showed her that Ma was making good money but she could be making so much more. She knew she was privy to information no one else was and she was loyal to Ma. She'd kept her own counsel and kept on working, doing any job Ma gave her. Except the one, of course. And they'd got over that in time. She thought about this place that she'd hated with a passion at first, but now loved with all her heart.

What looked like a simple row of cottages on the point of falling down, was in fact the front of a nice little empire. Behind the ramshackle frontage the cottages opened onto a courtyard with a raised walkway leading to a row of more substantial building that were invisible from the road. Two of the buildings were given over to the entertainment of gentlemen. They could have the company of girls or boys, depending upon their taste, and the size of their money bag.

Entry was through the cottage at the far left or by driving down a track that looked as though it led nowhere and into the courtyard and away from prying eyes. All the boys and girls that worked here were hand picked and willing to please. Bella still ran these houses and she'd become a good friend to Ruby over the five years they'd worked together. She was five years older than Ruby and had been responsible for a huge part of her education into the ways of the world and how to manage the men that ran it. Ruby had, in turn, tried to teach Bella to read but her friend was adamant that the skills she practised daily were far more use to her and she didn't have the time or need to learn more.

Another of the cottages was where the girls who were in trouble found sanctuary. They were fed and housed and then, when they'd given birth, Ma kept the baby, which she later sold. There were a dozen other pies Ma had her finger in, and Ruby knew she'd have to start paying a lot more attention if she was to maintain all of this.

"What I need is for you, my girl, to learn more than you know now about how I make my money and then take over for me, so, will you or won't you?"

"I'll do it Ma. You can trust me. But there's so much I don't know."

Ma slumped back and reminisced as Ruby sat quietly and let it all soak in. "This lot all started forty years ago when I lost the only thing I really cared about. I turned my mind over then to making money and nothing else."

Ruby sighed with satisfaction, perhaps tonight she'd have all her questions answered. She sat back and waited for the story to unfold.

"I vowed no one would ever have the power to make me do summat I didn't want to do again and I knew for that I needed money. I reckon when you first came here you had made the same vow. I could see me in you, your spirit, your guts and the fact that no one has ever made a fool of you since you got here. Birds of a feather, me and you."

Ruby was certain they were no such thing but if Ma was going to turn maudlin in her old age, well, perhaps she'd earned the right.

"I don't want you to make any mistakes here though, girls with no money, no class and even less education, like me, don't get as rich as I am now by hard work. They get rich by dirty dealing, and my dealings have been as dirty as you like. Still are to tell the truth. And I will tell you the truth, all on it."

"Not all dirty dealings Ma, you've helped a lot of girls like me."

“I'm no bleeding heart nor a saint though and don't you ever think it, I never did a thing without knowing what I'd get paid. Terrible things were done to me when I had no power, terrible, terrible things and I'm still making the world pay but I've lost the taste for it somehow.”

Ma's voice tailed away again and this time Ruby left her alone, she needed time to grasp that her life was changing through the course of this evening. She'd found sanctuary here at a time when she was terrified and alone and it had become everything to her. But to think it could all be hers and she would be able to direct her own future, now that would be something.

She was torn, though, this was what she'd hoped for, but Ma was sick and although she didn't love the old woman she trusted and respected her and the thought of her dying was horrible. Ma had saved her when no one else would give her the time of day.

Ruby couldn't keep quiet any longer. “Why choose me Ma? Why not John, he was with you before I came along?”

“I'll never give all I've built to a man, no matter who he might be, I'd sooner burn the lot down, it's men what's caused all the problems in my world. They might all get what they want when they come here, but by God I make sure they pay for it." She wheezed and cackled.

"John's not a bad 'un mind, he needed work at a time when I needed help and I paid him fair and square but he'll never get more than that and he knows not to expect it. Besides that he 'ent got but half a brain in his head. He wouldn't last long looking after all this, and them girls with Bella would eat him up and spit him on the ground inside a week. They can be as gentle as lambs with a man what's paying for it but there's not one of em who wouldn't tear him to shreds if he tried to tell em what's what. He's getting old an' all. In the old days if a fight broke out or some chap needed a smack John could take on all comers. He was a fine figure of a man then, mind you. She gave

Ruby a knowing nod that made her cringe. Not Ma, and John together, Ruby thought, that wasn't a picture she wanted to see. Ma laughed at her expression. "Nowadays he's more likely to sleep through anything short of a riot."

Ruby persisted. “Why not Bella then?”

Ma cackled again and waved her hand in dismissal. “Bella you ask, why not Bella? You know as well as I do she's only ever taken to one thing, and that's fucking. She's damn good mind you, no gentleman's ever left her room unsatisfied that much I do know, but she never even had the sense to charge em for it until I took her in hand. She's one of them as has a taste for it, she'll never be any use in business and you damn well know it.”

Ma shook her head at the thought of all that Bella had wasted.

“No, you're the one, you've had an education, you've got the spirit and when you was given the easy way out you wouldn't take it. You could have gone in with Bella and earned a nice life for yourself entertaining the gentlemen. You're as pretty as a picture, when you keep your mouth shut, and I know we'd have em lining up for a bit of time with you but, oh no, first gentleman in your room and I thought you'd killed him.”

Ma snorted and Ruby grinned as they remembered that night. Ma had come to see her later and explained that she wasn't entirely surprised at Ruby's reaction. As a rule the girls that found themselves in trouble and ending up at Ma's to have a baby normally fell safely into one of two categories. Those that had a choice would leave and make their lives somewhere else. Those that have no choice, like Ruby usually get on with the business in hand. But not Ruby, she couldn't or wouldn't do it.

“I didn't trust you to hold firm then, but now I know you better I can see you're made of stronger stuff than either of them two. You've got a good nature and you know what it's like to be in trouble and I reckon you're clever enough to know that the way I do business must change."

Ruby blushed, there were so many things here she'd do differently if she were in charge, she'd already made all kinds of changes in her head, late at night when she was alone and free to dream.

"I've never known how to go about making all of this respectable and to be honest I've never cared about being respectable anyway but I bet you've had ideas already. I'd let you have a free hand to change what you like as long as you leave me alone. I want a fire and me drink. Apart from that you can do as you will."

Ruby walked around the room thinking, then she began to speak slowly, "I'll do anything I can but I'll need a lot of help."

"Aye, maybe to start with you think you will, but not for long. As soon as you get the bit between your teeth you'll be off and running. I've got the measure of you my girl, you'll wake up tomorrow morning full of ideas and itching to get started."

Ruby blushed again, in truth she was ready to start now.

"You've dealt with everything since you got here so well that I started thinking a long time ago about giving it all to you one day, so long as you didn't let me down and you never did. Now then you can take that daft look off your face, I'm getting sick not soft. I want a home with a fire and enough food then I want to be left alone. The time hasn't come yet but it's nearby and I want your word that I won't be put out."

"Of course I won't put you out." Ruby was defensive instantly. "What ever you need you'll get. You say you're no saint but you saved me and you saved dozens more like me and I'll make sure you don't have anything to worry about at all. I give you my word."

"All right then my girl, let's see what you can make of all this."

"Will you tell me how you started it all?"

On Sunday last died David Moore, Master of the Old Coffee House, Worcester. He was valued and esteemed by the nobility and gentry that frequented it, for his obliging behaviour, and is much lamented by all his acquaintances.

(Copyright and courtesy of the Worcester News)

CHAPTER TEN

Ma poured herself another drink, spat again into the fire and nodded, she thought back to a time forty years ago when her twenty year old self was both fascinated by, and envious of, the glorious doings of the rich people that lived in the same town as her but on such a different level to hers she could only watch from the outside.

Everyone loved to gossip about the rich and famous, partly through envy and partly because it brightened an otherwise dull life. It was a simple fact that if a rich man had a servant he did not have a secret. It was not possible to keep both and the servants of the very rich had a great many friends around the inns and taverns of Worcester. One particular event had captured the interest of the entire city.

Caroline Mallory was famous for being the most exquisite beauty for miles around. The perfection of her features was said to be something to behold. Poets wrote of her and painters longed to copy her. Her family were courted by the great and the good simply for the honour of having Caroline dance at one of their balls. She was one of those blessed few that others love to look at. Her sweet nature meant that the girls in her circle rarely felt jealous of her beauty at all and besides having someone so lovely as her grace their parties guaranteed to attract all the single men for miles around.

She had smooth, silvery white hair that sparkled in candlelight, flawless pale skin and bright blue eyes, she almost seemed to shine. She was tall for a girl but so slender and graceful that she appeared delicate and nymph like. If she was nearby one could not help but look at her and few were untouched by her beauty. Great things were predicted for her.

The Mallory family were gentry, real quality. Caroline was destined to make a good marriage, and normally a girl like that would expect to attract a title. The only problem was Dukes rarely marry girls with no money and the Mallory family secret was that they had no money left at all.

Taxes, gambling and the risk taking of ancestors long gone had left the current Mr Mallory in urgent need of a sizeable windfall. His struggle to maintain the family houses and a terrifyingly expensive lifestyle was taking a toll. Mr Mallory knew he couldn't keep his financial worries hidden much longer. He was living behind a marvellous facade, but cracks were starting to appear.

The family had a manor house in Worcester that required immediate, and extensive, attention to the roof. There was a place in London that took an exorbitant amount of money to keep up to snuff and yet another vast property up in Scotland that was falling to rack and ruin.

Added to the property concerns that worried the poor man half to death, was a wife with a taste for Parisian style and two unremarkable younger daughters soon to be in need of husbands.

Old man Mallory was resigned to the knowledge that his most valuable asset, in truth his only asset, was the incomparable Caroline. She simply *had* to marry money. A title would have been agreeable but a fortune was imperative. And preferably in the not too distant future.

In order to preserve the illusion that all was well, the Mallory family would move from home to home according to the seasons, as did all in their circle. The latest fashions in dress and transport had to be displayed and at least one large ball and several suppers were expected.

This was a costly way to live but the least sign of financial ills would scare off any potential suitors and some of their creditors were already becoming testy, a solution must be found urgently.

The social round made for relaxed and happy company but also meant that the Mallory family mixed only with the usual people, all of whom were looking for the same, or very similar, things. The rich ones wanted a title and the titles wanted money.

Into this rarefied world had gradually edged one George Sansome. He was an upstart, but an extremely wealthy and clever upstart. He'd made his money in all sorts of dubious ways, some a bit cleaner than others. No one quite knew where he or his money had come from but he seemed to have been around for a long time.

He was polite and charming, he knew how to speak well and he had enough money to at least be worth talking to. His precise background was not important to these men, they had no interest in him as a person, it was not as if there was any chance of him becoming a friend. He was tolerated because the top drawer wanted to know how a man who was clearly not one of them had managed to amass such a fortune. That knowledge could be very useful indeed. Perhaps his Midas touch could be replicated? And he was damned useful to know in a pinch.

George charmed the older ladies with his good looks and slightly forward flattery, he could dance elegantly and his manners at table were impeccable. He impressed the men with his daring at cards and his willingness to attend the bare knuckle fights and horse racing they so loved.

He was invited here there and everywhere, so much so that he felt that he was almost, but not quite, accepted at last. He had a burning desire to be accepted by society and the more time he spent being held at arms length by the favoured few the more compelling his desire became.

He'd achieved everything in life he needed except their genuine approval and that became his obsession. He was determined to be a gentleman. He couldn't think of anything but how to gain admittance to the elite.

He was a clever rogue and eventually his opportunity presented itself, as he had known it would. He had been on the fringes of society for several years when tales of the exceptional Caroline reached him. Her launch into society had caused a storm of admiring chatter and raised the hopes of a legion of eligible men.

George had his first sighting of Caroline when he attended a ball, a tedious overblown affair thrown by a man to whom he had loaned a considerable sum of money. He witnessed a room full of supposedly intelligent men fawning like fools and suddenly he knew what to do. The one thing no one else could bring themselves to do.

He didn't take any special notice of Caroline. Not at that ball or for the remainder of that season. He wasn't ever rude or unkind to her, he simply wasn't dazzled by her as others were. Now, young Caroline had grown up knowing what was her due and being ignored was an entirely new and unwelcome experience. It was one she was not prepared to stand for, everyone she'd ever met fell under spell and she was furious that George seemed impervious to her charms. He became her target and she was determined to stop at nothing to bring him to heel.

He was clever and ruthless enough to make her work very hard for what he wanted. He sat back and let her labour. She took on her family and their bitter disapproval single handedly. Yes, they agreed, he was rich, but even in these dire circumstances he simply didn't come up to the mark. They all wanted so much more for her. No one knew where his money had come from, they could not and would not have that in the family.

She was shipped of to the country for a year, where she screamed and raged and sank into a decline. She refused to eat and became thin and withdrawn and her poor father was driven half mad with worry. Her looks were being ravaged and without her looks he had nothing. He reached a point where he would do anything to bring the old Caroline back.

Once he agreed to her demands she began to eat sensibly and to take the air. Her recovery was quite remarkable. A small supper party was planned to celebrate her return to full health. She drew up the invitation list and the seating plan herself. A new gown was made, silk stockings were purchased and something very special from the goldsmith was fashioned to adorn her wrists.

At the supper she sat opposite George Sansome and flirted and teased to such an extent that for the sake of decency there was only one thing to be done. Her father, and George, gave in gracefully and an arrangement was made. Work began on the roof of the manor less than a week after the wedding to end all weddings had taken place. No expense was spared on either.

Caroline and George both got what they thought they wanted and neither one ever knew more than a moment of happiness there on in. Caroline did everything she could to make him fall in love with her, but in vain. She would gaily proclaim her joy in the marital state to all that would listen and at first few realized that she lied, but soon the strain of pretending to be deliriously happy to friends and family, all of whom had disapproved of the marriage, began to tell and she once again became thin and anxious.

George felt so guilty that he vowed to be kinder to her, after all she'd played into his hands and given him exactly what he wanted. It was not her fault that what he thought he wanted had left a bitter taste. He owed her something after all was said and done. It was quite painful to see her desperation and he knew it was up to him to make the best of what he had. She must not be punished for his selfishness. He arranged a voyage for them. A luxurious trip to every exotic place she could name. They both got pleasure planning the trip and then duly set off in high hopes, both determined to make a success of something that could not be reversed.

Several months later they returned to Worcester, having reached a happier level of understanding. Caroline glowed, she was with child and had found joy and peace of mind. She became, if possible, even more lovely and her genuine delight in her impending motherhood was celebrated by all. Her family were so happy to have her restored to them that peace reigned.

George, to the outside world was an extremely fortunate

man. Inside though he was still in turmoil, nothing was as he'd hoped it would be. His money meant that on the surface all was well but he knew it wasn't and he also knew now that it never would be. He was not a gentleman and would never be one. Even his own servants, who showed the utmost respect to Caroline, somehow showed something less to him. He couldn't quite put his finger on what it was, but it was real enough for all that.

Yesterday was married at the church of Ombersley, Christopher Bethel, of Hanover Square, London to the Hon Miss Sandys, youngest daughter of the Lord Sandys - a most amiable and accomplished young lady, as eminently endowed and adorned with the good qualities and disposition of mind, beauty and gracefulness in her person as she is distinguished by her high birth and noble extraction.

(Copyright and courtesy of the Worcester News)

CHAPTER ELEVEN

Ma sat up suddenly and coughed violently again. She nodded her head towards the half empty bottle and Ruby handed it over. It was clear that Ma was worn out but Ruby really wanted to hear the rest. She was afraid if Ma stopped now she might never finish the story

"Do you need to have a rest Ma?" She asked.

Ma shook her head and drank some more. "No, you've made me rake it all up with your questions and I shan't rest now until it's all said but then we'll let it lie."

Ruby stoked up the fire and sat down again. "Then tell me how you know so much about it. Gossip is one thing, but you know so much that would have been private. How?"

"Ha, you mean cos that's top drawer stuff and I'm just an old whore running a bunch of good time girls and drunken nurses?"

"Did you know them Ma?" Ruby wouldn't be diverted.

"I knew George, or at least I knew him years before all that happened, when he was called Joe. I knew him as well as I know myself, and I loved him even more. We were together as babies in a rats nest outside Foregate,"

What could she mean, Ruby wondered. Was she saying he was her brother? Ruby wanted to know but was afraid of stopping Ma by asking. She bit her tongue and hoped the answer would come.

"The how and the why don't matter, we grew up starving and stealing together and let me tell you, when you're hungry, really truly hungry and desperate you'll do anything for food. Anything!"

Ma drank deeply and sat quietly for a moment. "We did things I hope I never have to tell you about, but we got by. Jess and Joe against the world, that was us. I'll tell you how it was."

Joe was a brave, sturdy boy and he grew into a strong, handsome man. He learned to be quick and clever, crafty and ruthless enough to spot an opportunity and make something of it. He could look a person in the eye and lie through his teeth and steal their money bag at the same time.

After years of almost starving and living like animals together Joe and Jess had developed the skills to survive, usually she was the diversion and he was the thief. His strength and her agility got them in most places. Whatever happened around them, Joe could turn things to their advantage.

He considered Jess his responsibility and he was fiercely protective of her. He couldn't remember a time when they weren't together and neither could she, he wanted to make enough money to ensure that they would both have security. She just wanted them to be together.

He was clever, determined and totally without morals. In the space of fifteen years he took them from the gutter to considerable wealth. Certainly enough to stop doing the dirty work. But that wasn't ever enough for Joe. If he'd stopped then they'd have been comfortable, prosperous even, but he had this compulsion to be up with the gentlemen. He'd been running in the gutters and looking up for so long he was convinced that was where he belonged.

As a boy he would fetch and carry messages for men between the coffee shops and the coaching inns, he learned what was important to them and he learned who was influential in the town as he studied what they wore, what they ate and how they spoke.

He copied how to dress and ride and eat with fancy manners. He thought that men with short names must be poor, Joe, Tom and Will were names for stable lads. The names he heard called out to the men he ran errands for were different, longer. Samuel, Richard or William were names with weight. He decided not to be Joe any more, he was ready to change.

He listened to the chat, picking up valuable gossip and

learning far more than anyone ever guessed. He studied how to play cards and watched the best as they cheated. He listened and learned who needed money and might sell something cheaply to raise capital quietly. He discovered who was likely to get stupid drunk and gamble a home or carriage once all his cash was gone.

One of the things that all these men were endlessly fascinated by was royalty. What was King George doing now and who knew about it. Joe decided to become George, because no one could ever say that was a name that belonged in the gutter.

He was knowledgeable enough to arrange certain things for these men, things they wouldn't want each other or their families to know about. He made himself useful in countless ways. A few pounds loaned here, a debt written off there. No one could pinpoint when and how he had got himself involved with them, he'd simply always been there and they all just accepted him for his usefulness and discretion. And for his money.

As he matured he found he could learn a lot from the lonely wives of those very men whose dress and manners he was mimicking. He also found that those neglected wives could be very generous once they were sure of his discretion. Somehow he knew when they were alone and in need of diversion and he never failed them.

His life was slowly turning into the one he'd longed for, his only sadness was that Jess seemed happy to stay in the gutter, in fact she refused to leave it, she mocked his fancy manners and false airs and she flatly refused to call him George.

She was happy having fun with the inn keepers and their customers. She wanted laughter and dancing, drinking and singing, and she would not, indeed could not, pretend to be something she wasn't. He knew their parting was not far away.

They still told each other everything and tried not to judge each other although it was a dark day when he told her he intended to marry Caroline. She begged him to just have his fun and move on, she could see his spirit was being sapped but he couldn't. She felt he was putting himself in gaol and she knew that once inside he would never get out again but he wouldn't listen.

They both realized it was time to part and they sadly divided all they had. Joe gave Jess a couple of tumbledown houses, a pony and trap and a pile of money. He made John vow to stand by and protect her and get word to him should she ever be in dire need. They spent one last night together, curled up against the world as they used to and in the morning their lives continued on separate paths.

Jess opened her bawdy house up in the tumbledown cottages with two girls she trusted and proceeded to enjoy her life to the full, she was earning money and was beholden to no one. She did what she wanted when she wanted and, apart from the sadness of losing Joe, she was happy. Finding girls was never difficult, this was a better life than that of a laundry maid or a kitchen helper if you had a mind to try it.

She was unruffled when she realised that she was going to have a baby, it was not an entirely unexpected event for a woman making her living in the way she had chosen to. She didn't think it would make any difference to the way she lived her life. She worked on for as long as she had customers that would pay her and then she sat back and waited for her baby to come. Money was coming in from the other girls and it gave her time to think. She realised that what was happening to her was happening to women all the time. Some were happy about it, some were not, and some thought it was the end of the world. She began to think she might have an idea to make more money.

Jess wasn't concerned about having a baby herself, she didn't intend to allow a baby to make any difference to her life, good or bad. It was just a case of waiting till it was born then getting on with things. When the other girls asked what she might name the baby or whether she'd want a boy or girl she had no answer for them but it did help her realize that as well as women like her who found a baby an obstacle there were as many women who longed for one in vain. There was a way of making money here if only she could work it out.

Worcester Races are to be held next week and to prevent accidents happening to the horses in their exercise or at the time of running, it is desired that all persons would keep their dogs confined and away from Pitchcroft, and as the sheep are also a great interruption it is hoped that the owners will be so obliging as to have them removed.

(Copyright and courtesy of the Worcester News)

CHAPTER TWELVE

George meantime had married his Caroline.

Preparing rooms and finding help for when the baby arrived gave them a shared interest. George liked the idea of being a father and knew that whatever his own issues with acceptance had been his child would have no such problems, he, or she, would be born to it. His child was the grandchild of Mallory and that would get him in anywhere. George may never be one of the gentry but his child would be and that would have to be good enough.

Once the novelty wore off Caroline begun to find her advancing condition thoroughly unpleasant. She hated her thickening waistline, swollen ankles, morning sickness and the fact that her hair refused to shine as it used to. She felt ugly and unloved. Childbearing was a long, slow and uncomfortable experience for her and it was made more difficult by George who continued to socialise as though there were no tomorrow.

The long awaited birth arrived and was as painful and distressing for Caroline as it was potentially damaging for the child. The doctor, a man provided by Mallory, was very concerned and tried to talk to Mallory and George together. He explained that the boy was feeble and would probably not survive. It was, in his opinion, only a matter of time.

George was entirely out of patience, nothing had worked out the way he'd intended and he would not suffer any more over educated, pompous fools telling him this, that and the other. He threw the man out, convinced his mutterings of doom and gloom were yet another attempt to let George know he wasn't up to the mark. He ordered Mallory to leave him to his own business and set about putting his world back the way he wanted it.

Ma stopped speaking suddenly and Ruby could see that she was upset and very tired. Ruby herself was torn between wanting to leave Ma in peace but needing to know what happened to George and Caroline.

Her need took over. “Ma, what did he do?”

“He come back here to see me, the only person in the world he could truly trust, and we talked it all over. There was something wrong with his son, he didn't thrive as he should and the doctor didn't expect him to live more than a week or two. He just seemed to go from one sickness to another, each time getting a bit weaker."

Ruby held her breath and waited.

“My boy had been born a few months by then and he was a proper bruiser. Fat and happy he was, a lovely, lively little fellow, trying to sit up and look around him way before his time, he was that special.” Ma smiled quietly then and just looked into the fire.

“Ma, what did you do?”

“We swapped 'em of course. He took my little bruiser and I kept his little one.”

“Joe gave me more money and that bloody great piece of wilderness where we get our drinking water from. The Talbot's mine an all and them cottages up by the brook. Parsons pays me a sum once a year for the Inn and I've let a couple of my old girls rent the cottages."

Ruby was stunned. Ma was saying she gave away her baby and in exchange now owned all the land between them and Worcester, and all the houses and inns along the way. If she was speaking the truth, which she didn't always do, she was rich, far richer than Ruby had imagined. Which might mean that Ruby was about to be rich. Now she felt really sick.

"Joe said he'd always look after me but we both agreed that we wouldn't see each other anymore. The money and the land were like a goodbye and thank you all in one. I knew my boy would thrive with him and he didn't want any ties to me, for the boy's sake. It was best for me to forget about them both. I suppose that was the first baby I sold, cos like I said he gave me a pile of money and a fair bit of land. It was enough to buy this row of houses and get a few little things going. I never did anything with that God forsaken patch of land though."

Ruby didn't dare speak for fear of breaking the mood.

"Young George Mallory what drives about town in his fancy carriage with the big black horses, he's my son, I know it and so does fancy Miss Caroline and I reckon it was trying to deny it that turned her funny, she wanted him and she loved him but she couldn't quite convince herself that he was her son. George, my Joe, told her what he'd done but she just couldn't or wouldn't accept it. She tried to believe he was really hers, but she couldn't let go of the one she lost. Well, you never do really, do you?"

"I don't think you ever could."

"No. She hated the fact that she loved him even though he loved me." Ruby realized she was talking of the man now and not the baby.

"She drove herself mad trying to find out what we were to each other. That was a damn fools errand, cos even we didn't know what we were to each other, could have been brother and sister, could have been cousins or could have just been two bits of shit what landed in the same ditch. All we knew was we had each other and needed nothing else. While we were kids we was comfort enough for each other, we never worried about who we was. She never worried about anything else, poor little bitch."

"You started off envying her but in the end you pitied her?"

Ma laughed and coughed again, she spat out then rinsed her mouth with the drink.

"After a time Caroline started to act strange and folk love to talk about things like that. You know, servants and tradesmen, they know everything that goes on with the toffs, they hear something fresh and they love to pass it on. Apparently she started carrying on and they were forever calling in doctors and hiring nurses and what have you. I paid a lot of attention to the talk because her boy is my son after all, and I wouldn't have left him where he wasn't safe but she was just sad more than anything else I reckon."

Ruby added yet more fuel to the fire and got herself a drink. Ma talked on and she listened but with only half her mind. She was thinking of how much Ma was worth. Why was she living as she did when she could be living in comfort. It was beyond her understanding.

“My Joe died when the boy was twelve or so. He fell down some steps drunk, so they say. I kept a closer eye on them after that, for a time, but the boy was sent to boarding school and I knew he was out of harms way. I always wondered if she had something to do with Joe falling down like that, but that's cos I hate her and all she stands for in truth.”

Ruby knew that the old lady had just about told her story now but there was one more thing she wanted to know. “You said all this started when you lost the only thing you loved. Did you mean your son?”

The old lady cackled with delight. “You know me better than that, girl. Any old whore can have a baby, it was Joe I couldn't bear to lose. Babies a woman can get any time, men like Joe are rare.”

“How many more secrets have you got Ma?”

“Forty years’ worth my girl, I could tell you stories about all the grand families around here, in fact one day I will. Not today though. I'll tell you one thing more today and it's the most important thing I ever learned. “Listen to everything but keep your mouth shut. Knowing what's really what, well that's worth more than gold. And don't fritter what you know, treat it like gold. Don't tell anyone you have it and only spend it if you know what you'll get in return.”

For the benefit of Mr Pembruge on Thursday next at the Guildhall in Worcester will be performed a concert of vocal and instrumental musick, to begin at six o'clock in the evening. After the concert will be a ball. Tickets to be had of Mr Pembruge, at both the Coffee Houses and at the Hop Pole in the Forgate, at 2/6 each.

NB no admittance to the ball without a concert ticket.

(Copyright and courtesy of the Worcester News)

CHAPTER THIRTEEN

Henry Daventor was a man who strode through his life with a finely developed sense of his own importance. He was a wealthy man who owned everything around him as far as the eye could see and he wanted more. He lived in the finest house in St John's and almost every man for miles around had a living because Henry allowed it. He owned most of the St John's side of the Severn and had many financial interests over the river in Worcester. He was not, however a contented man, life had been a disappointment to Henry since the day he'd married.

A man, in Henry's opinion, took a wife for one purpose only, procreating the next generation. When that generation appeared the wife had done her duty and could, to a greater or lesser extent be forgotten. It was up to the man of the house to take responsibility for shaping his heir. Henry had dutifully taken a wife, after his father had put his foot down and insisted, and that had been the start of his problems. After five years of struggle and loss and doctors - damned expensive doctors - Elizabeth did finally manage to provide him with an heir.

Before she had though, Henry, thinking she never would, had adopted his second cousin's orphaned son, Hugh. Elizabeth then proved the expensive doctors to be the idiots that Henry had always known them to be by proceeding to carry her own child to full term. She delivered him safely, then promptly died, leaving Henry alone with two small boys to care for. Hugh, a toddler, and his own new born child William.

Henry made sure to provide everything for both boys that had, in his youth, been supplied for him. Food, shelter and a woman to look over them through babyhood. Susan Morgan was hard working and could manage his two boys easily, her twin daughters had never seemed to be too much for her and after all she owed everything she had to the foolish generosity of his wife.

During these early years Henry travelled the country talking to the men who were involved in pushing the canal building movement forward and was firmly bitten by the bug. He learned everything he needed to know and spent many months in Northumberland alongside the engineers as they work on the Duke of Bridgewater's great experiment.

He'd come home at decent intervals and, when Hugh was eleven and William eight a tutor was employed to live with them and prepare them for school. In due course they went to school and now their education was almost complete Henry had come home for good and was ready to take his boys in hand.

He'd reached a point where he was ready to build his own canal and it would change the face of Worcester forever. He'd never made his mark on the city in the way he wanted and this was his moment. He intended the name Daventor to be spoken with the same admiration that Brindley currently enjoyed.

He had returned home full of exciting plans that he and his boys would embark upon. They'd both enjoyed the best education money could buy and Henry was taken aback to find lazy, arrogant strangers where he'd hoped to find two willing young men. The fact that they were practically strangers to him wasn't the issue, no man knows his children when they are children, but he'd assumed that once he was home and they were grown up they'd fall in with his plans and things would move forward a pace. It had proved a false assumption.

His irritation today was because he was alone and he'd dearly wanted to have his son William with him, he was looking for men to start his working on his grand project and he had wanted embark on the project, shoulder to shoulder with his boy and it was not to be. William was not at home, he'd gone to Worcester last night and, once again, failed to return.

Today was the day of the Mop Fair and Henry had

planned to go there and hire the first team of workers, he was ready for some labourers to start breaking ground. He had wanted to be in a position to show William off and to ensure that the workers could see what a fine man his son had grown to be. He also wanted to teach his son how to go about hiring men and keeping the upper hand with them from the very first.

Henry stomped around the church-yard in an effort to clear his mind and dispel his temper, he had work to do and must pay attention to the job in hand. He would have to sort the boy out, but for today he needed working men and that must be his priority.

He reached the family plot, his usual destination when he needed solitude. Generations of his family lay here and it was the place to strengthen his resolve to teach the boys' responsibility and duty. From this favoured vantage point Henry could see the Severn marking the boundary of his own land. On the far side of the Severn lay Worcester and from this raised position he could see the spires and towers of the Cathedral, the Bishops Palace, Warmstry House, St Andrews and All Hallows.

Henry's father had always been content to be an admiring neighbour to Worcester but Henry had a need to dominate it in some way. He could remember his father talking to him when he was a boy. Teaching him what was right and what was expected. Or at least what he expected, Henry was honest enough with himself to admit that in fact he and his father had not agreed on very much as he grew up.

One thing in particular that they never could agree on was Dr Wall. Henry's father had laughed when he had heard about the plans that Dr Wall had to open an infirmary in Worcester that would offer care to all regardless of their wealth. He declared the place would be torn apart by the street rabble and could not possibly thrive.

When the infirmary became so successful that funds

were easily found to build a new larger facility in the town, he then became adamant there must be some sort of political conspiracy afoot because the whole idea was clearly unworkable. Free medical care, how could it work? Profit and charity cannot work hand in hand, any fool knows that.

When Dr Wall went on to create a porcelain manufacturers in the town with the declared aim of creating a product so distinctive as to be instantly recognisable, whilst at the same time helping to alleviate the grinding poverty in the town, Henry's father had shaken his head in disbelief and declared that Dr Wall was a romantic fool and he wanted to hear no more of him.

Henry, who was a young man at the time, had no doubt the man must be some kind of genius and longed to be able to do something similar. Not, it must be said, for altruistic reasons but because Henry thought nothing could be more satisfying than knowing that every man in town knew his name and would do his will.

He felt the same today as he had all those years ago. He wouldn't rest until everyone in Worcester knew his name and by God he'd make sure his boys worked alongside him to achieve that aim. St John's village was fine place for a home but he and his family had to be a part of the commerce in Worcester. It was unthinkable that he could look at it from here whenever he wanted but not own some of it. Unthinkable.

William must be brought to heel, and quickly. Henry had proved with Hugh that a severe punishment was effective and he'd do the same with William. Clearing up after them was taking up too much time and was beginning to reflect on Henry himself. Five years ago there had been that dreadful business with the slut who'd worked in the kitchen. She was gone the instant he realised which way that wind blew, but he'd never quite regained his faith in Hugh.

Young Hugh, who he'd taken in and given shelter and

an education to, had fallen at the first hurdle. He'd proved unworthy and had been packed off to a failing part of the business and told to make of it what he could, he was the spare, after all was said and done. After a very unsteady start he was now doing an impressive job. But he'd let Henry down once and Henry was not a man to forgive easily.

And now William, his own flesh and blood, had changed from a happy go lucky, willing child into a truculent and lazy nineteen year old. Just at a time when Henry was utterly dependant upon having a second pair of eyes. He had tried to interest him in his many dealings but William lacked any enthusiasm, his only interest seemed to be in chasing off into Worcester and gaming the nights away.

Henry had to face up to the fact that William couldn't be trusted. On the surface he'd agree with his father and be suitably apologetic when his misdemeanour's came to light but this latest business convinced Henry that his son was in fact a fine actor and, possibly, a first class liar.

He toyed with the idea of sending William off to the tannery and bringing Hugh home, now he'd begun to start showing some signs of maturity, but William was his heir and he couldn't give up on him just yet.

The epidemic of intestine troubles being now happily extinguished, it is thought proper to make a general application through all parts of this county on behalf of our infirmary at Worcester, and as is not doubted but all well disposed persons will readily concur in supporting this very useful charity, an addition has been made to the minimum number of beds so that, if possible, no person may be refused admittance for want of a room.

(Copyright and courtesy of the Worcester News)

CHAPTER FOURTEEN

Henry walked on briskly, his temper abated and his resolve strengthened, until he reached the site of the fair and could proceed with the business of the day. As a child Henry had loved to go to the annual hiring fair in St John's, the Mop, as his father's generation called it. It was a meeting place for those who wanted workers and those who needed work. The two parties could look each other over, perhaps wait to see if a better option was available and then reach an agreement.

Those seeking work carried a token to show what their skill was; a housemaid carried a broom, a milkmaid might carry a bucket while a shepherd often had a tuft of wool tied to his hat. Anyone who was prepared to turn his hand to most things carried a mop.

The sons and daughters of large, poor families would attend in the hopes of finding employment that offered a roof, food and a bit of warmth. Once people had found whatever it was they wanted and the deal was sealed the rest of the day was to be enjoyed. The fun could begin. Hawkers and pedlars were free to display their goods. Food and ale was available and there was always music.

Later there would be dancing and singing and then, later still, when the respectable women had gone there was fighting to bet upon; men, dogs and cocks. For boys who were confident enough to find a hiding place and wait there was an abundance of entertainment and education to be had.

As a boy he'd loved the whole thing, but as a man Henry found it a necessary evil. Men who were hiring people were usually doing well and it always paid to know who they were and what they were planning. By talking to those looking for work he learned a lot about who was not doing so well and that could often be even more lucrative.

Today for example Henry met a couple of good, strong young men who'd been let go from a landowner along towards Bransford. An old man had died and his son intended to move to the city.

As he spoke to the men he made a mental note to get along to Bransford in the next day or so to see if he could pick up some land at a good rate. He thought with some irritation that this was exactly the sort of thing William should be off and doing for his father.

He needed men to start clearing a vast swathe of his land, the first step in realising his own canal dream. He assured them both that if they worked well he'd see to it that they were taken on as part of a permanent gang when the actual navigation works began.

Worcester was a vital part of Brindley's Grand Cross Canal plan that would link the great rivers of England, the Severn, the Trent, the Mersey, and the Thames. Henry intended to build his own canal to run the length of his land down to the Severn before the Grand Cross plan was complete and thus be linked to the great rivers himself before anyone else.

Henry owned all the land the canal would run through, everything from the church all the way down to the Severn and each way further than the eye could see. He had the licences and finance all in place, all he lacked was an engineer that he felt he could work with. And a son he could depend on.

Yesterday one of those disgraceful scenes called bull baiting was exhibited in the neighbourhood of Worcester. It is really grievous to reflect that men who have not totally lost all feelings of humanity well be present at scenes like these which expose human nature in its most degraded state

(Copyright and courtesy of the Worcester News)

CHAPTER FIFTEEN

Henry hired the two men to begin the ground clearing work the following morning. He resolved to spend a few days with them himself and give William the job of working alongside Chambers to see if he could make something of himself.

If he wouldn't agree, convincingly, to knuckle down and work then he'd be sent to the newspaper with Sam Thatcher. Perhaps if William suddenly found himself with no allowance, but simply pay for work done then he might face up to his responsibilities.

Henry tried once more to talk sense into the young man but as he spoke he knew he was wasting his time.

"It's essential that you ride the length and breadth of our land every single day and make sure every man on it knows that you are the master. Those bastards will rob us blind unless they understand that we know every move they make. You must question everything you're told and, once you know, not think, but know, what is happening I want you to come and report to me."

He paced the room in frustration, seeing the blank and uninterested look in Williams eye's.

"This is your last chance to shape up and get a grip on our holdings. If you hear of any wrong doing you absolutely must punish the wrongdoer in the most public and brutal manner. It's unpleasant but essential. Word will quickly spread that you are not a man to trifle with."

"Really father." William groaned theatrically. "We have Chambers overseeing everything. Surely he's at fault if we are being robbed." As he spoke William was looking about for Chambers, he'd ordered his horse to be made ready, where was the damned man? He needed to be away before his father really hit his stride.

Seeing that his words were making no impression on William Henry saw red and he lost his temper. "I'm not offering you a choice here, you are my heir and this is your responsibility, the men must be made to respect you. If they don't they will take liberties, it's in their blood."

William sighed. The old man had smelt blood, he'd have to stay for the full lecture now. Damn Chambers, when he was in charge Chambers would be the first to go. He almost smiled at the thought, but his father's voice droned on.

"I intend to spend some time on our canal project, as you know that will make a big difference to our futures. I want you to take control here and oversee everything else. We've been over it often enough, let's see what you can make of it."

"I'll do my best but really I feel sure Hugh is the man to work with Chambers on this not me. I'm not so keen on the land, I see myself more a man of business." William declared.

"You'll damn well do as I say you pathetic, whining cretin. God damn you, to think your mother died giving you life. What a waste!"

This is to give notice that John Dale, living in St Johns near the city of Worcester, doth scale and cleanse the blackest and yellowest teeth and make them white as ivory, and that without pain to the party, he hath likewise and extraordinary water and powder which cures the scurvy in the gums and preserves the mouth, teeth and jaws to great satisfaction. He likewise draws teeth with great ease and safety. He will wait upon gentry or others at their home, if desired.

(Copyright and courtesy of the Worcester News)

CHAPTER SIXTEEN

Worcester was bracing itself for the Pitchcroft fair and the excitement in Ma's house, like most homes in the city, had reached fever pitch.

Ma's houses – and many of the other business's in town - would be closed for the duration. There was far more money to be had mixing with the crowds on Pitchcroft and no one for miles around would be found anywhere else.

Ma's party was a big one this year, Bella along with three girls and two boys from her side of the business were raring to go. They'd all been up since dawn trying on their best outfits and primping each others' hair and the whole house rang with laughter and teasing.

Every one of them loved the music and the dancing that went on and were grateful for the fact that as long as they shared some of their earnings with Ma she closed her eyes to a lot else they got away with. It was a holiday for them all and they would enjoy it, every single moment was one to treasure and remember.

John and the two kitchen girls were going as a group, they would buy the goods that would keep the entire household running for another year. They'd also made up pies and pastries that they would sell and again Ma would let them keep some of their profits. This was the one time of the year John allowed himself to have a drink and the girls knew they'd be carrying him home tomorrow. It was all part of the fun.

Dumb Sal tagged along with them because, as Ma said, she might be deaf and dumb, and she's certainly ugly as sin but there's bugger all wrong with her eyesight and she's as entitled to look as anybody else. The two lads who worked in the stables also came along for the ride although Ruby lost track of them very early in the day.

Ruby was expected to stay close to Ma's side and watch and learn. Fun was all well and good but now she was officially Ma's apprentice, learning how the money was made was more important, nevertheless she was infected with the same excitement as the others. Work it maybe but it was also a non stop party and she loved the entire thing.

As the happy group neared Pitchcroft the sound of the music greeted them, this was soon drowned out by the noise of the hawkers calling out the virtues of their products and they in turn were drowned out by the good natured jeering of the listening crowds. The music surged again and then the smells of all the food being prepared whetted their appetites and they made haste.

People came to this spectacle from miles around, some rode on horseback, or arrived by boat but many walked. Carriages and coaches delivered the wealthy, while boats and barges were moored at the rivers edge for miles each way, all delivering working people dressed in their Sunday best.

The ferries travelled back and forth bringing people from St Johns and Hallow. The Hallow people began their three day break in the traditional way by arriving at the Camp Inn in at Grimley and proceeding to drink that establishment dry as they waited for the ferry to take them across the Severn to Pitchcroft. The owner of the now dry inn would come across with them.

The fair was held on an area of lush common land lying along-side the river and was packed with so many people and attractions that it was impossible to see from one side to the other.

Cooks and housewives were calling to each other and the traders, all anxious to secure the best deals before too much drink was taken. Music came from all directions and singing could be heard coming from one of the covered areas. Horses were neighing, dogs barking, and children shrieking with excitement.

Ruby saw a very grand family group look with distaste at Ma and her followers who were all giggling and looking for fun. As the father of the smart family pulled his wife and daughter back in order not to touch any of Ma's group

Ruby tossed her head and, with a show of defiance, put her arm through Bella's and they leaned into each other and laughed. This was her family, these were her people, they'd offered her shelter and never judged her and she would stand proudly with them.

She felt a rush of excitement as they joined the crowds of people, most were laughing and all were pushing forward, desperate not to miss anything and determined to have fun. These three days were the highlight of the year for all and every second was to be relished.

There was something here for everyone. Stalls and tables were in lines as far as the eye could see decorated with all that a trader could provide. Ruby stopped to look at a cart weighed down with lush fabrics and shiny ribbons in rainbow colours all in a tumble with silver buttons and buckles. Behind her was a man selling clips and pins and the prettiest bits of lace and satin. Great lengths of fabric were hanging across boards and men called out the prices and would try to throw the gaily coloured material across a pretty girls shoulder if she stood still for too long.

Ruby's head was spinning in no time.

The Dent's glove makers had a display of the most exquisite gloves for all occasions. They ranged from simple lightweight gloves solely designed to protect rich ladies hands from the sunlight, through to delicately embroidered elbow length gloves to wear with evening dress. They even had a novelty walnut, which, when opened contained the finest imaginable pair of gloves. These delicate items were only ever used once and were considered an acceptable gift for a lady. Cutlers stood side by side with men selling pots and pans, all assuring passers by they had ready made goods or could provide something special to order. Richly decorated china was piled up on some stands, while plain and functional pottery was laid out on others. Underneath were piles of pewter ware. Kitchen equipment and furniture was set out as though in a room with the maker there ready to sell to any who would buy.

The tantalizing smell of food and drink hung in the air and was enough to make a mouth water all day long. Whole pigs lined up in rows strung up over fires, meat pies of every description were ready to eat, hot or cold. Sausages and cold meats could be served on hunks of bread. Also sweetmeats and custards, baked apples and hot wine were ready and waiting.

Along the river side was a line of wagons offering such delights as jugglers, magic men, freak shows and fortune tellers to entertain the folks as they ate their food and then, set a little way apart could be found huge boxing rings marked out with makeshift fences for the bare knuckle fighters that would be on later.

There was a cock fighting circle ready with the cocks lined up in their cages and covered with cloths until the fighting was due to start at dusk. A little further on the men from the Dog and Duck were already cutting the tendons in the wings of caged ducks. They'd do their best to draw a crowd and then throw the hobbled ducks into the river, men could then challenge each other and wager on whose dog would get them first.

The great and good trod the same path as cooks and housemaids. They rubbed shoulders with beggars and thieves and the whole thing was played out against a background of laughter and music. At every turn there was something to delight or amaze and gradually a giddiness took over the crowd while the traders and hawkers rubbed their hands together in gleeful anticipation.

Ruby had been in to the fair as a child but her mother had been seeking bargains that Ruby and her sister Ellie had to help carry across the river and home. In those days the fair was just hard work with a very long walk both at the beginning and end for a couple of little girls. She had never been able to appreciate the sheer excitement of it as she could nowadays.

The acrobats and entertainers would begin their shows

later in the day but the medicine men were already in full flow, selling cures for everything a man could think of. She couldn't bear to pull herself past any of them until she'd heard which miracle they were selling. She believed them all and marvelled at how she had ever lived without such things for so long.

The freak shows were opening up and offering delights such as the two headed lady and the snake man. Everywhere she looked ale, brandy and rum was being consumed in vast quantities and everyone seemed to be happy and in good spirits.

The reasons people came were as varied as the modes of transport used to get there. The wealthy people came to see and be seen. Business men and gamblers came to make deals, lovers came to do what lovers do as children squealed with excitement and youths were torn between bull racing, bare knuckles and the dark eyed girls like Bella who were deliciously frightening.

People of modest means came to source bargains, either for themselves or to save and sell on later at a premium. The hotel and inn owners came to buy the unlicensed liquor that their customers demanded. Opportunists came because when there's a crowd there's a chance, and a chance is all you need if you're quick enough.

There were fine linens and household goods to appeal to wives and housekeepers, whilst fashionable young ladies were anxious to see the latest offerings the dressmakers could suggest. There were Parisian hair artists and corset makers. Gold and silver smiths had wonderful creations made especially for this event.

It was a glorious, noisy, exciting free for all and Ruby had no doubt that heaven could not be better than this. Ma could see she was dizzy with excitement and tugged her arm gently, "Come on this way for a while. Over here is where the folks looking for work come to and you know I always like to see what's here. If I think there's a likely looking girl I tell Bella and she'll come and talk to the girl.

It's important to have something new to offer the regular gentlemen."

Ruby spent the day following Ma around and she saw sights she knew she'd never forget. Once she thought she saw Henry and she flinched and turned away but Ma noticed and took Ruby's chin in her hands and spoke firmly to her. "Don't you worry about hiding yourself away from him my girl, he's got a lot more to worry about than you have. You don't know your strength properly yet but he does. Mark my words he'll be trying his best to keep out of your way. Come on now, chin up and look the world in the eye. You're worth twice what he's worth."

She drew Ruby's attention to a handsome couple dressed in the most fashionable clothes and attended by three servants. With all the riches and comfort that the couple had it was clear that neither was happy. "I read when them two got married and I knew it wouldn't take, you mark my words. That's a mistake there, right in front of you." Ruby stared unabashed, he was an ordinary looking man, a bit solemn maybe. His clothes were good quality and she could see at a glance he'd never worked a day in his life. The woman with him was dressed in the latest style and should have looked wonderful but her perfection was marred only by the sadness in her eyes.

"Who are they?"

"That's Henry Cecil and his bride." Ma tossed her head in disgust as it was obvious Ruby was no wiser. "You ought to pay a bit more attention to what's going around you if ask me. Not at what nonsense to spend your money, I mean who is getting up to what. It's all gold my girl, knowing about folks. Gold it is."

They continued walking and taking in the sights until hunger dictated that they make their way to one of the covered areas, drawn there by the smell of food cooking and the sounds of laughter. They grabbed a bowl to share and found a corner to sit in and just watch the comings and goings as they rested and ate. Ruby noticed someone waving their arms about and she saw it was Mary, her friend from the Hop Pole Inn.

Mary skipped over to sit with them for a while and it was clear to Ruby that Mary had been a favourite of Ma's when she'd been with her. Ma smiled and closed her eyes as the two girls rushed to tell each other everything that happened to them in past few weeks.

Once Mary had heard Ruby's news she told them a story Bill had told her, that he'd heard from a traveller from Pershore way. This fellow was calling on a man who he'd sold to before in Berrow. The talk of the village was of a whole family that had been murdered in their beds. Father, mother, daughter and the mother's brother all hacked to death and found in a pool of blood. No word on who did it, or why. "Make sure you keep yourselves locked up tight at night, until they catch whoever did it." She advised.

Ma was having none of that. "Pershore's a damn long way from here." She declared. "And any road locked doors at night are no good for my business. Tell us something to make us laugh, that's the sort of story I like."

Mary's words and laughter tripped over and through everything. The other two leaned forward as they laughed at a scandalous titbit Mary had picked up from one of the porters at the Hop Pole. Mary always had the best gossip in town because the Hop Pole was where all the big wigs stayed. Ma looked at the two pretty girls, laughing and holding hands, both faces lit up with intelligence and humour.

"I might have known you two would get on well, you're both nosey little things with too many ideas of your own. What trouble you'd cause if ever you have the time to put your heads together."

"Don't worry Ma, whatever we get up to won't bring trouble to you, that I do promise." Ruby said with a laugh.

Ma looked around and saw Bill casting glances towards them.

Ma nodded her head once at him. "Get on your way

now Mary, I can see him over there looking for you and you don't want him worrying about you coming back to me, and your old ways do you? Oh, and when you've sweetened him up a bit, tell him I want some of that Jamaica Rum he's been telling all and sundry he's got hidden in his cellar."

Ruby laughed to see how quickly Mary turned and skipped across the grass towards her pet innkeeper. Ma nodded in approval.

"She's clever that one, knows how far she can go and where she's well off. I reckon you're a step in front of her though my girl."

They spent a few more happy hours together with Ma passing on her wisdom to Ruby until the sun sank low and the air cooled. Ma decided she and Ruby should make their way home. Ruby was tired out but buzzing with the excitement of the day and longed to stay and sample the late night entertainment but Ma didn't want her to.

"The thing is, Bella and her girls know what's going on and they can handle any trouble that comes their way. If you stay they'll want to look out for you and that might slow em down a bit and it 'ent fair on em, you should come home with me. The fun tonight 'ent really for the likes of you and we don't want any feller misunderstanding you and getting a black eye for his trouble, now do we?"

Ruby couldn't sleep much that night, she lay in her bed for hours and replayed every sight, sound, smell and taste of the best day of the year. When she did at last drift off it was with a smile on her face.

On Sunday about noon, his Royal Highness, the Duke of Gloucester, accompanied by the Hon Colonel West and other persons of distinction arrived at the Hop Pole Inn, Forgate Street, Worcester. After taking a view of the cathedral and other places they returned to the Hop Pole and there dined. On his Royal Highness's arrival here his Right Worshipful the Mayor sent his most dutiful compliments, intimating that his worship and the rest of the corporation proposed paying their personal respects, to which his highness returned a most polite answer of thanks.

CHAPTER SEVENTEEN

After three glorious days of freedom and debauchery at the Pitchcroft fair William Daventor had been forced to make his way home to St John's. He'd managed throughout to avoid his father and have a wild time but now he needed clean clothes, a shave and something to take the pain away from a black eye that was there when he woke up one morning and was throbbing like the devil. He'd lost much of his bravado along with the last of his money on the card tables and was hoping to be left undisturbed for a while.

He was caught, however, sneaking into the Great House via the kitchen and now father and son stood facing each other, both silent and both determined not to give way. William had the feeling his father had reached the end of his patience and he was a little nervous, but remained unrepentant. He was the only son of a rich and important man and he mixed with similar young men and lived as they did. Who, in their right minds, could take exception to that?

The fact of the matter was, his father was getting old and feeble and he simply didn't understand the way the modern world worked. It may well have been different in his day but his day was over and had been so for a long time. It couldn't be much longer before he was ready to give up any way.

William was almost eighteen and he was ready to make his own choices in life. It was only a matter of time until he inherited everything anyhow. Until then he'd just have to put up with the old man's crazy ideas and keep him as quiet as he could. Today could become a bit of a trial though, he'd been unsettled to see one of Sadler's men ride away as he rode in and he knew that didn't bode well.

His father began by shouting. "William you have sunk as far down as I'm prepared to allow. I have been approached by one of Sadler's men, it would appear he's owed a considerable sum of money that is now overdue. I understand he made you a loan when you were in some difficulty, and, as you've failed to honour the debt I find that I'm now expected to pay!"

William blustered. "Nonsense, that's a simple misunderstanding. I've got it all in hand."

"You have nothing in hand you idiot. That bill is now paid and your line of credit with Sadler is cut. He will not loan you another penny under any circumstance whatsoever, I've made quite certain of that. You have no idea how hard it would be to shake off a leech like him and I will not allow all that I have built up to be put in peril by a fool like you."

William put his hand up, wanting to stop the flow of anger heading his way, the old man was getting a bit out of hand.

Henry carried on, too angry to stop. "Today I plan to take steps to let people know that any debts in your name are no longer my responsibility and I am assured that no one will permit you credit in town. You *will* learn to live according to your means."

"Oh for heaven sake..." William stopped speaking almost as soon as he'd started and quickly leaned backwards, but not quickly enough. Henry's meaty fist had swung out and he was caught a massive blow on the chin which caused him to drop like a stone onto his backside. He sat still in shock as Henry once again spoke.

"Stand up and listen to me!" Henry barked in a savage tone that William hadn't heard before. "Tomorrow you will report to Sam Thatcher at the newspaper, as his assistant. You'll be paid for the work that you do and you'll learn to live on that pay. You were warned and you disregarded my warning. There will be nothing more for you until I decide that you have grown into a man that I can work with and depend on. Do you hear me?"

William was too shocked to speak. He looked at his father in amazement, the old man had always been distant and a bit tough, but this was all a bit much and the thought of going to work with Sam, that dull, bookish bore, was humiliating in the extreme.

Satisfied that he was not going to hear any more whining, Henry ordered William to keep silent and follow him. They saddled their horses and rode down to the ferry and then across the river and into Worcester with not a word spoken between them.

Henry was still too full of rage to trust himself to speak and William was still smarting, not so much from the blow to his chin, more from the fact that his father had knocked him down and shouted at him as though he were a stupid child, or an untrained dog. It was dawning on him at last that he may have pushed his father too far and he was afraid of what could happen next.

They left their horses in a stable-yard in the shade of the Cathedral and then went into Henry's favourite coffee house where he greeted a few friends and then, armed with a newspaper, a pot of coffee and a bottle of brandy he made himself comfortable. Henry raised a glass of brandy to his lips and at last spoke to his son. “Pay attention to your surroundings boy, this your first piece of training, a little test for you.”

“What do you mean, test?” William was smarting, from the blow before and now from being treated as a child in front of his father's cronies.

“Take that petulant tone from your voice now, this is your last chance, as I have made perfectly clear. Sit quietly, absorb and observe.”

Henry shook out the newspaper and spent an hour or so reading, drifting and calming himself down. He was aware that William, sitting opposite him was torn, he was angry and ashamed and wanted to rail at his father but at heart he was coward and he lacked the spirit to demand an explanation and the gumption to get up and leave. He sat and glowered but did nothing.

Henry drained his coffee and folded the newspaper at last. “Now then, look around you and tell me what is happening here.”

“We're in a grubby, sour smelling coffee house, surrounded by dull old men talking to each other and nothing, as far as I can see, is happening at all.”

“You are still such a child and you lack even the most basic awareness. The men you see here are far from dull and old and your opinion is simply an indication of your youth and stupidity.

“These are the men who are making things happen in this city. They are all, in some part, inspired by notices in pamphlets and newspapers. When something great happens somewhere in the world, someone else passes that information on and these men, and dozens more like them, decide that's the very thing that is needed in their own part of the world.”

Henry waved his arm about in a grand sweeping gesture.

“Information and ideas are what drives the world we live in and this place is alive with both. Someone must gather the information and pass it on to the people who write and print the papers.

“You said once you see yourself as a man of business, well, if you are to succeed you must be a person who can converse easily with all men, you should be quick witted and able. You need the ability to walk into a place like this and glean what is going on in an instant.”

Again he swept the room with his arms.

William was stung. “I am as quick witted and able as I need to be and if there was anything going on here I'd know.”

Henry sighed and shook his head. “We've been in here now, for what would you say, an hour?”

William nodded. "At least."

“So tell me, what are the gentlemen on the table to my left talking about?”

“I wasn't...”

“Very well, the group that are talking very loudly and

leaving now, what were they discussing?"

"I think it was about, ah..." William gave up.

"You have no idea what they were discussing because you are not mature enough to be interested. That is a fact. In time you will, I trust, become interested in your surroundings and you will care more. You may even want to contribute something. Indeed with a little maturity you might have appreciated that both groups are made up of men of considerable importance in this town."

William heard a snort from somewhere behind him and he realized with disgust that he was providing entertainment for some of his father's cronies. He turned scarlet with shame and humiliation.

"Consider this your first lesson. Men of importance rarely sit and chat idly, that is something that your generation enjoy because they know no better."

Henry picked up a drawing of the town that had been left on the table beside them. "Those men were discussing matters that will affect us all for many years to come. I mean us as a city, but also us as individuals, let me explain. Those men are all involved in the china manufactory at Warmstry House, they have a found new investor and are looking for larger premises and intend to increase their production."

He called for another pot of coffee and waited in vain for any sign of intelligence from his son. He sighed sadly, the boy was dull and there was no hope for him. Sadly he carried on speaking, still hoping to spark some sign of intelligence.

"These men are all, however, very worried about one thing. The transporting of their fragile goods. For much of the year the roads out of Worcester are impassable, due to rain damage and mud as indeed they are in the rest of the country. When the roads are dry they are so cratered and pitted that the goods are being badly damaged as they travel over the obstacles. There is no point in those men moving to a larger premises and increasing production if their delicate product is destroyed before it leaves our town. That was the core of their discussion. They have a big problem and so far no possible idea of a solution."

Henry paused for breath and waited for William to speak, he just shook his head, bemused.

"We have the answer to their problem, don't you see? At least we shall do once these canals are ready which would be very soon if I only had your help. By paying attention now we'll know who to approach when we're ready. We could move their goods on our canals."

William nodded slowly in a semblance of understanding and Henry thought perhaps there was a slim chance for this boy.

"The other group that I drew your attention to are the men behind the building of our new bridge, they are in the final phase of works and the new bridge will be open next year. From then on everyone who crosses that bridge from Worcester steps onto our land. Think about this, that bridge will be one of the finest structures for miles, people will come from all over the land to see it and copy it. They will travel on roads we own through tolls we profit from, are we ready? Do you know, do you even care?"

William began to bluster because the truth was he hadn't known and he certainly didn't care. Money came in and he spent it. Surely the responsibility for ensuring that the situation continued was what Chambers, the agent, was paid to manage.

"I can't understand how you heard so much of other people's conversations, when you were reading the papers and dozing." He said.

Henry shook his head again at his son's ignorance

"It's because these things are of interest to many people, myself included and they are often talked of. Think how much difference a new, strong bridge over the Severn will make to us, it could encourage people of Worcester to come out and invest in us. Business my boy, I thought you saw yourself as a business man. Your eyes and ears should be your most hard working tools if that is the case. Almost anything that happens in a town has an effect on people one would not immediately think of."

"I see, I didn't understand but now you've explained it to me. But surely we pay Chambers to be on top of all this change."

Henry almost gave up. He could do no more, his son was stupid and there was little hope for him. Sam Thatcher was his last chance.

"You're a young man, you have no concern about a second bridge or if the factory needs a better transport system so you don't even hear the conversations and this is why I say you're a boy and not a man. But now it's time to be a man. You'll work here, in town with Sam on the newspaper and you'll give him all the help you can or by God you'll be cut off without a penny."

Henry stood up at this point but William made one more attempt to change the way things were heading. "But you can't simply cut me off, I'm your heir." He protested, knowing as he spoke that his shout came out as a whine and would change nothing.

"I *can* cut you off if I so choose and I will, so make no mistake. You need to give me a damned good reason not to do that. Since Hugh took over at the tannery he's impressed me very much. He didn't want to go but he got on with it and has made a success of himself. I'm giving you that same opportunity. Sam Thatcher is a good man and a sound tutor, as I'm certain you recall. If anyone can teach you the newspaper business it's Sam. You'll start with him tomorrow."

"But..."

"Start with him tomorrow or leave here now with nothing. I mean it William, my business is too important to be turned over to a boy. Become a man and impress me or go and make your own way, I won't pay for you to idle your life away."

By the Warwick Company of Comedians on Tuesday next at the Town Hall in Stratford-upon-Avon will be acted a celebrated Comedy called the Merry Wives of Windsor written by the famous Shakespeare. The profits from this play (after paying the charge of printing, music and candles) are to be appropriated towards repairing the monument of that justly esteemed author in the Great Church in Stratford-upon-Avon.

(Copyright and courtesy of the Worcester News)

CHAPTER EIGHTEEN

Henry was more distressed than he would ever admit at his deteriorating relationship with William, he'd hoped that Sam Thatcher would be able to help the boy see sense, but he was beginning to have doubts about that. During his conversations with William he'd seen the expected lazy and dismissive attitude, but what he had not expected was the fact that William had looked him in the eye and lied at least twice. He'd hoped all along that his son was just young and careless, now though he wondered, perhaps the boy was really bad and would never prove trustworthy. He'd give him more time but his faith was being severely tested.

Certainly now was the time for Henry to build bridges with Hugh and see if he really had matured. There was no doubt that when they had last met, some two months ago to review things at the tannery, Henry had been very impressed with the promise the lad had shown. He'd handed him a business that was failing, and all the signs were that he'd turned things almost completely around. A surprise visit and inspection today would be a good idea, just in case he needed to bring him back into the fold.

The excitement and confidence Hugh had shown in the tannery the last time Henry visited was genuine then, and had increased since. He'd obviously recognised he'd been given a wonderful opportunity and had fully embraced it. He had several ideas that he put forward, and, while one or two were patently ridiculous, one or two others were sound suggestions and Henry encouraged him to push forward with them.

One particular project Hugh was trying to pull together was an idea he had to get the local glove makers all together in one place, rather than all working from home on different parts of the process. He'd had trouble making them understand that he could and would help but only if their standards were of the highest. He'd witnessed the success of the porcelain manufactory and saw no reason why the glovers couldn't benefit from the same working practice.

He also wanted to work with other materials but was facing opposition from the guild, who currently prohibited the use of sheepskin, being of the opinion that hair bearing skin is stronger and more elastic than wool bearing skin.

There were men, Hugh included, who wanted to prove the guild wrong and felt that the rules were holding them back. Hugh was being tested daily but he found he relished the challenge. He would make gloves and they would be as good as those made by Dents. If he had to fight for what he needed then so be it.

“I'm trying to find a way to help the glove makers see that working together will help them all. The work is all so spread out and difficult to control and it doesn't need to be. I also want to help them distribute more widely but it's hard, trying to change the minds of men who've worked one way for twenty or thirty years. Moving the leather from place to place is costly and several loads have been lost recently in different ways.”

Henry remained silent, but there was the ghost of a smile on his face.

Hugh strode about the room as he got carried away with his own enthusiasm. “One load got buried in mud before it had reached Birmingham. The whole wagon slid into a pit so deep it was impossible to recover everything. The driver has ruined his legs and what was recovered from the wagon was spoiled. Another load was stolen while the driver was resting."

He looked at Henry and saw he was nodding in agreement and so, feeling encouraged he continued. “It's a problem I want to resolve for them if I can, the men are starting to listen to me but they are still suspicious of my motives. They only need time, as they begin to trust me more I know we can be much more successful.” He couldn't have picked a better way to convince Henry that he was a changed man.

“Hmm, interesting." Henry said. "I've been studying transport for several years now and that's why I've been going against the grain and begun building our own canal. Something to connect us with the rest of the country is going to be priceless in time. In fact I've taken on a couple of fellows and they've cleared a huge swath of land in preparation. I intend to cut a straight line from the old barns through to the river.”

“I've wondered what you were doing there but it's obvious of course, I see that now. So, were you able to spend much time in Northumberland when you were travelling? The talk of what Bridgewater is doing has reached us of course but I wonder how true it all is.”

“It's the most incredible thing to see Hugh, the man's a visionary. His canal's not open yet but he's already demonstrated how dramatically his profits will increase. The speed at which heavy goods can be moved around is astonishing." Henry banged his fist on the table in his need to impress upon Hugh the importance of what he'd seen and learned. "Trust me, the canal network is the future for England and we can be a driving part of it. Not like all these short sighted fools who are watching and waiting to see if the whole thing will work. It will work, and we can steal a march on all of them."

Hugh poured them both a drink. He was uncertain of Henry's motives in talking to him, was this talk a sign that he was about to be brought back into the fold? He'd been banished years ago for something he hadn't done and his appeal had been dismissed out of hand. He'd had to work hard to overcome his feelings of bitterness and learned to stand on his own two feet. However, if the door was being opened to him...

"Just think how many days it takes to get a wagon from here to London. How many horses you use with every fresh team of horses adding to the cost, then add in the dangers that have to be faced." Henry was caught up in his own dreams and assumed he had Hugh's full attention.

"As for using pack horses, well that's fraught with danger and takes far too much time to be of a commercial use these days. But a canal changes everything, do you see? Two horses can pull a loaded barge ten times the weight of a wagon in a fraction of the time over water. All those goods can be moved without worry about mud or ruts or tolls. It's the way of the future and I want us, our family, to be at the forefront."

Hugh nodded enthusiastically, those crucial words, our family, had reassured him. One day he hoped he'd be in a position to show Henry he was innocent of the crime he'd been punished for, but not today. Today was a day to consolidate his rapidly improving prospects.

"Just think of the consequences for all our business interests, when the entire country is opened up to all of us." He said to Henry, striking exactly the right note.

"So you're with me in my efforts to move the idea forward?" Henry asked him.

Hugh assured him that he was with him but felt obliged to let Henry know what the feelings amongst the men he worked with day in and day out were. The idea of good land being ripped up worried the men with herds and crops and no one knew how much damage might be done to the rivers once the canals were ready to be filled. Added to this, over the years there had been attempts to canalise rivers at great cost and no benefit. There was a great mood against the canals from the ordinary man.

"They're looking at it from the wrong point of view. Henry spoke impatiently. "Rivers are subject to tides, and are already choked with craft. When you add in the lack tow paths and the natural bends and curves in rivers, well it's preposterous, that idea could never have succeeded. Canals are quite different, there are no tides, they'll run straight and a tow path will be put in place at the same time as the canal. We'll be in a position to transport goods anywhere."

Their conversation carried on into the night and before morning Hugh was as committed to canals as Henry was and he would begin immediately on a mission to convert the nay sayers. When Henry was ready to go public with his plan he wanted all obstacles to be behind him.

A new England was being shaped and they, in the landlocked Midlands would be landlocked no more. Henry felt much of his confidence return. Hugh, dear Hugh had managed to restore some of his faith. If banishment would only show a similar change in William he'd be a very happy man with no concern over the future.

The negligence of butchers and persons employed by them in the slaying of beasts frequently results in cuts and gashes to the hides and skin to the great detriment of glovers, shoe-makers curriers, saddlers, collar makers and other artificers in leather.

(Copyright and courtesy of the Worcester News)

CHAPTER NINETEEN

Self protection had caused Ruby to adopt the habit of questioning every story Ma told, and when the old woman showed an inclination to ramble pull her back in with a question. She had to keep reminding herself that Ma had made her way in the world by lying, cheating, and selling babies. She couldn't be trusted, and for that reason Ruby wanted to have some paperwork drawn up. Something to confirm that she owned a stake in all this, she felt she needed a bit of protection now she had even more responsibilities. She was going to talk to Ma about that. She'd always known she needed to make a place for herself in the world but since being with Ma she hadn't had to worry about anyone else.

Now the reality had set in, she was working very hard and Ma was getting more tired and less interested by the day but still there was nothing on paper to say she would one day own everything. Ruby decided to broach the subject one evening as sat together going over the accounts, as had been their habit for the past year or so, which usually meant Ruby spent the evening totting up numbers and coins while Ma dozed and drank herself into a stupor. Tonight though she wanted to talk to Ma so she made sure the bottle wasn't filled and ready for Ma when she reached out her hand for it.

Ruby seized her moment. "Ma, I need to talk to you, seriously..."

A pounding on the door surprised them both, no one ever visited Ma's private doorway. Ma flapped her hand as Ruby looked at her. Unexpected visitors at this part of the house were not welcome.

"Go on, you sort it out girl. I'm too tired to be bothered."

Ruby sighed. "Well don't start on the drink as soon as my back's turned, you know I want to talk to you." As she headed out the passage way she heard Ma shuffle across the room to where the drink was kept and she sighed. She'd lost Ma for the night.

She threw open the door in some frustration at the interruption that had ruined her plans for the evening, prepared to give the unwanted caller a lecture in manners. Banging out such a racket at this late hour, frightening folk to death. The business houses were open night and day but this was their escape and no-one was admitted.

The light was poor but she could see to her surprise that a lone woman stood there, she raised her lantern and cried out in surprise when she recognised her twin sister Ellie standing there.

Six years ago when they'd been separated they were like two peas in a pod and they'd not seen each other since. The intervening years had wrought such changes that at first glance they now only resembled each other in the vaguest way. They stood and stared, drinking the sight of each other in.

Ruby saw a girl her height with the same rich, brown hair, but that hair was glossy and coiled around her head in the latest style, a world away from her own scraped back, pinned up style. Ellie had a healthy roundness and a pinkness that spoke of good food, soft soap and kind words. A working girl, yes, but one the years had been quite kind to.

Ellie, in turn, saw a thin woman with no curves and no softness, all lines and angles, strong and fierce looking. Broad shoulders and a straight back suggested a strength and a hardness Ellie had never needed to find.

It took only moments before they reached forward as one, kissed and held hands, Ruby was instantly aware of how capable her own rough hands were compared to the delicate, shaking hands she was holding. Ellie saw a tougher version of herself.

“Oh Ellie, I thought I'd never see you again." Ruby gasped, so emotional she could barely speak. Ellie was as affected, she just squeezed Ruby to her as the tears rained down. Ruby gathered herself and held Ellie at arms length and looked into her dear face. "You're looking so fine. How on earth did you find me?"

"Let me in and I'll tell you all." Ellie spoke at last, half laughing and half crying.

Ruby ushered her in and closed the door. Ellie looked a world away from herself and her life here and Ruby thought that meeting Ma might be a bit of a shock to her fine sensibilities. She showed her into a small side room that was cold as the fire hadn't been lit in there for days.

"Sit here, Ellie, it'll only take a moment for me to get a blaze going then we'll have a drink and you must tell me all your news. You'll stay for a while?"

Ellie nodded her agreement and watched as her sister efficiently built a fire. It was plain to see she was used to working much harder than Ellie was. She'd have struggled to get a blaze like that going in such a short space of time.

"I'll go and tell Ma, my employer, what's happening and I'll be back." Ruby said once the fire was cheerfully burning.

Ellie looked around the room she'd been shown into, it was small but clean and the furniture was of a better quality than she'd expected to find from looking at the outside of the cottage. The wooden table near the window glowed and the wall hangings were bright and smelled fresh.

Ruby came back into the room carrying a tray of food and a pot of coffee. She sat next to Ellie and for a few moments they sat and held each other. After six years of separation touch meant more than words and both girls were so thankful to have been given this time together.

Once again Ruby pulled away first and began fiddling with the food on the tray as Ellie recounted her tale. "I'm in trouble Ruby and I need some help. I went out to them at St John's but she said I couldn't stay there, Henry wouldn't allow it, and I didn't know where else to go. Chambers told me how to find you."

The sisters sat up all night as Ellie explained the situation that had brought her to Ruby's door.

After Ruby had been forced to leave home Henry wasted no time in finding a place for Ellie. He said that their fathers bad blood must be running through their veins and he wanted them nowhere near his boys. He had no doubt Ellie would get into the same kind of trouble as her sister had if she wasn't put to work without delay. Susan, their mother, could stay but the girls could not.

Ellie was sent to a large family house over in Kempsey to be trained as a lady's maid. She'd been homesick and nervous at first but soon came to realize how lucky she was, it was a dream position.

"They told me you'd gone to Birmingham." Ruby interrupted sadly. Thinking back to all the travellers that passed through that she'd questioned or begged to carry futile, wasted messages back. Always praying one day someone would know of Ellie and they would be re-united.

At her new place Ellie was taught how to dress hair and was also given instruction in how to help a lady look her absolute best at all times. She learned to make a potion using beetroot or rose blooms to colour cheeks and lips and how to apply the sooty end of a candle to darken lashes, or the odd grey hair. She knew how to trim and attach mouse fur to hide sparse eyebrows and she'd been taught how to add this seasons flourish to last seasons gowns and hats.

Her employer gave her clothes that were too out of date to be useful for a lady of fashion and as a consequence Ellie now knew how to act and dress almost like a lady. It was a paradise on earth for a girl with a background like theirs and she'd spent some very happy years there.

Things had begun to change over the last year or so though, the entire household had to watch out for the old lady's rapidly changing moods. She'd become confused with age and was ever more difficult to please, however, she was the mistress so everyone just watched their step around her.

She'd started to go about the house spying on the other inhabitants, servants and family alike. She treated her own family the worst and her son's wife in particular was singled out. Having always had a good relationship with her in the past, the young woman was distressed that she couldn't do anything right recently.

The old lady started telling lies about things she'd heard or seen, and sometimes she would move small personal items from one room to another. Sometimes someone would get upset but the household had got into the way of helping each other along, mostly out of loyalty to the old lady who had been so kind for so many years and who had been dearly loved. Her recent illness of the mind was something the entire household wanted to help her through.

One night the old lady woke up and felt cold so she walked into the room where her daughter-in-law slept and began to build a fire with her clothes. Only by chance had someone heard the old lady squealing in fright and burst in to the room, only to find her naked and crying, while desperately trying to stamp the fire out with her bare feet. She was badly burned and it was a miracle that the house was still standing. Her son was forced to accept that the situation called for action and outside help. The doctor was called and then another came in, there was a lot of coming and going, with different family members visiting and then having meetings with the son.

Eventually the young master got everyone together and told them all his mother was very ill and that they had decided that someone must be with her at all times, therefore a nurse would be arriving and her job; her only job, was to stay with his mother all day every day.

The nurse duly arrived and, as arranged she took care of the old lady through the day but refused to stay alone with her at night, insisting that if she was to do her job properly she needed her own rest. As the old lady fell asleep the nurse would go to bed and one of the maids had to sleep in a bed next to the old lady. This they took in turns. That was when things became much worse.

Two nights ago it had been Ellie's turn to spend the night watching the old lady. At around midnight she suddenly sat up in bed and announced she wanted to go for a walk. Ellie took hold of her hand and asked her to stay in bed for a little while longer but she pulled away and climbed out of the other side of the bed. She was across the room and through the open window and screaming in seconds. Ellie ran towards the window but the old lady screamed out that she would jump if Ellie came any closer.

The noise had roused the house and everyone went running towards the noise. The old lady told them she'd woken up to find Ellie going through her things. She said that when Ellie noticed that she was being watched she attacked the old lady and she was trying to escape through the window.

"It's a wicked lie though, Ruby. I never did, I swear." Ellie broke down in tears at last.

"Of course you didn't, and no one would believe such a thing." Ruby tried to sound reassuring.

"He said I can't stay there anymore. He's a nice man but he has to take his mother's side. The old lady has taken against me and it just upsets her each time she sees me. I've lost my place and I didn't do any wrong. It's not fair, but I don't know what to do."

Ma sat quietly listening next morning as Ruby relayed the tale to her while Ellie slept in her bed. "It seems to me as if we've got another bleeding stray in the house. If she stays she'll work hard mind you. I 'ent having you tied up covering for her, understand. And I 'ent feeding her for nothing neither."

"Ma, it'll only be until we can find something suitable for her."

Ma spat on the fire and grunted. "Yes, cos a course

this'll do while she's got nowt else but we 'ent *suitable* enough for her to stay are we? 'Ent it lucky she knew where to find you when she was in trouble."

On Friday evening last, a servant girl of this city threw herself into the river Severn near Diglis and was drowned. The cause of this rash action is supposed to be the rough usage she received from a man who pretended to court her. A short time before she destroyed herself she went to her sister who lives in service in this city and told her she should not live long, that as she loved her sister better than anyone else, she had bought her the best part of her apparel. She also asked her sister for sixpence to pay a person she owed that sum to, told her what wages she had due from her master, and then departed. Her sister, however, paid little regard to what she had said, imputing her behaviour to lowness of spirits, and little suspecting she meditated her own death. However since the above shocking event the sister had been in a very melancholy state.

(Copyright and courtesy of the Worcester News)

CHAPTER TWENTY

It was with some apprehension that Henry made his way over the bridge into Worcester. He'd neglected Sam Thatcher after leaving William with him at the newspaper printing office earlier in the year and he was feeling uncomfortable about that, he was in the wrong and he hated to admit it.

The truth was, both the newspaper and William were a nuisance to him. One showed little return and the other was becoming more of a worry and distraction than he wanted to cope with.

His father had bought an interest in the newspaper with a partner many years ago. The partner had subsequently died and the whole thing was left to his father. As a boy Henry had loved to visit the office and now he thoroughly enjoyed reading the end product and was proud of it. It was the hard work that had to go into producing a well written newspaper that didn't hold his interest added to that there was insufficient profit for Henry's taste.

When Henry had first learned that Samuel Thatcher, who had once been a tutor to William and Hugh before they went to school, was in need of a position, Henry had seen him as a life saver. He'd wasted no time in offering him the chance to work on the paper.

Sam accepted the offer with alacrity and it quickly became apparent that he loved the paper, he did a fine job from the very first, and almost single handedly. It was certainly one of the best decisions Henry had made and he'd found that he could get away with going along once a week for an hour or two and things ticked over very well.

Sam was too grateful for the opportunity to do a job he loved wholeheartedly to complain about his workload, he simply worked more and more hours in order to get the job done. Henry had hoped that by sending William to help him out with the work that the boy would pick up some of his old tutor's fine habits. A bit of pride in a job well done would do that young man a lot of good.

Once the arrangement had been made Henry thankfully put the whole business out of his mind, until today that is. The newspaper had, as well as the local news and announcements to cover, two very important stories to feature in the paper.

The Worcester Porcelain works were moving from their original site in Warmstry House to a larger and more suitable site on Severn Street. The move was a clear sign that the investors now felt confident enough in success of their venture to expand. The Porcelain works was to be a permanent feature in Worcester and everyone in the city knew someone who worked for them. Dr Wall may have retired but his legacy would live on forever if the good people of Worcester had anything to do with it.

The other big story of the day was that at last the new bridge was complete and a grand opening ceremony was planned. The building of the bridge had provided work for a great many of the men of Worcester for more than ten years now and their families, along with the rest of the city were justifiably proud of the new river crossing.

Worcester was becoming once more, a prosperous and important city and it was vital that the good news was spread as far afield as possible. The newspaper would tell all of England of the prosperity and forward thinking to be found in Worcester.

Although the paper was circulated locally, once a man had a copy he carried it with him and it was normal for papers from other towns to be exchanged. News might be slow getting through to everyone, but it got there in the end. And there lay the problem, Sam could not be out and about talking to people and gaining personal insight and still be here in the workshop, writing the copy, managing the press and taking care of a dozen or more things at the same time. He'd coped so far, but it was taking its toll on him. In order to do the thing properly he'd worked night and day and the strain was showing.

Henry was frustrated and became unusually indiscreet. "I don't know what's to become of that son of mine Sam, he's not taken to the work here as he should have has he?" Sam looked down at the floor, reluctant to reply.

"Oh I know you don't want to speak out of turn and I understand," Henry said as he looked around for a seat. "But you've been with me for quite a few years now in one capacity or another and I'll thank you for a straight answer, is he going to be any use at all in this endeavour or must I find a place for him elsewhere?"

Sam coughed nervously, Henry was not known to take kindly to the bearer of bad news and Sam had no good to say of his son. Fortunately Henry had enough to say for himself and did not yet require an answer "Here we are today, the town overrun with planners and architects and Lords and Ladies, all clapping each other on the back and all with a tale to tell and where the devil is he? I'll tell you now Sam, he'll turn up when the hard work is done. Am I right?"

Sam simply nodded his head and Henry laughed grimly.

"You don't need to worry Sam, I'm no fool, I can see I must find something else for him to do and then we must find someone more reliable to help you out here. It's too much for you and I can't give it the time needed. I take you'll be content to continue here if help is available?"

Sam took this opportunity to confirm that working on the paper was everything he hoped it would be. He *was* over stretched and in need of help but he planned to marry soon and he wanted his wife to work with him. The two of them would manage very well together.

Henry was surprised, but pleased, particularly when he heard that Ann Yeates was the bride to be, she had worked in his house alongside Susan when the children were small and he'd felt a little regret when he sent her away when the boys went to school. He knew his wife would never have done that, she would have wanted Ann to continue teaching in the school she had begun.

Henry threw his head back and beamed at Sam, he clapped him on the back and assured him he would arrange for a wedding gift to be paid to him in the next quarter to start his married life in style.

"This paper has become very well respected and that is entirely through your efforts Sam. I've never had cause to doubt you or your ideas and if Ann is willing to work alongside you I couldn't be happier, I shall leave you, and your good lady to continue the good work here and I will try to find a solution for my wayward son."

Tomorrow the Act for laying an additional duty of one halfpenny on every newspaper printed in this kingdom takes place. We shall therefore be under the painful necessity next week of advancing the price of this Journal to threepence. Our numerous readers must be convinced that the extra charge cannot be of the least advantage to the printer but may probably prove an injury. We cannot but embrace this opportunity of returning our most grateful acknowledgements to the public for the very generous encouragement they have hitherto given to the Worcester Journal.

(Copyright and courtesy of the Worcester News)

CHAPTER TWENTY ONE

Ruby had known from the very first week that she arrived that Ellie would not be staying long at Ma's. Ellie had been desperate when she had turned up that night and she was very grateful that Ruby had given her a place to stay but they both knew that long term it couldn't work.

She wasn't happy in the rough and tumble house, it wasn't what she'd become used to and she struggled. It was dirty, it smelled strange, the girls were coarse and the food was poor. She couldn't stay here.

However it was unlikely that she would find a place in another smart house as a lady's maid. While Ellie had done no wrong in her previous position she would need a reference to secure another position as no one would give her a moment of their time without written confirmation that she was who and what she said she was. References would be hard to come by because the family were quite determined that no word of the decline in the old lady's mental facility spread to the outside world. Were she in her right mind she'd be expected to be the one to write the testimonial, if it was written on her behalf people would wonder.

Ruby was at her wits end, she had no idea what she could do for Ellie and her mind was constantly going over her options. It was something offhand that Bella said one day that got Ruby thinking on a different track. "Where's the duchess Ruby, I want her to have a go at tidying up my hair?"

Ruby watched with interest as Ellie set about combing out Bella's hair and in almost no time she had turned a tangle of yellow curls into something sleek and shiny. Bella bounced out of the room declaring that she didn't know how they'd managed before the duchess had come to stay with them and what's more she hoped she'd never leave. Stuck up though she was.

Ellie replied that the sooner she went the better, but she

could easily show Bella how to do her own hair if she wanted her to before she went.

Ruby realised the answer was there in front of her. She fetched a couple of other girls down and the rest of the day was spent testing Ellie on her skills and her patience. It was fascinating to see that as each girl was made to feel prettier, Ellie herself glowed with satisfaction. At the end of the day she told Ruby it was the best day she'd had since she'd lost her position.

There and then Ruby announced that Ellie would style the girls' hair every afternoon before they started work if that was what they wanted. She encouraged them all to experiment with the styles they saw in the fashion sheets.

Before many days had passed Ma noticed what was happening and soon became vocal with her irritation, she couldn't see anything but time being wasted. “What's going on now with your sister Ruby? We've got the smartest whores in Worcester, I'll grant her that, but it 'ent bringing in any more money so it 'ent worth it."

Ruby smiled happily and let Ma have her say. She was currently overseeing a clean up of the living quarters and was working hard alongside a couple of girls she was trying to train to be maids. Getting the upper hand with Ma was a welcome diversion, this would something she could enjoy.

“Your sister's still here and living off of us but I don't see her doing a hands turn of anything useful. I know I put you in charge but I wish you'd tell me what you're up to, cos I'm damned if I can see any good coming our way from her.”

Ruby flung open a window and shook her cloth vigorously before she replied. “I'm testing her Ma. I know she can't stay here, she won't do any of the work we need help with and everyone who meets her calls her the duchess cos they think she's more of a lady than the rest of us.”

“You could soon knock that out of her.” Ma folded her

arms and waited for an agreement.

"No, I'm going to use it. In fact I want her to be even more high and mighty."

Ma cackled. "I knew you'd have a reason for letting this nonsense go on. Tell me."

Ruby pulled up a couple of chairs and made Ma sit and listen properly to her plan. She knew her idea would work but she wanted Ma's approval. "I'm going to take a few rooms, as near to the Hop Pole as I can and our Ellie is going to become Madame Eloise. She's going to help the fine ladies of Worcester be even more fine, she'll style their hair and, for a price, she'll teach the fine ladies maids how to do the same."

Ma grinned and nodded her head. "And will she do it?"

"I'll see to that. It'll take me a bit of time to set it all up and I haven't got everything straight in my head yet, but it's a good idea, don't you think?"

"Aye, respectable too. I'll leave you to it."

"Not a word though Ma. We can't have any talk that will link Madame Eloise to this house, she must be thought to be from the gentry, fallen on hard times. No one must know anything until she's gone from here and ready to start."

"I taught you all you know about keeping your mouth shut, I 'ent forgotten me own rules." Ma snapped.

Ruby watched her sister flourish as the weeks passed, she was never too tired to help someone with their hair or clothes and she loved to teach the girls the tricks she'd picked up to help a plain girl look prettier. What she didn't know she made it her business to learn.

At Ruby's suggestion she started teaching the girls how to do their own, and each others, hair. This proved more difficult, requiring both time and patience but Ruby knew that long term it would be the teaching that had greater value.

The girls were very quick to let Ellie know when her directions were unclear and she soon found a confidence that she didn't know she had, she enjoyed sharing her knowledge and felt a tremendous sense of achievement when one of them did something they were proud of.

One of the girls, Hannah, who was due to have a baby in the next month, intended to go back to live with her family out near Bevere once a home had been found for her baby. Ruby intended to see if she would be interested in working with Ellie when the time was right. She was a pretty, delicate little girl. She spoke well and was not the type to ever want to go into Bella's profession.

In the meantime the right set of rooms had to be found and Ruby knew that by using the Hop Pole as a guide she'd be safe. All the best people stayed there and it was thought to be a very respectable place. Wealthy women would be reassured by their proximity to such a well known establishment.

Soon enough she heard about the perfect location and she wasted no time going to meet a Miss Peters. She was a gentle old soul who made her living sewing for those who didn't need to do their own. Her sister had shared her house making hats but was now unable to work due to poor health and as a result they now had a lot of empty rooms and an urgent need for money.

Miss Peters was anxious to find a respectable woman to take on half the house and share the expenses which were proving far too burdensome for her meagre earnings to cope with. Once she heard the plans for Madame Eloise she was delighted. Both she and her sister had been terrified at having to share their home with a stranger and possibly even have men about the place. The idea of a lady styling hair was something the sisters found quite bemusing but had no objection to at all.

It was agreed that Madam Eloise would take three rooms, a bedroom, a dining room and a work room. Miss Peters would provide breakfast and a hot evening meal while Madame Eloise would have to take care of her own laundry requirements.

Ruby and John set to work right away, whitening the walls and scrubbing floors and windows. Suitable furniture was taken from Ma's and either scrubbed or painted. Ellie began training Hannah and kept her fully occupied making things like nail polishers and hair bolsters from horse hair. Ruby sent John to place a smart advertisement in the newspaper letting the citizens know that Madame Eloise was now happy to meet and discus with any lady her requirements. Discretion assured.

At last they were ready. Ellie moved in and became Madame Eloise, frequently seen around town in the smart shops or at the theatre, always dressed in the latest style and as well groomed as any lady. Her hair was always fanciful and faultless, she was the perfect advertisement.

All that was needed now were one or two ladies who had an excess of money and a lack of natural ability with such devices and Ruby knew there were plenty of those walking the streets of Worcester. She was happy to sit back and wait for the floodgates to open.

At Mrs Ruston's in the Forgate Street, Worcester, is lately come to reside, one Mrs Fulon, French teacher, who assures such gentlemen and ladies who please to favour her with their commands that she will wait on them in their houses or at her own lodgings and teach them by an easy and expeditious method the French language, on reasonable terms.

(Copyright and courtesy of the Worcester News)

CHAPTER TWENTY TWO

Ruby tossed and turned restlessly in her bed. She dreamed of a snake slithering into her room and crawling over her shoulder. It hissed in her ear and she woke up, slick with sweat and trembling, knowing that someone, or something, was in her room. She opened her mouth to scream, then she heard Bella whisper. “Don't make a noise Rube, it's only me. I need your help, come with me quick. There's a gentleman in my room and he's in bad trouble.”

Ruby rubbed her eyes and groaned, she never had a moment to herself it seemed. She padded after Bella from the warmth of her room across the crisp mud in the courtyard through one pool of moonlight to another until they reached the warm fug of Bella's room by which time Ruby was juddering with cold. As her eyes adjusted she saw a young man, fully dressed but mud and blood stained, lying on Bella's bed.

He was mumbling nonsense and struggling with John who was trying to keep him still. He obviously didn't know where he was and was struggling to break free and although he appeared to be much younger than John he was losing the battle. He eventually gave up and slumped back down which was when Ruby noticed that one of his arms was soaked in blood and he had several nasty gashes on the side of his head. She moved closer, ready to help him and at last saw his face in full. She clapped her hands across her mouth and looked at Bella.

Bella nodded at this confirmation. “I thought I knew his face, that's why I wanted to come and get you. I don't want anything to do with this business.”

“Just tell me what happened then you can go.” Ruby said.

John explained that he'd been heading home from a card game and seen the young man staggering about the courtyard in front of the house and calling for help. He declared he'd been set upon and a man was killed.

Knowing Ma wouldn't want the sort of trouble that talk like that would bring if word spread, he bundled the man inside and out of sight and called for Bella, thinking at first he'd found a drunk who just needed to sleep it off but then he realised the man was badly hurt and not drunk as he'd first supposed. He could tell from the way he was dressed that he was a man of quality. He insisted he didn't know who the man was and he didn't want to know.

"You both go and get on with your business now, I'll sort this out. Send Sal to me with some water and rags." Ruby said as she took over from them.

John wanted to stay and help her but Bella was out of the room in a flash. John stayed, he was no nurse but he was determined not to leave Ruby alone with this potential danger. She started to sit the injured man up and knew immediately that his injuries were serious, but she thought he would pull through. He was in a terrible confusion in his mind though. He was like a child, turning where she pushed him and not resisting in any way but he was still muttering almost incoherently.

His head was cut and badly bruised and there was a nasty gash that ran from the bottom of his eye down to his chin. She did all she could to make him comfortable then sat quietly and waited for him to calm himself. It was dawn before he sat up and began to look at his surroundings, he was taking in the gaudy little room and clearly struggling to get his bearings, when his eyes found her sitting there quietly waiting. "Ruby? Good God what are you doing here?"

"I live here Hugh, the question is, what are you doing here?"

He looked confused for a fleeting moment but then it was easy to see whatever had been upsetting him flooded back into his mind. "Oh God, Ruby. I killed him. I think I killed William."

He told her they'd gone out the previous evening to talk and try to mend a relationship that had been fractured by so many years of being pitted against each other by Henry. They had been as brothers in childhood but were now almost completely estranged.

The celebrations in the city at the opening of the new bridge and the civic pride at the continuing success of the Worcester Porcelain manufactory had caused a mood of general goodwill and so when Hugh had received the invitation to dine with William he accepted gladly, seeing it as a gesture of goodwill, perhaps their years of separation might be ending.

William however, was still full of bitter resentment that he was expected to work and, once he realized how content Hugh was he began to drink heavily and his talk turned bitter. He insisted he'd done nothing but try to work with his father, even to the point of willingly going to work alongside Sam who was struggling with his workload on the paper, but to no avail. Nothing he did was good enough for the old bastard.

He felt that as Henry's son he should be able to choose what he did. He wanted to get Hugh on his side and as the evening progressed it was clear to Hugh that this was the only reason he had sought out his company. William could never understand why his father was harder on him than he was on Hugh.

Hugh bristled at this, he'd been banished for something he'd not done while William had been given chance after chance, he struggled to keep calm in the face of such petulant whining. “Try to remember you're his son, I'm just a nephew, he naturally wants more for you.”

Hugh was confident in his new relationship with his uncle and felt he must do all he could to help father and son understand one another.

“Well, I want the freedom you have, I'm sick of being held to account all the time. He respects you, have a word with him for me would you Hugh? I'd be grateful.”

He was, like his father, looking for a weakness, a chink that he could exploit for his own ends. Realising Hugh had no information or help to give, William declared that he needed a woman to round off the evening. The whorehouse in Sidbury didn't suit him as that was his father's favourite bolt-hole but he knew of a place outside of Barbourne, at the opposite end of Worcester where they could go. As they were at the Hop Pole at this time Barbourne was the better place to choose to visit, though Hugh would much prefer to go home.

Ignoring his protests William had cantered off and into the darkness and Hugh, knowing it was far too dangerous after dark for either one of them to be alone out there, felt forced to follow his wayward cousin. When he finally caught up with him there was no light to be seen nearby. This area was open wasteland used only as a grazing ground. They rode together out through The Tything, where there was an inn that was known to be a haven for anyone up to no good. Hugh felt sick as they passed this notorious hell-hole, they'd be in trouble if any of the men who frequented it saw them in their fine clothes and full money bags.

Once they'd put enough distance between themselves and the Talbot, Hugh asked William how he'd heard about this place that was so far away from all that was clean and safe. William told him that this was the place Ruby had been sent to in disgrace. He said he thought it would be an interesting experiment to try her out again and see if she'd improved her lovemaking skills in the intervening years. She'd had seven years to practice in so she should be better at it by now.

Ruby shook with anger as Hugh relayed that portion of the story to her.

"I felt sick when he said that, I saw red and lashed out at him with my fists. He laughed at me, called me all kinds of a fool and tried to hit me. He knew I had always wondered where you'd gone and why we never heard from you. He laughed at me again, so I hit him as hard as I could, he hit me back and we fell down and fought brutally."

He slumped back on the bed and she could see he was feeling the anger again. He was feverish and she wiped his face again with a damp cloth and urged him to be calm.

"It was so dark Ruby, I stood up when he stopped hitting me but when he didn't get up I kicked him, hard, twice. I thought he was playing the fool, you know how cruel he could be. He didn't move so I bent down to grab him, his face was in water, or mud and he wasn't breathing." Hugh began to shake and his teeth chattered.

Ruby sat quietly for a moment then spoke. "He's no loss."

"He didn't deserve to die."

"Was he worth hanging for?" She demanded of Hugh.

"No, but..."

"He's no loss. I'll help you get out of this safely, but you need to decide now, do you want to confess or do you want to get away with it? It's nothing to me, I owe Henry and this pays the debt. Whether you hang or not..."

"What's made you so hard Ruby?"

She laughed bitterly. "That you even have to ask me that shows me you're a Daventor through and through and could never understand me, so I won't bother to answer." The look of disdain she gave him was chilling.

"I'm sorry, I wasn't thinking clearly. Has life been terrible for you since, ah...?"

"Since I was raped? Since I was handed over to a brothel keeper as a small girl? What do you imagine my life has been like Hugh?"

He hung his head in shame, knowing that nothing he could ever do or say could close the gulf between them.

She nodded and stood up. "Daylight's coming and it's time for you to decide, is it a fresh start or a hanging for you?"

Hugh chose life.

Last Monday in the morning, Mr Wynniat of the parish of Broadway in this county was found in a field near his house almost senseless, with several marks of violence upon him, in which condition he continued till Wednesday and then died, without ever being able to declare, intelligibly, any particulars of the misfortune which had befallen him. The jury at the Coroners inquest which afterwards sat on his body brought in a verdict of "wilful murder against some person or persons unknown."

(Copyright and courtesy of the Worcester News)

CHAPTER TWENTY THREE

It was obvious to all that knew him that Henry had taken a mortal blow when his son died. He'd cursed and railed against his indolent nature for years but when all was said and done his son had been all the world to him. The day he had heard that his boy was dead he called for his legal team and formally informed them that he wanted to hand everything over to Hugh as soon as they could sort out the details. He wanted no more to do with any of his business's and the doings of Worcester were of no interest to him any more.

It was an immense burden to place on the shoulders of Hugh, who was still recovering his own health, but he rose to the challenge. He suffered greatly with feelings of guilt over Williams death but he consoled himself with the thought that perhaps this was his chance to make something good come of the tragedy. He'd strive to maintain the reputation that Henry was so proud of, he was now the heir, subject only to the paperwork, and he would protect and enhance all that Henry had built. He vowed he would never give Henry a day's worry in future. It was the least he could do.

He instructed Susan, the woman who had worked in the Great House all her life, to be sure to put good, hot food on the table at regular intervals for Henry and keep the house going as normally as possible regardless of what Henry may say. The estate manager, Chambers, was a decent hard working man that Hugh had always had a great deal of respect for, and Hugh asked him to make a point of seeing Henry every day on one pretext or another and report back to Hugh.

A notice was put in the paper, announcing the death of William and offering a reward to anyone who helped in the capture of the murderous robbers who had attacked him whilst he was out with his cousin and caused his untimely death.

Hugh grasped all the family interests and soon made them his own. He never felt tired or overwhelmed, he relished every challenge before him and in very little time people began to see he was every bit the man his uncle had been, if not more so.

He never knew exactly what lengths Ruby had gone to in order to help him that dreadful night. She'd given him a drink and he'd slept. When he woke the following morning it was to find a parish officer by his bed in the infirmary asking him for a description of the men who had attacked him and his cousin. They told him, with all due respect and solemnity that his cousin had perished in the night.

Ruby now a power over him, but there was nothing he could do about that. He knew he owed her his life and if she called in the debt one day, then so be it.

We are assured that a cock match is agreed on between the gentlemen of Worcestershire and Herefordshire against the gentlemen of Warwickshire and Staffordshire for £10 a battle and £200 the odd battle. The first match is to be fought at Birmingham and the second at Worcester.

(Copyright and courtesy of the Worcester News)

CHAPTER TWENTY FOUR

"Well, well, well." Ma said as she slapped the newspaper down on the table and looked around to see if anyone was paying any attention. No one was, so she waited a while and picked up the paper again.

"As I always say, you never know when one of your little secrets might turn into a nugget. How many times have you heard me say that Ruby?"

Ruby gave up, sometimes it paid to ignore Ma and sometimes it didn't.

"So many times that I think I'll bloody scream if I hear it once more. Is there something in the paper you want to tell me about?"

"Oh hell Ruby, you're no fun any more. Yes there is something in the paper I want to tell you about so, if it pleases you your highness, stop totting up numbers and pay attention to me."

Ruby sighed and laid down her pen. "I'm all yours Ma, tell me a nugget."

"Young William Daventor is dead, attacked by robbers they say, not a great distance from here it happened. Only nineteen years old he was, eh it's a cruel world."

Ruby didn't speak but sat bolt upright, looking straight ahead knowing that Ma had only just begun.

"He was killed outright and his cousin Hugh was left for dead, but them bloody quacks have patched him up. They do say there's a reward to be had by anyone who saw anything. Don't you think that's worth knowing girl?"

"The Daventor clan have been nothing to me for a very long time."

"Aye, you say, but we both know you was across the courtyard taking care of someone, not many nights ago. Now was that Mr Hugh you was nursing, I wonder? I only asks because it says here that Mr Hugh was left by the door to the infirmary by a man on horseback who rode swiftly away. If that was our John you better be straight with me girl."

"Leave it alone Ma." Ruby said as she paced the room.

"I will not. " Ma folded her arms and planted her feet. "I told you this was all yours to do with as you would and I meant it. But if you're putting fools like my John in harms way I want to know about it. He'll do as you say until the cows come home cos he trusts you. He might need my help though, someone reckons they saw the rider as he rode off. And I won't stand by and see John in trouble."

"No one saw John ride away Ma because it was me."

This time it was Ma who was surprised. "So what's been going on here girl?"

"Hugh came to the door, he didn't know I was here, he saw a light and needed help. He'd been out with William and they were set upon, robbed and beaten. I patched him up and then took him to the infirmary and left him."

"Why did you have to leave him there, you could have a reward for helping him, why hide it?"

"He wouldn't want any of Henry's circle or the other toffs in town to know they were coming here when they were set upon, now would he? I thought it might pay me to help him keep it a secret."

"Set upon! There's more to it than that." Ma was still suspicious.

"Ma, I'm not going to talk about this, I helped him out for old times sake but I want nothing more to do with him or his family." Ruby took up her pencil and began again to tot up her figures. Ma watched her for a moment or two then spoke again in a sly voice.

"So you're ready to cheat your sons out of what's theirs by right then."

"What a wicked thing to say, I'm not cheating anyone out of anything. What are you talking about Ma? This has nothing to do with anyone but me."

"Did Henry Daventor rape you and put you with child or did he not? Tell me the truth now"

"Oh my god Ma, is that what you thought? No, of

course he didn't, once again you've got it all wrong. I'll tell you what happened."

A few days since, a widow woman of Whittington near this city took a large dose of poison which in just a few hours despatched her. This rash action was occasioned, as supposed, by a quarrel with her sweetheart, in which he signified he would not marry her, notwithstanding marks of a particular intimacy between them began to be visible.

(Copyright and courtesy of the Worcester News)

CHAPTER TWENTY FIVE

Henry's wife Elizabeth had discovered Susan and her newborn twins hiding in the barn the day after she'd given birth and had brought the woman into her home. Once she heard her story she insisted Susan, who had lived in the village all her life, stay and work for her. The babies were to be kept out of Henry's way but they could all stay together.

Elizabeth doted on the baby girls and they were a comfort to her over the following months as she lost several of her own babies. When she gave up at last on the idea of having her own child she and Henry adopted Hugh, a distant cousin. He was the same age as the girls and they were all cared for together.

It was then that Elizabeth carried a child safely and gave birth to William but lost her own life. Ruby, Ellie and Hugh were almost two years old and William was less than six months old when Henry set of to travel the country leaving them in the care of Susan and Ann. They ate and slept together, and later explored, learned and fought together. They loved each other and were a team for almost eleven years.

When William was eleven years old and Hugh thirteen, Sam Thatcher was appointed by Henry as the home tutor for the boys, they needed to be made ready for a formal school education, their childhood was over. Henry was rarely seen, he found children and home life boring and dull so he continued his life of travel and devoted himself to business.

Because it kept the girls out of her way, Susan often made them sit in on the boys' lessons with Sam who was a firm supporter of the education of girls and welcomed them with open arms.

Sam taught them all so much more than simple classroom lessons, he taught them to respect themselves and each other, he taught them how to behave with other people and generally gave them any small amount of polish they had.

He put a structure and a discipline into their days and Ruby in particular blossomed under his care. He made lessons and learning fun and opened her eyes to the magic of reading. He treated them all the same, as did her mother. So much so that Ruby hadn't realised how very different they all really were. Until the boys were ready to go to school, that is.

She remembered the excitement in the house, new clothes and shoes were being delivered and plans were being made. Two great red leather trunks with gold initials stamped on them were delivered. They had shiny brass buckles on black leather straps. Ruby thought them beautiful but couldn't imagine actually owning enough things to fill one of them.

She had excitedly asked where her trunk was and even today she could still feel the cold, desperate, choking feeling of shame and confusion as her mother laughed at her and said that her learning days were over and it was time for her to start earning her keep. She wouldn't be going to school. That was only for the young gentlemen.

Sam understood her desolation and, in an attempt to comfort her, gave her a small wooden box. He'd carved her initials on it and inside were two books that she had not read but that he told her she must one day. Also inside was a blank paged book and he urged her to continue to read everything she could get her hands on and write her thoughts down each day. This, he said would be as good, if not better than school for her in the long term.

When the boys went away, so did Ann, to another position in the village, and Sam went back over the Severn to scratch out a living offering lessons from a rented room in Sidbury.

Ruby took over the cleaning of the Great House from her mother while Ellie was given responsibility for the chickens, ducks and a vegetable patch. Hard work and nothing else became their lives.

During the first school holidays the boys came home and things were more like old times, but William had started to change. After a year or so he became cruel in the things he said and was different towards her somehow. He seemed angry and impatient and he never wanted to talk to Ruby. It seemed that at school he had learned that his boyhood friends were not the same as him, not as good as him.

Ruby thought he'd just been away too long and the old William would be back soon. She loved him and Hugh and still felt like they were her brothers, whatever they, or her mother might say.

Until the day William cornered her in the barn. She kicked and screamed and fought like a demon, partly through anger and fear but also partly through shattering sadness that the boy she loved so dearly would hurt her so badly. The agony was as bad in her heart and mind as it was in her childish body. She felt the fight go out of her, there was one more savage, burning pain, a drop of blood and it was all over. Hugh found her some time later and helped her tidy herself up.

Ruby leaned back and sighed as she remembered, absently pushing her tongue into the gap that had been left by the tooth that had been knocked out in the struggle.

"Henry saw us walking out of the barn together, my clothes were torn and I had blood on my face. Henry being his usual self lashed out at both of us, Hugh and me, with his whip."

"Pig of a man, he is." Ma sounded almost satisfied.

"I ran to find my mother but she'd seen Henry whip Hugh and had made up her mind what had happened. She asked me nothing, just thrashed me, then stood by as he threw me out. All I had of my own was my little wooden box, and an old shawl. And two babies in my belly."

At this, she picked up the box and opened it showing Ma the books Sam had given her, along with a piece of faded ribbon that Ann had tied her hair up with once and then, in the bottom a folded piece of lace with an R embroidered in the corner was wrapped around two glass beads.

"Until Ellie turned up here last year I've never seen or thought of any one of them. And to my knowledge not one of them ever thought of me either. Until Ellie needed my help, of course, then she came to me 'cos she knows as well as me there's no help for us two over in St Johns."

Ma relaxed visibly, she'd had a look of horror on her face when Ruby denied Henry had fathered her babies but that had been replaced now by a crafty, greedy glint that Ruby knew of old.

"Well I thank God it was a Daventor what did it cos I've been keeping summat from you for a long time and it would have all been for nothing if it hadn't a been one of em. I should tell you about it now. I've kept a secret for all these years and I want it off my mind now.

At Mr Joseph Baddiley's apothecary in the High Street, Worcester is to be sold a parcel of extraordinary good French brandy at a very reasonable rate, either wholesale or retail.

(Copyright and courtesy of the Worcester News)

CHAPTER TWENTY SIX

"Do you remember Mr Watkins, Ruby?" Ma spoke quietly.

"Ma, he's the man who took my son, I'm not likely to forget that name am I?"

"No, but he didn't exactly take your son, that's the thing I've got to tell you."

Ruby was impatient, she didn't know where Ma was going with today's story and was, for some reason nervous. "I saw him carry my baby out with my blessing, do you think I'd have made a mistake about that. I had nightmares for months after as you well know, I couldn't sleep without laudanum. What are you talking about?"

Ma had the grace to look ashamed. "I don't know what I was thinking of at the time so I 'ent surprised you don't believe me now. I'll try to explain it. As soon as I knew you was having two babies I started to think how I could get more money for em. I knew you'd come from Daventors and I couldn't let a chance of having a double dip into his pockets go by."

Ma knew Henry Daventor from way back and though he'd deny knowing her she still burned with hatred for him. "I didn't have anyone I could talk to about you and your babies see, and I couldn't think how I could work it on my own. It was when he, old Watkins, asked you who the father was, it suddenly hit me that I had a prize if only I knew what to do with it."

Ma looked at Ruby and waited for a response but Ruby sat in silence, biding her time. She could tell Ma was uncomfortable and wouldn't risk putting her off finishing the story.

"He liked you, Mr Watkins did, and he liked the idea of you being the mother, so I let him keep the idea but not your baby. I gave him the baby Lily had birthed a week before you had yours."

Ruby gasped in horror. "So what the hell did you do

with my baby for God's sake?" She had to grip her hands together for fear of hitting Ma.

The first born boy, now called Tom, had been sent to a foster mother that had done wet nursing for Ma for a long time. Jane, the foster mother, had never been able to have a baby of her own though she tried more times than was good for her health. Being a wet nurse and foster mother helped keep her mind at peace.

When Ma had asked her to keep Tom for her she was more than happy, it meant she had an income from Ma and a boy she could make her own. Ma had never intended it to be a permanent thing, she simply needed time to work out how best to profit from having the Daventor twins in her care.

She felt certain she'd have a clear plan by the time Richard's leg had straightened but as time went on she began to enjoy seeing Richard about the place and never came up with a plan and never found the right time to tell Ruby.

Ruby shook her head from side to side, not quite accepting what she was being told. Ma was a liar and a cheat, as she well knew, but surely this was too much, even for her. She dashed the tears from her eyes angrily.

"Now don't get so upset Ruby. I didn't think it would do any good telling you before, you're happy, he's happy and Richard's happy. I didn't know what to do so I did nothing. But now, well your two boys are all he's got now. They'll get everything if we play it right."

"I don't believe you sometimes Ma. I hardened my heart to them both on your instructions. I've never let Richard get close to me and I needed Laudanum to sleep for weeks after they were born and now you tell me it was all for nothing?"

"I know, I know. To tell the truth it was making that mistake that made me start thinking that I'd gone a bit off track. I've never made any money out of your two babies and that's never happened to me before. I knew I'd have to tell you one day and today's the day."

"Does Bella or John know?"

"No one from here knows, nor would they care. Come on love, babies are ten a penny around here, who can even tell em apart? I wasn't deceiving you deliberately, I honestly wanted to get rid of both of them together, that's what I do after all. But you know Richard's leg was all twisted when he was born and I wanted to wait for it to straighten out and that was the truth. But I thought I was doing right but I didn't know how to make it work."

"Have you ever told the truth about anything in your life Ma or is it all lies and tricks and whoring?"

Ma pulled herself upright and planted her hands on her hips. She didn't like apologising, in fact she never had before but she was not going to have her nose rubbed in it. "Well now then Lady Muck, it's thanks to liars like me and whore's like Bella that you and your brats have all had food in your bellies for all these years so don't get too high and mighty now, cos it'd be a damn shame to see you fall back into the gutter."

"Oh shut up Ma, you know I'm thankful for most of what you've done for me. But you live in a web of lies and I don't know what to think from one day to the next. I swear Ma, I'm that close to belting you right now."

"No need for violence now. Nothings spoiled."

Ruby shook her head in despair, nothing spoiled the crazy old woman said. She now had two sons to be responsible for, she knew neither one of them and had no idea what she was going to do next.

Ma had more to say and Ruby let her run on. "Old man Daventor owes you, don't you reckon?"

"There's a great many folks are owed by him I dare say."

Ma slapped the table in anger. "Get of your high horse and start thinking straight Ruby. You're a sharp girl, sharp enough to know you've got summat all the others haven't got. He's going to be burying his only son tomorrow and you're the only person who knows he has two grandsons. Think what that's worth."

Ruby looked away. She didn't want any more lies or fuss or trouble because when the truth came to the surface it was all too hard to cope with.

"I don't say we go off half cocked but I do say, let's agree they owe you and think about how to get the best out of it for you and your boys. Just think about it."

On Thursday, Count Czernichew, the Russian Ambassador and his Lady, Baron Diedin, the Danish Ambassador, and Prince Cantimir from the Russian Empire, attended by a grand retinue, dined at the Hop Pole Inn, the Forgate, Worcester, on their return to London. They having been on a visit to the Right Hon Lord Lyttleton at Hagley in this county.

(Copyright and courtesy of the Worcester News)

CHAPTER TWENTY SEVEN

Ruby thought about nothing else, she walked to the spring and back and mulled over this new situation. She went across the courtyard and found Bella and asked her advice. Not hearing what she wanted to hear she took the trap and went to visit Mary, this also left her unsatisfied, she knew what she had to do and no help or advice was going to change that.

The following day Ruby and Ma headed out towards Worcester for a short distance but then turned left and headed up to some higher ground where there was a little cluster of dwellings that Ruby had never seen before tucked away.

Two or three cottages were up there and precious little else. One building looked as though it might have been an inn at one time though it was not very appealing now. As they walked past the middle cottage a small boy ran about and was playing at helping a woman spread some white linen out on a hedge to dry. They were laughing and chattering together with not a care in the world.

Ruby gasped at the sight of him, he was exactly like Richard. The woman with the boy watched them as they passed by and then she pulled the boy close and they walked together into the house.

"Let's go home." Ruby said to Ma.

Ruby mind was in turmoil, she'd lived for almost ten years denying her sons, making a life without them and now she found she was responsible for two young boys, both in need of an education. In order to try to distract herself she spent as much time as she could with Ellie, having learned a long time ago that getting on with some honest hard work was always the best way, an answer would come.

Madame Eloise and her services had become very highly sought after amongst the great and the good of Worcester. The little enterprise that Ruby had hoped would make her sister self sufficient had turned into something that was showing a good revenue and offering employment to several other girls.

In their quiet times Madame Eloise and Ruby were both enjoying rediscovering their closeness. It was different now, they were adults and there was a lot about each other they didn't know but they were both happy re-discovering each other. Ruby told Ellie all that Ma had been keeping from her.

“I don't want to get involved with all of them in St John's again.” Ruby said after finally telling Ellie what was on her mind.

“Well you know I'm not as keen on Ma and all that lot as you are, they are a proper bunch of... well you know what I mean. Bella and the girls are good fun but it's not decent really is it? If you can get something from Henry then you could leave Ma and we could even live together again. You could come here and live with me.”

Ruby was startled to hear this, she'd never led Ellie to think she was unhappy with her situation, surely. “Oh Ellie, I'll never leave Ma. I know what people say about what she does and I know what you think of her but I honestly don't think there's anything wrong with what we do. If she hadn't taken me in I don't know what would have happened to me. I *do* know I wouldn't have been able to help you when you were in trouble. She provides a haven for girls like me and service for the gentry."

Ellie thought she was mistaken to view Ma in this charitable way, every girl that crossed Ma's path earned money for the old witch, how could Ruby be so blind as to be grateful?

"All those tender little virgins who come here with their mama's to have their hair done prettily, well they're safe in their beds at night cos of Bella and the girls. They can sit on their honour and wait for the right man to offer them a wedding. We do all the dirty work for them while they breathe in lavender scented air. There's no shame in having a dirty job and truth be told most of the milk fed misses in Worcester are grateful that we do the heavy work for them, they just can't admit that they know about it."

Ellie collapsed in laughter as she acknowledged the truth in that statement. "So why do you keep looking for respectable work then, if you believe that?" Ellie finally said.

"I want Richard to grow up to be someone, I don't know what, but I don't want him to be known as just a boy who grew up with whores and baby sellers."

"Not even if the whores and baby sellers work for you?"

"Not even then Ellie. It's good enough for me, it's not good enough for him."

Ellie smiled. "And what do you want for you?"

"Freedom. I want to make my own way in the world. I don't want to be hiding behind some man doing what he says I must do. I want to be important enough to mingle with people who think they're better than me." Ruby's face lit up with animation. "One day I intend to rub their noses in it, but there's a lot to be achieved in the meantime. I want to secure the best possible future for Richard, and now Tom, of course before I can think about me."

She was speaking the truth, she had no shame about what Ma and the girls did. She was grateful for the chance they had given her and she felt comfortable among those people, but by God she would not be looked down on by anybody.

Ellie nodded her head, there was no doubting Ruby's sincerity.

"Ruby, I can't help you out with advice, my life's just how I want it now thanks to you. I've got all the freedom I need. I know you want more but I don't know what more there is. That's something you've got to figure out for yourself."

"I want more than to just not have to worry. I want to hold my head up. Just look at the so called respectable men of this town, you know the ones, they look down on us in daylight hours but come crawling around at night. They're the dirty and dishonest ones. Henry Daventor looks down on the likes of us, yet it's the likes of him that's put us where we are."

"So go and see the old bastard then, and make him pay. Go and get what you can, after all, Ma's right about one thing, he owes you."

Mary, the wife of Richard Hemming the younger of Castlemorton in the county of Worcester, has absconded from the family home and is not to be trusted. She hath since by fraud been in the possession of divers goods and chattels of the said Richard Hemming, she being concerned in carrying of the same to divers disorderly persons etc.

(Copyright and courtesy of the Worcester News)

CHAPTER TWENTY EIGHT

Ruby stepped off the ferry and walked steadily uphill, she passed through the dairy fields that she'd once known so well but were now changed beyond recognition by Henry's canal works. She strolled through the remains of the old copse and then, as she reached the top of the slope she saw the Great House looming over all that lay below, its darkened windows giving the impression that the old house was looking down on all the rest of the world in judgement. She shuddered, then straightened her shoulders and moved briskly forward.

After seven years away she'd noticed a few changes to the village but nothing that compared to the changes she felt within herself. She had a job to do here and, once it was done she'd never have to come back.

As she walked under the archway at the start of the walk to the Great House she took the path that led to the side of the house, a servants entrance was just fine by her. She turned the corner and there right in front of her, arms full of clean white linen stood Susan, her mother. Exactly where she'd been standing the night she'd watched Ruby being taken away all those years ago.

"Ruby! What are you doing back here?" Susan dropped the linen in the mud, her surprise and fear at seeing her daughter here on Daventors land was so great. She bent and struggled to pick up the now soiled linen.

Ruby stood and watched her. "It's been a long time, aren't you pleased to see me Ma?"

"You can't be found here today Ruby, Mr Henry is away burying his son and you should show the man some respect. Go now, before he finds you here."

"Is that all you want to say to me Ma? It's been seven years since you watched as he threw me away like last nights shit. Did you never give me a thought in all that time?"

Her mother kept twisting the bundle of linens. "Ruby,

don't cause trouble for me."

"My business here is with him, not you. Trouble or not, I couldn't say. You'll have to ask him when I've gone. I thought you might want to see me, as I'm here."

Her mother wouldn't reply, she just shook her head and turned away.

"You're so worried about him coming back and finding me here aren't you? Well it'll happen, so go and hide in the chicken run if that's how you feel, but here I am and here I stay until I've said my piece." She was so enraged at her mother's lack of interest in her that she hadn't heard Henry walk up behind her.

"Well here I am Ruby Morgan." He boomed. "Standing right behind you, so say what you will then go. Your mother has work to do and you're keeping her from it."

She turned round and looked directly at him, he was still tall and arrogant looking, but now he was thin and so much older. She could smell the drink on him and noticed the way he leant on Hugh for support. He's an old man, she thought with surprise.

Hugh held Daventors arm steady but his attention was fixed on Ruby. He was white faced and with panic in his eyes.

She took a deep breath and began. "Mr Daventor, as long as my mother lives here she'll have work to do and I don't think that will ever change. I'm sure that when she gets too old to be any use you'll shoot her in the head as you would an old mule, then use her skin for gloves. Can't waste food on those that can't work, I remember hearing you say."

Henry looked about him and called for Chambers but Ruby carried on, she had something to say and was determined to finish it now.

"I came to remind you that you have an heir, he's seven years old and you've never met him, but I wouldn't want him to entirely slip your mind. You've neglected him shamefully of course, but don't worry, I made sure he came to no harm."

"What trick are you trying now you whore? After all that I've had to deal with."

"No trick, I heard that William was killed and thought it was time you met his son. Of course he never knew his father but he's always had me. It's sad that he was cheated out of knowing his grandparents, but that was your choice and he's happy enough."

"What are you saying? I'll have you whipped, telling such lies about my dead son. Don't sully his name on the day I buried him." She smiled suddenly, shocking him. She realized he was afraid and she had no need to be.

"Your son raped me years ago and you threw me out. You didn't give me a chance to tell you, and I know that William never would. He was far too much of a coward to ever let you see what he was really like. However, I am the mother of his son, and *you* are his absent grandfather. I want nothing from you, I have all I need. The knowledge that I'm bringing up your heir is satisfaction enough. I have him and you never will."

She nodded her head as Henry staggered and Hugh struggled to hold him upright.

"Ruby, stop this now." Her mother pleaded as she rushed to take Henry's other arm.

She shook her head and continued to speak. "You thought it was Hugh didn't you, but once again Mr Daventor, you got something wrong."

"It was Hugh!" The old man shouted and looked at them both with a strange, pleading light in his eyes. "I saw you both together with my own eyes, you were dragging my nephew down into your gutter. That is why I sent you both elsewhere. Hugh, please?"

Hugh shook his head, he couldn't speak, he was so afraid that Ruby might tell Henry that he'd killed his son, it was all he could do to stand here.

"What you saw was Hugh trying to console me after your son had brutally forced himself upon me. You saw that and reached a conclusion. The wrong one. And you threw me out without a second thought."

Finally, with a nod of acknowledgement to Hugh, she turned and walked away from the silent group. When she reached the gateway she turned and looked back, her mother and Henry were standing side by side staring after her in shocked silence while Hugh now had a look of ill disguised admiration on his face.

"If either of you would care to meet your grandson, you'll have to come to us. We can usually be found in the best brothel in Worcester. It's where you sent me and it's where I stayed. I'm sure you'll find us with no trouble."

The three of them watched in silence as Ruby marched proudly out of the courtyard with her head held high. Once he was sure she had gone Henry went into the house with Hugh close behind. He exchanged not a word with Susan. The death of William had knocked the life out of him but somehow knowing there could be a child of his out there somewhere had revived him to a degree. Some off Henry's spirit was still in there and ready for battle.

"Tell me what you know of this business, all of it." He demanded of Hugh.

"She spoke the truth, Sir. William had forced himself on her, that was what she was crying about when I found her. I was just helping her. It was no more than that, I swear."

Henry blindly grabbed for the back of a chair and sat down heavily. He reached for the brandy bottle and poured himself a large measure then shook the bottle towards Hugh in invitation. One he accepted with alacrity.

Hugh tried to speak but Henry held up his hand for silence. "William left me a son." His voice was low but there was a hint of question still there.

Hugh nodded.

"Do you understand what that means? I have a grandson, my own flesh and blood is being brought up by sluts in a cheap brothel. This changes everything don't you see?"

Hugh looked at Henry, his future as the heir was going to slip away from him before it was really there, gone in a heartbeat. He helped himself to more brandy and resigned himself to being forever at the mercy of Henry and his whims.

Henry broke the silence. “We must make haste to Worcester. I want to meet my grandson and I want you with me. You're my family Hugh, you must be with me. This won't change things for you though, I've given you my word, so don't you worry. This is yours and I won't be changing that. But this boy, if he's ours, will take over when you're done. He might be no good, her blood's poor and to be truthful I was worried about William ever shaping up. There's not a lot of chance that he'll be worth much but blood is blood. He's ours though and we will have him. We need to plan our way carefully, that slut was devious as a child and she's spent years mixing with the scum of the city so she'll be tricky.” Hugh breathed a little easier, perhaps all was not lost.

There followed several days of planning but at last they were ready to reclaim their boy. Henry had consulted his lawyers and thought long and hard about what he might have to do in order to claim his blood. The lawyers had urged caution, the girl could be trying to trick him. But in his heart he knew what she'd said was true, he dismissed their concerns and proceeded in his own way.

Together Henry and Hugh rode briskly down the sloped ground and rang for the ferry to cross them into Worcester. The new bridge was open but was still drawing crowds of onlookers and a parade of local business men and landowners were all there, accepting the plaudits being bandied about as though they had built the damned bridge themselves.

Henry wanted his private business dealt with as quickly and as quietly as possible and should he cross the bridge someone would see him and either delay or question him. The ferry man knew enough to do the job in hand and to keep his mouth shut about Daventor and his comings and goings.

The ferry reached the other side and they headed up the slope that led from the rivers edge up to the new porcelain manufactory. Once here they re-mounted and then rode on up, passing behind the cathedral and into the town.

They rode briskly through the main thoroughfare and many people stopped to look and nod an acknowledgement to them as they passed by. Henry nodded graciously to anyone he thought worth his while and ignored the others. In this manner they travelled the length of Worcester and out through the other side. Once they were clear of the City they paused for a rest and Henry looked across to his left and saw the river glinting in the sunlight as it passed through Worcester, teeming with all manner of craft bringing goods in and out and adding to the riches of his city.

It was a heart warming sight, all that commerce being conducted before his very eyes. He shook himself out of his day-dream, he had work to do and he needed his wits about him. He nodded to Hugh and they continued their journey past the odd scattered building to at last find themselves at the ramshackle collection of houses on the far side of Barbourne that had proved a haven to so many lost souls over the years.

Henry stood with his feet planted apart and glared at the buildings as though to intimidate them. He nodded to himself after a moment and approached the biggest door in the centre of the buildings. As they got within touching distance the door swung open to reveal Bella in all her glory waiting to greet them. Bella, who could smell a full money bag a mile off, and would be first in the running to relieve the owner of his gold, given half a chance. “Come along in gents, let me find you a drink and a companion each. I hope you'll be spending the evening with us.”

“We will not, slut." Henry began to bluster. "We have other business in mind. Where's your mistress?”

Bella grinned and licked her lips. “I'm all the mistress you might want Sir, just tell me what you fancy and I can provide it. You won't be disappointed I swear.”

Henry pushed her away from him with a sneer of disgust. “I've come to get my grandson, now stop wasting my time. Where is your mistress?”

Bella stood up straight and looked him proudly in the eye. “I'm the mistress here and I don't know anything about no grandson. But I will say if he's old enough to have found his way here, he's old enough to be left alone to enjoy himself. You're welcome to stay and enjoy a drink with me if you wish, but I will not be showing you where any of my customers are.”

Hugh stifled a smile at her games but Henry had no patience left and marched forward, brushing past Bella towards a door he could just see tucked away behind a curtain.

Bella screamed at the top of her voice. “John, come quick.” Within seconds the door that Henry was making for crashed open and the doorway was blocked by John. He said nothing, just stood in silence with his arms folded.

Henry cursed and turned back to Bella. “I want to see Mrs Jebb now.”

Bella smiled sweetly at him and curtsied, then she left the room as Ma made her entrance, smiling and simpering,

“Oh Mr Daventor, this is an unexpected honour. I don't believe you've been here before, but don't you worry, we'll find someone to suit your tastes I'm quite sure of that. You'll just have to be patient while we get to know you. And your fine young companion here, how good you are bringing a new face to us. I don't think we've seen you here before have we young sir?” She winked as she smiled up at Hugh and he flushed.

She tutted as she fussed about with a bottle of spirit. “Hasn't Bella even offered you a drink, my goodness we must put that right. That girl has no manners at all.”

“Oh stop your ridiculous nonsense at once you old hag,

if it's not one of you playing the fool it's another. I've come for my grandson as you well know, where is he?"

"Old hag now is it Mr Daventor." Ma spat at him, all hint of simpering gone. "It's not only Bella who has a lack of manners I see. You say you want your grandson, no doubt that will be the child that was born here some eight or nine years ago to young Ruby."

Henry waved his arm in dismissal of Ruby's role in anything important. "Yes, yes, my grandson, now where is he?"

"The thing is," Ma continued. "She was sent here when she was but a child herself and I took care of her and her little bundle of trouble, as I've taken care of so many before, because I heard that you didn't want her in your home. Now you've changed your mind it seems. Well I have to tell you I don't make it a habit to pay all the bills for food and clothes and shelter for years on end just to give my investment away Mr Daventor. If you want your grandson back it's going to cost you a lot of money."

Hugh gasped as he braced himself for Henry's reaction. He was not a man to tolerate this kind of disrespect and Hugh knew how dangerous he could be when roused.

"Do you seriously think I'm going to *buy* my own flesh and blood, from you?" Henry's outrage was fearsome as he towered over Ma with his whip in his hand. His rage was terrible to see but Ma had faced worse and was more than a match for him, she was also secure in the knowledge that John and the boys were simply waiting for her signal and she'd be out of harms way.

She stood her ground and looked up into Henry's face. "You couldn't wait to see the back of that bit of trouble and so I took it on. Do *you* seriously think I'm going to give him back to you for nothing now."

"If I can be convinced he's mine we can come to some arrangement."

Ma laughed at this. "You know he's yours, you wouldn't be here otherwise. No sir, we come to an arrangement first, then you can see him. You know full well he's your blood. You wouldn't be talking to *me* if there was a shadow of doubt."

She nodded with satisfaction as Henry turned to Hugh and the two exchanged a few muttered words. What they might say to each other was neither here nor there. Ma held the ace and they knew it.

Henry turned back to Ma. "So what do you want from me?" He spat the words.

"I want you to come back here tomorrow, with a sack full of money. A large one mind, I'll let you decide how much the boy is worth to you, but by God if you insult me with a piddling amount there will be no deal. If I'm satisfied then you can sit down with me and Ruby and we can come to an agreement that suits us all. And just so we all know how the land lies, your grandson is not here and if you don't do exactly as I ask then he never will be and I shall make sure you never find him."

Henry stormed and shouted and shook his fists but Ma stood firm and he had to accept that he had no choice. Ma was in control and he must dance to her tune. He rode away at a far brisker pace than he'd come with Hugh trailing nervously behind him.

Someone would pay for the treatment Henry had just been forced to swallow and right now his horse felt the brunt of his mood but Hugh was in no doubt whatsoever that it would be his turn once they reached St Johns.

Ma watched them disappear from view and then walked through the doorway and into the darkened room where Ruby had been sitting in silence, listening.

"Perfect Ma. You're quite a performer." Ruby declared with a laugh in her voice.

Ma nodded, accepting her due. "Aye well there was no danger of me giving the game away, cos I still don't know what the bleeding game is. You'd better tell me what you've got planned though, he wasn't happy, leaving like that, and he's no fool, he'll be back."

"I depend upon it."

Her intention was to take all the money that Henry brought with him the following day. That would cover the initial expenses for Richards education. Then she intended to have the paperwork written up, and legally notified, to make Tom the heir to all that Daventor had.

Henry would be expected to enrol Tom in a good school and would be able to have him stay during alternate school holidays. The other holidays Tom was to spend with the people he knew, as he matured he would no doubt want to spend more time in St Johns and Ruby would encourage that.

If the plan worked both boys would soon be enjoying a good education and would both have the chance to make a future for themselves. Tom would eventually have all Daventor business while Richard would have all that she could build. As long as Henry didn't realize there were two boys she would always have the upper hand.

She wanted the best for her sons but she didn't need to have them close, she'd shut down those feelings years ago and would not let them re-surface. Daventor should pay for the harsh treatment he'd meted out to her when she'd done no wrong, he'd pay and she'd profit. It was a simple as that.

"My sons will be quite a force in Worcester when they are grown up."

"You're a clever girl Ruby."

"I was taught by the best." The two women looked at each other and laughed.

"Now then, Richard must be kept hidden tomorrow. I want Daventor to have all the time he needs to do the right thing before he sets sight on anyone but me."

"I'll get one of Bella's girls to take him out for the day, leave that to me."

Ruby nodded approval. "We'll stay here and do the business with Henry, then, when it's done and we've got as much money as we can we'll send John to go and bring

Tom and his nurse over for a walk nearby. I'll take Daventor out and he can see Tom but not talk to him. He'll have no doubts left then 'cos he's the image of William."

"Be careful Ruby, he won't like doing things your way you know."

"This is his grandson though and that's the key. Tom really is his grandson, so he'll see he's getting exactly what he's paying for. I know him enough to know he demands ownership of what's his but he can't stand children being around him. They irritate him so he'll be quite happy to have his heir kept at a distance, you'll see. He's a bully but he's not a very clever man at all. He's no match for us, we can pull this off Ma."

"We'll do it or bust trying my girl. What a day, revenge on Daventor and both boys provided for. I'm looking forward to the battle." Ma rubbed her hands together in gleeful anticipation.

Worcester Bridge - The trustees appointed by Act of Parliament for building a new bridge across the Severn in this city give notice to all such persons who are willing to undertake the masons' carpenters' and ballast work of the said bridge to give their attendance at the Town Hall on Thursday next at 10 o'clock in the morning.

Signed: Michael Brown, clerk.

A plan, elevation and drawings of the said bridge plus further particulars mat be now seen at his office in broad Street, Worcester.

(Copyright and courtesy of the Worcester News)

CHAPTER TWENTY NINE

There was a lot of bluster and bluff from Henry the following day, he argued and threatened the women but eventually the business was settled exactly as Ruby had planned and Tom's future, funded entirely by Henry, was now secure. He would remain with Jane until a school place was arranged for him. He could spend his holidays with Jane but would be introduced to Henry and the Daventor way of life at intervals over the coming years. At that point he'd be given the option to choose whether to stay with Jane or to live with Henry.

All that remained was for Ruby to arrange was the education of Richard and that would be make easier now she had taken every penny she could from Henry. However she faced a problem that money couldn't entirely resolve. Money and lots of it was essential to get a boy a place in a good school. But what was a good school and how would she know? Also she had no doubt that having a mother like her would be an obstacle to getting Richard into the sort of place she hoped for. However, as she paced and puzzled and snapped at anyone who came near her she began to formulate a plan.

There was one person that she knew of who could help her and thanks to Hugh and his night of horror, she knew where to find him. She'd never asked anyone for help before but this time she would beg a favour from an old friend.

To do this meant a walk into Sidbury, which was the far side of Worcester from where Ruby lived. It was walk she loved as it showed off all of Worcester, the good and the bad, the rich and the poor.

When she'd lived in St John's all the local children talked of the city and it's imagined delights and she'd longed to see it for herself. Occasionally they had been able to escape across the river in a boat belonging to one of the tanners, but it was always on pain of a whipping if they got found out and the terror of being found marred any pleasure.

Her mother, Susan, had always considered Worcester to be a den of iniquity, it was after all where her husband had regularly come to meet his partners in crime. Here it was that they would plot and plan and agitate for change, and where eventually he was to be hanged for his trouble. After that Susan had vowed to never set foot in the cursed city unless ordered to by Henry, and neither would her girls.

Since living and working here Ruby had grown familiar with the town and she loved it. All of it. Leaving the familiar little houses that were home she passed through the area that she'd named the water fields, this was the area that George had given to Ma in exchange for her son, all those years ago, and where Ruby came to collect water whenever she could. Ma insisted it was a God forsaken place but Ruby felt sure it was blessed. It was wild and rough and uninhabited, that was true and somewhere out here William had lost his life, but Ruby knew it to be fresh and clean. There were wild herbs growing which scented the air and attracted birds and butterflies. There was a small spring that supplied the water for their household, and cooled and freshened the air on hot sour days and passing through the area never failed to calm her.

Walking on into the outskirts of the city itself the first buildings of any note she came upon were the charity hospitals, one for men and boys was here. Women and girls were offered shelter a few miles away. These places were feared by some but they provided a last chance for many and the people of Worcester were proud to have such facilities available for the poor and infirm.

Next she came to Forgate, once an imposing opening in the vast city wall though the gateway itself had been demolished as it proved to be a constant bottleneck for the ever increasing amount of traffic that pounded through the city day after day. The gatehouse remained though and this heralded the start of the business area. Tradespeople had their work shops and store fronts here and all was bustle as men and wagons dodged around each other as they headed to and from the river in a constant stream.

Madame Eloise had her establishment here, cheek by jowl with the best wig makers. The seamstresses and jewellery makers traded from here as did the coach makers and leather workers. When searching for the right location for Madame Eloise, Ruby had become familiar with some of these businesses but could never imagine spending her own money with them.

The Hop Pole was one such establishment. Ever open and ready with fresh horses, a clean bed or a hot meal for travellers. Local people were also catered for here, in the evening great banquets and musicals were often hosted. Men could find cards and spirits in a room towards the rear, whilst nearer the windows women could take tea and rest from the rigours of shopping. In the evening banquets were often held. The Hop Pole was the social centre for a great part of the city.

A little further down the road were the tradespeople Ruby was more comfortable with. The butchers and bakers, the vegetable market and the apothecary were all in much smaller buildings, the ground outside them was usually mud and the crowds were more vocal.

Here was the infirmary that had been started by Isaac Maddox and Dr Wall, this was the dreaded place where doctors did the mysterious meddling that Ma was so opposed to. Here also were offices for merchants and clerks, legal and financial.

Ruby was curious to read a new sign she watched being put in place. For a small fee a Mr Hopkin, newly arrived here from London, would read your letters and compose a suitable reply.

On her left she passed the track that led to St Martins House, this building used to be another gatehouse that protected the city from the wilderness beyond, nowadays it was where the city sent poor orphan children, they were given work to do and in exchange were fed and given a roof over their heads. If any man wanted help in his workshop he could come here and pick up a strong looking child for a few pennies, so long as he would agree to feed, clothe and house the child.

On her right was the fearful area known as St Andrews, a terrifying maze of hovels and shelters where people sewed gloves in their homes for a living. The place was foul with the stench of poverty, human excrement and untreated hides. It was said to be a den of thieves and rabble. Ruby could see naked children playing in the mud, but as she stopped to look they stared back at her with huge eyes and hard faces. It was a place best avoided unless you belonged there and Ruby thanked God that she didn't as she hurried by. It seemed to her to be a place of utter hopelessness.

Next came the majestic Guildhall placed on the ground above St Andrews. This was the very place where her own father had been sentenced to death, at the assizes. It had been designed by Nash, who usually designed for Royalty, so people said, and that went to show there were people in Worcester were as important as those surrounding the King.

Opposite the Guildhall was the ground where a fruit and vegetable market had been held three days a week for as long as anyone could remember.

Set a small distance away stood the Cathedral in an area of greenery and not too much mud and filth. Ruby found a shady area and sat down to rest and collect her thoughts. The Cathedral sat perched up on its own patch of serenity at the head of the main thoroughfare of Worcester and appeared to Ruby to be standing guard and ready to offer protection to all the citizens.

By the side of the Cathedral was the old castle which was nowadays used as the city gaol, this was where her father had been held whilst he awaited his trial. She sometimes wondered what it must be like to have a father and then told herself if he was anything like her mother she was lucky to have not known him, he'd died on the day she was born and all she knew was the local tale that her mother had been a young and lovely girl with a smile on her lips all day long until that very day. Ruby found that impossible to believe.

Her mind clear and her feet rested she left the Cathedral grounds and picked her way carefully downhill heading away from the town and through the muddy tracks to her goal.

Sidbury was a settlement that had popped up outside the city wall many years ago as a place for travellers from London to rest at. When the city wall was used as a protection outsiders were not admitted after dark in those days and so lodgings and food on the outsides of city walls were in great demand. Nowadays though anyone could come and go as they pleased and there was scant need for the services Sidbury used to provide. A few folk managed to scratch a living but it was a poor place.

There was something here that Ruby needed though and she held her head high as she tamped down her nerves and bravely walked in to a dingy looking building opposite the Commandery.

To her surprise she recognised a voice from her past sing out a greeting. “Morning Miss, what can we do for you today?”

It was Ann Yeates, her mother’s friend, and the only person that had ever showed Ruby and Ellie any warmth or love as children, here, in this little newspaper works. She'd not seen Ann since that day she'd been despatched in tears from her home and seeing her now lifted her spirits instantly.

“Don't you recognise me Ann?” She asked, her voice wavering.

The woman looked directly at her with a frown that soon turned into a smile. In a second she was across the room and had both her arms around Ruby.

"Is it really you Ruby? My lord girl, it's good to see you here after all these years. Oh Ruby I'm glad you're back, I missed you and Ellie so much." She began to cry and dashed her tears away impatiently. Ruby was also struggling to control herself and eventually she gave in and let her tears fall. It was some moments before they pulled apart.

"Little Ruby, all grown up. It looks as though you've done well for yourself though, it's clear that whatever happened to you in the past didn't seem to do too much lasting harm. Come and sit here, tell me how you found me and why it took you so long?"

"Ann, in truth I didn't expect to find you here, I'm really here on business. I'm looking for Mr Thatcher. What are you doing here?"

Ann laughed happily. "I'm working alongside my new husband."

Ruby gasped in surprised delight. "Oh Ann, you married Mr Thatcher?" The two women hugged each other and giggled.

Ann pride and happiness was evident as she said, "Yes I did marry him, and you'll have to learn to call him Sam. But you must tell us where you went Ruby, and how you've managed. One minute you were there and then you were gone and no one would talk about it. Your mother, well you know your mother, she never did share much of herself but I swear she got worse after you went." She smiled and hugged Ruby. "Come on let's go and talk to Sam."

As they walked Ann kept up her dialogue of news without waiting for a response. "It is good to see you looking so well Ruby. I'll need news of Ellie before you go, there's so much I want to ask you, you must stay awhile. Sam, look who's here. It's young Ruby, Ruby Morgan."

Ruby was delighted to see that he looked exactly as she

remembered. When he had been the tutor to the boys she and Ellie had joined in their lessons and Ruby had soon come to trust and admire him and his gentle but firm ways. He insisted on good manners in the class room and she'd learned a lot just by watching how he conducted himself.

She felt instantly reassured, she had come to the right place. "Mr Thatcher, I promise I won't take up too much of your time but I need some advice and I would like to think I can speak to you and it won't go any further. I know you work for Mr Daventor and won't want to go behind his back, but I need help and I would like to ask that our conversation remain private."

Sam greeted her warmly, she'd been one of his most promising students and he was happy to see her looking so well and self assured now. He reassured her that she could speak in complete confidence. Mr Daventor was still the owner of the newspaper but he never visited and Sam was free to talk to who ever he chose.

He was overjoyed to see her and insisted on hearing the whole story, from her point of view as to why she went away. He and Ann remained silent as she told her story and both looked ashamed as she ended.

"No one would ever give me a chance to explain what happened you see. My mother and Henry both made up their minds and wouldn't listen to me. Everyone imagined they knew the truth and knew what needed to be done."

Ruby was re-living the desperate choking grief of those first terrible weeks, sleeping without Ellie. It had been months before she could stop stretching her hand out in the darkness trying to find her sister. All the love in her life had been taken away and, young as she was, she knew she'd never feel entirely safe again. She was happy now and she knew where she was going but every now and again she felt great sorrow for the children they had been and all that was lost.

Sam and Ann were both consumed with regret. Of course they'd known Ruby had done something to enrage

Henry. He was a man who told the world when he felt he'd been let down, and he was very vocal about Ruby and her failings.

Both of them felt that they should have done more to find her but they had lost their positions at the same time and their priorities had been to find work and shelter. Ruby, and Ellie, had been allowed to slip from their minds.

Sam broke the silence. "So how can we help you now Ruby? Tell us what you want and be assured if we can help you we will."

She told them all about her son Richard, how quick and clever he was. His kind nature and his willingness to run errands for anyone who asked him, and the fear she had that if she didn't get him out and away from Ma's he'd fall into that lifestyle. It was a good life for her and she felt no shame in it but she wanted something better for her son.

"All I want is some advice. I want him to be educated, properly and I don't know how to go about it. I do remember it was very hard for William and Hugh when they first went away to school and I don't want my boy to suffer any more than he'll have to, but he must go away."

This was Sam's field of expertise after all, and she knew as well as anyone that he was an advocate of education for all. He told her that in his opinion they should start now if possible. Their age wasn't the only reason for the bullying that William and Hugh suffered in their early years at school. Their manners were oafish compared to boys who'd been schooled from a much earlier age and they were behind the other boys in their studies.

He wanted to meet Richard for himself and then think where might be best to send him. "But Ruby you must understand that sending him away to school will cost you so much. Money of course, he'll need to be fully kitted out, but it will cost you more than just money, he'll change beyond all recognition and you won't. He may grow to be ashamed of his humble start in life, are you certain that you're prepared for that, he won't be your little boy any more."

"He's not my little boy now Sam. I've made sure of that all through his life."

She'd never wanted a child, his birth had been an accident and she'd never allowed herself to indulge in maternal feelings. He was an adorable little boy but she forced herself to keep him at arms length. He knew her as just another aunt, the one who'd give him jobs to do and was kind and encouraging when he did well. She was the one who pushed him to run and play, jump and climb trees and never to allow his limp to stop him. She was the one who made him practice his letters at night and he grew used to striving for her approval.

"I want him to be a decent man who can provide for himself. I believe, thanks to my lessons with you that a good education is crucial and I believe it's my responsibility to provide it. I want to be a better mother to him than my mother was to us."

Sam had a friend, someone he had been at school with himself, who had opened a preparatory school for boys in Malvern. This could be exactly the right place to start the boy's education properly. The school was still very small and yet to have earned a good reputation. This would enable Richard to benefit from close supervision of his overall attitude and manners. He could attend the Malvern school for a year or two and be brought up to speed quickly and effectively, it would then be a small step into one of the bigger schools once he was ready. Sam volunteered to act as a go between if Ruby would allow him a free hand.

Of course she agreed, this was more help than she had dared hope for. Sam's only concern was that once at school Richard would be questioned by the other boys, they would all discuss their own lives, homes and parents. It would be helpful if they could find some ready answers that would not isolate him.

"We've always told him his parents are dead and that

I'm his aunt, I've never wanted him to get close to me for both our sakes. I knew he would have to leave one day if he was to have a better life than me. He's starting to ask questions now and that's another reason to for me to get on and get him thinking about more important things."

Sam proposed that he meet Richard as soon as possible, assuming they liked one another, then Richard could stay with him and Ann until a place could be found for him at the school. This way when boys asked him things about home and family, Sam and Ann would be the people he could talk about. They could both also introduce him to the behaviours and habits he'd need to practice until they became second nature.

"Sam, thank you. I had hoped you could give me advice but I hadn't expected anything like this happening. I can see what an opportunity that would be and I'll do whatever you tell me I must. It's so good of you to offer to undertake all of this."

Sam put his hand up to stop her speaking. He apologised for letting her disappear as a child and not looking for her. Being able to help her son make his way in life would help Sam come to terms with the fact that he'd failed her. He went on to explain that it was extraordinary that she had chosen today to visit. He'd been putting the finishing touches to a story he would be running tomorrow.

Catherine Higgs had been brought to the goal at Worcester just a few days ago. She would stand trial for the murder of her baby daughter and if found guilty would hang. Sam had wondered at the desperation the woman must have felt to have committed such an act.

He gave thanks that, although he had not been there for her, at least Ruby did find a place of safety in her hour of need. Who knows what could have befallen her otherwise.

Worcester Stage Coach in Two days.

All persons that are willing to go to London from Worcester by land may repair to the Crown in Broad Street, Worcester, where they may be furnished with a good coach and able horses, which set's out every Monday and Friday for London and likewise the same days for Worcester, performing the whole stage in two days; each passenger paying one pound and five shillings and is allowed to carry fourteen pounds weight; all weight above to be paid at the raid of two pence the pound. All parcels taken into the carriage are there to be paid for.

Note the master of the coach will not be answerable for the loss of money, jewels, watches or plate.

CHAPTER THIRTY

Preparing Tom and Richard for their education and then sending them both on their way had caused considerable upheaval and excitement for the inhabitants of Ma's house and also for Jane, who'd loved and cared for Tom since birth.

Ruby capitalized on the general chaos caused by the various arrangements by implementing some changes she'd long been toying with. Although she was the driving force behind the business since Ma had asked her to take over three years ago and all major decisions were hers. Ma still made a fuss about every change she saw and argued day in and day out with Ruby. They both knew it was all show, Ma had lost any desire she had to keep building a business, she had everything she needed and was happy now to sit back and watch Ruby go from strength to strength. She argued with everything purely for fun, which usually Ruby played along with.

Ruby had the greatest respect for the empire Ma had built, and she intended to do all that she could to keep things going but she had far bigger dreams than those that Ma started out with. Ma's ways were old fashioned, people needed new fresh ideas. There was some unpleasant talk in the town about what happened out here at Ma's, and, although Ruby felt there was a need for all that they provided here, she accepted that most people wanted a decent face put on things. She would be that decent face. Times were changing and people paid a lot more attention to what was happening around and about them these days.

Firstly she turned her attention to the woeful building where the new born babies were kept until a place for them could be found. She'd hated it since her first days here and had always thought that things could be done better but the change needed to be a big one and she'd never had all that she needed ready at the same time. Now, she did.

When Tom left Jane to go to school Ruby saw right

away that Jane would need help or she'd fall apart, she loved the boy so much. He was all she had and she felt that with him gone she'd be left feeling useless and lonely. She could still be made to feel needed and Ruby knew exactly how to achieve that. The pregnant girls and newborn babies would all be moved out of Ma's and into the row of cottages where Jane lived.

Jane was to be the head of the nursery and Sal would work with her there along with Limping Lou who had waited long enough for her chance with the babies. Jane lived in the middle cottage of three and the new arrangement was that all the cooking and cleaning now took place in her cottage. The cottage on the left would house Sal, with the baby boys, and on the one on the right housed Lou with the baby girls. This way the babies were better cared for in a much healthier atmosphere, they could enjoy the benefits of fresh air and outside space.

It had taken time for Ruby to get the cottages ready, Jane's was in good order but the ones either side of hers had been empty for some time and needed extensive repairs. But it was done at last and the babies were moved.

There was now no evident connection between the two houses, the babies were one thing and the girls' something else entirely. Any interfering busy-body from Worcester could come and have a look at what was going on at Sansome Springs at any time and find nothing untoward.

Her next project was to improve the approach to main house, the brothels here were the primary income for all of them and Ruby was determined to increase the profitability here. Respectability was all well and good but she wasn't about to allow a drop in income and while Ma had always depended upon word of mouth amongst local men to keep trade going Ruby had bigger ideas.

Their location was perfect, being far enough from town to be safe from offending anyone with sensibilities but on the main track into the city from Droitwich, Ombersley and beyond. Ruby wanted to offer food and shelter to all travellers along with the other, more specialised, services they were famous for.

Local well set up regular visitors were a good foundation to build a business on, but travellers from nearby towns would often pay more for something they didn't have permanent access to. She wanted to attract people that would be prepared to travel some distance for what she could offer.

Now there were no babies or pregnant girls about the place they could ensure that a better service was available at all times. She could offer comfortable rooms suitable for an overnight stay and still continue to satisfy those who called for an hour of fun and relaxation.

Both these businesses, the brothels and the babies, brought in considerable sums of money and Ruby was happy enough with them and in her efforts to improve them, but there was one thing that had always played on her mind and those were what she called the lost girls.

These were the girls that came to Ma but didn't want to stay once their baby was born. If any girls wanted to stay and work with Bella they could, if they were pretty and obliging enough. But some of them either weren't suitable or weren't willing, They came, had a baby, then left. Sadder and wiser but still with no prospects as their reputation was often ruined.

Ruby wished she could do something for these girls.

To all Gentlemen, tradesmen and others of Worcester, James Collins takes this method to acquaint the public that he is now removing from the White Lion and Cheshire Cheese in the Forgate Street to the sign of the Rein Deer in Mealcheapen Street, which is now being fitted up in a very neat commodious manner.

Neat post-chaises and saddle horses will be available at the Rein Deer to go to any part of England upon reasonable terms.

(Copyright and courtesy of the Worcester News)

CHAPTER THIRTY ONE

As Ruby threw herself into re-shaping Ma's little empire into something she could depend upon for years to come, so Richard and Tom embarked upon their formal education.

It was year that proved to be exciting and challenging for Richard. The school at Malvern had been the perfect venue to begin the process of polishing him into the man Ruby wanted him to be and in no time at all he felt at home. With the help and guidance of Sam and his friend Charles Minet, who was the master at the school, he had managed to catch up with his own age group with relative ease.

There were four boys a few years older than him at the school, so much older in fact that for the first year they took no notice of him at all. There were also five boys younger than him and he spent most of his time with them in their lessons. These boys looked up to him because he was older and had displayed an unexpected knack for anything sporting.

His leg, though not quite as straight as it should be, was as strong as the other and he could run faster, throw straighter and swim further than any of them. This earned him respect from the boys rather than scorn for his lack of social skills, all of which were improving daily. He had a determination to succeed that radiated from him.

Ma and Ruby, along with Sam and Ann had done all they could to ensure he understood just how great a chance this was and he was proud, and grateful to know that they all felt he was good enough to do well. He would not disappoint them.

By the time his tutors judged him ready, academically, to move up a year he had become completely accepted by all the boys. Everyone knew that he'd been brought up by an aunt following the death of both his parents and no one even asked about his background any more.

He didn't miss his Aunt Ruby at all, they hadn't been close and he'd always been used to his own company, the girls at Ma's had treated him like a pet and he found being around boys and men more challenging but far more rewarding.

Sam, as promised, continued to visit him at school on a monthly basis and Richard looked forward to these visits hugely. Uncle Sam brought news and warm wishes from Worcester and in return took back a complete analysis on how Richard had spent the last month in the classroom as well as a report on how well he looked and how tall he had grown.

While Richard thrived, Tom found his new life much tougher to settle into.

Henry had sent him to the school his own boys had gone to and, as he had with them, he expected Tom to survive alone. Where Richard had lived with Ruby all his life encouraging him to read and write, practice his numbers and think for himself Tom had spent all his time playing with village boys and being petted by Jane.

It was hardly surprising that he encountered a fair amount of bullying in his first few months. He lagged behind the other boys both educationally and socially and was held to ridicule from them and the masters. He did learn, though it was a brutal process, and he became a much tougher boy. One great benefit he'd taken to school with him was the ability to fight that he'd learned from the village lads. He was not afraid to put his fists up if he felt riled enough.

He strived to keep his attention fixed on his books or the masters and avoid being alone with the other boys as much as possible, Jane hated it when he fought and he wanted her to be proud of him. Sometimes though the bullying became almost too much for a little boy to bear without lashing out. He missed Jane, who had been everything to him, very much. But before he left her she had told him so often how very lucky he was to have this wonderful education paid for by his unknown rich relative, something many people would like to have was being offered to him and she'd urged him not to waste a moment thinking about anything but his lessons and he tried desperately hard not to let her down. She told him that she would always be there to welcome him home but she wanted to be proud of him, so she trusted he'd be brave and work hard.

He kept his unhappiness to himself and focused on working as hard as he could. His pals in the village had teased him unmercifully when they found out he was going to school but he could see the envy on the faces of a couple of them who would love to swap places with him if they could. He had to make the best of things and then, when he next saw them he would be able to tell them all the good things that had happened to him.

He struggled with his lessons, writing and reading bored him but science and arithmetic fascinated him. He enjoyed sports but preferred music instruction. He also found that he could sketch very well.

When things got too bad he would sneak out at night distract himself by studying the night sky. He'd name the stars and remind himself how small he was compared to all that was out there. He developed the knack of keeping out of trouble and ignoring the petty bullying that persisted. Once his tormentors saw that their insults were ignored they began to look elsewhere for their fun and he was left blessedly alone.

The Academy in The Tything, Worcester. This pleasant and healthy establishment will re-open on Monday when young gentlemen will be liberally boarded, tenderly treated and diligently taught writing, English grammar and composition, the classics, mathematics, book-keeping, geography and the use of globes and maps by J Richards. The terms, which are moderate may be known by applying at the academy.

(Copyright and courtesy of the Worcester News)

CHAPTER THIRTY TWO

Bella and Ruby chattered happily as they linked arms and headed out for an afternoon of fun. Ruby was gradually learning how to enjoy life and act more like the young woman that she was and Bella and Mary were more than willing to help her in this quest.

They were later than planned as Bella had entertained a new gentleman that morning and was now describing his preferences to Ruby who could now laugh with genuine enjoyment at the peculiarities of men rather than giggle with ill disguised horror.

The improvements in the business that she had implemented had given her a confidence and lust for life that had transformed her. She worked every bit as hard as she ever had, shaping things her way, but now she played hard as well. She took a half day off each week and generally spent it with Bella. They would walk the town on fine days looking at the fashions women wore and talk about what they liked and didn't like and how these things would look so much better on them. They occasionally went to the theatre and copied, as closely as they could the women they saw there.

Today they were intending today to walk to the inn where Mary worked and while away a couple of hours with her if she could slip away. The Worcester grapevine made sure that between the three of them they knew pretty well all that was worth knowing about the city and it's inhabitants and there was always plenty of scandal and gossip for them to relish.

The last time they had met Mary they had been delayed by a fine carriage that had stopped in the middle of the pathway. They hid and watched as a solid, respectable looking man helped a delicate lady up into a carriage, being most solicitous of her welfare. Mary entertained them both when she told them what she knew about him, and what he got up to with the magistrate's wife on the one night a month when his wife visited her sister.

There was a five year span in the ages of the three friends, with Bella being the oldest, then Mary and the baby of the group was Ruby. Bella and Mary had seen a lot more of the underbelly of Worcester than Ruby had but with their help she'd all but caught them up. The threesome shared a trust and companionship that served them all well. They'd all faced the one thing that usually caused woman to be scorned for life and they'd come through it unscathed.

Bella had never before known anyone who wanted to be with her for herself alone and now she had two friends she considered herself rich. Ruby brought out all that was kind and good in her and in return she taught Ruby to laugh at people and their faults, rather than condemn.

Mary was the comedian of the trio, whatever happened she could make a person laugh and try again. She put up with Bill because it meant she didn't have to put up with anyone else and she knew she wasn't badly done by.

Time and circumstance meant that Ruby was closer to these two than she was to her sister Ellie who thought both girls coarse and vulgar. Ruby had laughed at this, "Of course they are, I am too." She'd declared happily.

Bella stopped her story telling suddenly and gripped Ruby's arm saying, "Ruby, there's a man over by the trees watching us."

Ruby laughed. "It'll be one of your regulars I expect. Will you tell him you're not working or will I be going to see Mary on my own?"

Bella shook her head. "No, it's that friend of yours. Look."

Ruby looked to where Bella was pointing and saw a rather nervous looking Sam approaching them. "Sam. Is it Richard..."

Realizing she was shocked to see him and fearing the worst he was quick to reassure her. "No, no. Don't worry there's nothing wrong with Richard." Sam made a poor attempt at a smile. "The last report I had from Malvern was very good. I was just passing and I wondered if you had time to speak with me but I can see you're off somewhere..."

Ruby turned to Bella, who grinned and said, "That's all right my wench, you go off with your gentleman caller. You can tell me and Ma all about it later." She flounced away throwing a practised smile and a wink at Sam, who turned crimson.

Ruby smiled and took pity on him. "Come in and tell me what's on your mind. I must say I never thought the day would come that I'd see you all the way out here, but you'll be quite safe. I can't think what your fancy friends would say if they saw you though."

He coughed and smiled nervously. "I'd prefer to talk outside if you don't mind." Ruby shook her head.

"Now that would be impolite Sam, come in. Surely you know I wouldn't invite you into where the girls are working. I have a separate little parlour where I keep my own things. We can sit in comfort and privacy."

She walked into the house and within a few seconds a somewhat shamefaced Sam followed her in. The first thing he saw was the little box he'd given her all those years ago, polished and in pride of place by the fire. She saw him looking and she touched his hand briefly. "It's my most treasured possession Sam. The books you gave me are still in there and I've read them both many times and I've kept a journal, just as you told me to."

"I meant no insult outside Ruby, since getting to know you again and listening to the things you've told me of your life here and how much help you've had from these people, well, I have to say that whatever my friends might say, they would probably be wrong about the girls here."

She nodded acceptance of his apology. "Yes, they almost certainly would. Sit down Sam and tell me what's wrong. It's something important because no one ever passes by here from Sidbury."

Sam explained that Henry had, quite suddenly, decided to withdraw his support totally from the newspaper. He'd gone to see Sam earlier that week and announced that he intended to free himself of all his business interests. He was grieving for his son and in the process of handing everything over to Hugh, but the newspaper, as his least profitable enterprise was not something they felt able to continue with.

As far as the Daventors were concerned, the newspaper had served its purpose and so, it seemed, had Sam. Without Henry's backing Sam couldn't see how the newspaper could survive. It was successful, in that it had done exactly what Henry had wanted it to do, and that was to generate good publicity for him and his cronies and not to cost him anything. He could control an awful lot as head of the only newspaper around. He hadn't worried too much about making it a highly profitable enterprise, he'd just wanted it to be effective as a tool until his son was ready to take over.

That, of course would never happen now and so Henry had decided to simply walk away. As a gesture of goodwill, and with a nod to Sam's many years of service, he'd signed over the printing machines to him but that marked the end of his interest.

In order that the paper continue Sam needed credit, or money, to pay people, to buy paper and ink, the runners had costs and then the landlord had to be paid. The sort of people who had allowed Henry credit would allow Sam none. Within a day of his going the landlord had arrived, demanding payment in full within the week if Sam was to remain in the shop.

"I had hoped, in my heart of hearts, to one day in the future to own the paper, but not yet. I don't have the funds available. I could sell my books perhaps, but that would take time, and it will break my heart. And, though they are my pride and joy they wouldn't raise anything like enough money." He looked terribly sad at the thought and took a moment to gather himself. "I have a collection that took my father a lifetime to gather but has very little monetary value. Some of my books were his most treasured possessions and now they are like old, treasured friends to me, Ruby, selling those books would be like selling my father."

"But surely there is something else you can do. You have friends and family, can no-one help you?"

"It's impossible, I can't see a way out. My family have no money to spare and as for friends, no, I'm afraid I don't know anyone who'd be in a position to help out. I only came to talk to you because I needed to get away for a while and I took a long walk. I found myself at the Tything and I thought I'd continue out here when I saw you and your friend. I'm not expecting a solution, I simply wanted to talk to someone who would understand."

He was terribly worried about Ann who was beside herself. She'd hardly come to terms with losing the much longed for baby she was carrying. At forty years of age losing the first baby she'd ever conceived broke her heart and she knew her chance of carrying another one was slim. He wanted to keep her free from as much concern as he could, which was partly why he was out and about. He knew his own worry was written across his face and he was trying to walk himself into a better frame of mind.

"Mr Piper, who owns the building we've been working from has said he'll accept the printing press as payment but if I handed that over to him then I'd have no way of earning a living and I would be forever beholden to him. Everything has gone so horribly wrong in such a short space of time. There's no answer that I can see."

Ruby was no longer listening, she had long since learned by personal experience that sitting and pulling a problem apart did no good at all, often in fact it made things worse. Doing something, even if it was the wrong thing could at the very least make things seem better and help pass the time. When things felt better a solution could be found.

She gave Sam a drink and told him to wait a while. She then marched briskly into the room where Ma spent most of her time now, pretending to be looking over her accounts but in reality dozing and daydreaming. "Ma, I've got Sam here with a problem."

Ma laughed. "We get a lot of fellows here with problems Ruby, I didn't think that was the sort of thing you wanted to be bothered with though, and Bella's gone out for the day."

"Seriously Ma. I wondered if you could think of anywhere he can move the newspaper printing office to. He's having a problem with the landlord, he's got no money and nowhere to go."

"I'm in the business taking money away from toffs not rescuing em."

"Sam's no toff, he's a friend, but he does need rescuing. Henry's dumped him with debts, no credit and no way of earning a living. No home either as they live on the premises."

"Henry!" Ma sniffed and spat into the fire.

Ruby waited quietly, biding her time as Ma grumbled on. "Why does it matter so much to you? I know he helped with your boy, but you've paid for all you had, this is no concern of yours. You 'ent gone soft on him have you?"

"Ma, the day I go soft on a man is the day I trust you'll slip me some poison. No. I can see a profit here for us, if we play it right. Let me tell you what I'm thinking."

Owning a stake in a newspaper would be a respectable business venture, Ruby reasoned. A business that in time her son could have a part in. If suitable premises could be found, that would enable Sam to continue with the newspaper then in time Richard would have a going concern to take over.

"Ha, you don't miss a trick do you, you're a good girl and you'll be a force to be reckoned with in no time in this town. I got myself a good one when I found you, you could almost be my daughter." Ma cackled. "Except if you had been I'd no doubt have sold you."

Ma pondered on this concept for a moment. "Course girls don't fetch as much as boys. Never have and never will, amazing it is, that one little flap of useless skin is worth so much to them. Ha, and all it does is cost em when they come back here all growed up." She laughed so much she began to cough and before long she was choking and spitting.

Ruby watched in dismay as Ma spat, missing the fire and splashing the floor. At last she slumped, exhausted, back into her chair. Her chest rattling and her hands shaking.

"Ma, take it easy, please." Ruby tried to give the woman a glass of spring water but she waved it away in disgust.

"All right, all right." She struggled upright and pushed Ruby away. She struggled for breath for a moment or two and then spoke slowly. "I do know of an old small holding out there past Sidbury on along the road to London. There's a bit of a cottage and a barn or two. It's a shabby old nest though, too far out for me to bother with. Not a penny's been spent on it for years mind, they'd have to do a lot of hard work to patch it up but I think it might do."

Ruby leapt up in excitement as Ma went on to explain that an old chap works the land there, he was a herbalist who was always trying to find a cure for something or other. He grew all manner of herbs and plants and then sold them for drinks or potions that could cure anything and everything. He was an old friend of Ma's and she was adamant that he was to stay, in peace and safety, but if Sam could work around him then they could come to some agreement. The old man lost his wife and son many years ago and lived there with his grandson.

"Go and get John to fetch the wagon out, we'll go and have a look at it now, it's been, I don't know how many years since I've seen the place, it'll do me good to get over there again afore I die. Let's see whether your Sam can get along with old man Whitehouse."

She raised her eyebrows as Ruby made no move. "Well don't just stand there looking at me like a half wit Ruby, do you want a place for your blasted newspaper or don't you? Look lively."

On Monday began the selling by auction at the Talbot Inn, Sidbury, of a collection of several thousand volumes of the best English books, among which are the works of Milton, Pope, Swift, Shakespeare, Gay and a great many more of the best authors. All the volumes are in good condition, most of them neatly bound with gilt lettering,

Also on sale are family bibles, pocket bibles, prayer books, maps, prints and pictures. The sale begins at six o'clock and there are seats for the ladies.

(Copyright and courtesy of the Worcester News)

CHAPTER THIRTY THREE

Sam and Ann spent many months of back breaking work and hand to mouth living as they struggled to knock Ma's neglected and tumbledown cottage and barn into a workable state at the same time as keeping the newspaper in production.

Somehow they succeeded, but it was an experience neither would choose to repeat. It was with a considerable feeling of pride that Sam declared he was ready to let the good folk of Worcester know that the local newspaper was now being produced from new offices at the top of the hill just past Sidbury gate. All local business men, traders and gentlemen could be certain of a warm welcome, should they care to visit.

Ruby had settled all the outstanding debts and had also managed to negotiate better prices for all the supplies the newspaper needed. The offer of an instant cash payment on delivery had secured huge discounts as most business people expected time to pay.

Sam would continue to run the newspaper in his own very successful way but Ruby was now an equal partner. She'd made a considerable financial commitment and retained ownership of the premises. She had vowed that she wouldn't interfere unless Sam wanted her help as she had more than enough to keep herself occupied. Today she was making her first visit to the newly opened premises and Sam was nervously showing her around.

He had been hugely relieved to find that Ruby was in a position to help him so much but there was also, somewhere in the back of his mind, a small niggle at the speed with which things had happened and a concern about the degree to which Ruby might expect to become involved. Their relationship had completely altered and Ruby was far more comfortable with the change than he was.

He'd confided his worries Ann who had sensibly pointed

out that without Ruby's intervention the paper would have closed down anyway, and they'd both be reduced to depending upon friends and family for sustenance.

Ruby had given them a future and they must both be thankful for that. It was inevitable that their relationship would change, she was now a successful business owner and their partner, it was up to them, Sam and her, to make that change as easy as possible for them all. Because after all was said and done Ruby had done more for them than anyone else had, ever.

Ruby walked slowly around the work space that Sam had cleared for himself, she looked at everything and questioned its purpose. She nodded now and again. “Well, this is looking so much better than the first time we saw it. You've worked miracles, both of you. When Ma first brought us here I thought it was a bit too far gone but it looks entirely suitable, and quite respectable, now.”

Sam nodded happily. “It's perfect Ruby, we've more space than we had before and much more light. People can find us just as easily, and it's a better place for Ann to feel safe in when I'm away."

"And the space outside will be wonderful when the baby comes." Ann had come to join them and was linking her arms with Sam's.

One look at their glowing faces told her all she needed to know and she congratulated them both heartily then, having given up a few moments for chatter Ruby pulled the conversation back to business.

She fully intended to let Sam continue working his own way but she'd had some ideas of her own and wanted to talk them over with him. She'd learned well from Ma, a thing was worth doing only if it made a profit and she had high hopes for this, her second venture into legitimate business.

As they sat and discussed the way Sam planned to take the newspaper forward Ruby was reminded once again of how passionately proud he was of the role the newspaper played in the lives of the people of Worcester.

"Things are improving now all around, I'm enjoying a freedom that I'd not enjoyed before, being able to decide what should go into the paper for myself and that's all thanks to you Ruby. I swear you'll never regret joining forces with me." Sam smiled proudly as he led her around, pointing out things.

"Sam, I know and trust you, when I came to you for help you were very generous to me and I won't ever forget that. When you came to me for help I listened out of friendship and talked to Ma for the same reason. I won't deny though that I saw this newspaper a fine business opportunity and a chance for me to be a part of the respectable side of commerce."

"That's a good thing Ruby, you've invested money for sound business reasons, I wouldn't have expected anything else and, on that very note, I must tell you that I pursued one of the suggestions you made to me some time ago and I've been pleasantly surprised."

"Tell me?"

"A few of the local inns have agreed to let me carry their advertisements on a regular basis. One or two other merchants, a barber, and a coffee house have also made a regular arrangement, I followed your advice and gave them better rates for a longer commitment."

"I knew it." She was jubilant. "I've found it relatively simple to secure a good price reduction on most things I buy because I will insist on paying cash and I felt certain that it would work the other way." She was thrilled.

He went on to tell her he'd been approached by a couple of people who had never advertised with the newspaper before because they had problems with Henry in the past. Now the word was spreading that he was no longer involved Sam had been contacted by several people and held quite a few interesting and possibly profitable conversations. The coach builders out near Barbourne had spoken of spending a regular sum with Sam and he was greatly encouraged.

A lot of people had said they wanted to wait and see how things went but he had enough firm promises to make him feel very optimistic. "We already have a profit and that will increase steadily now, I'm certain of it."

Sam had struck exactly the right note for Ruby, he clearly understood that it was crucial that the newspaper showed a profit constantly now that Daventor was around to cover any shortfall. Her only concern was seeing that promise turn into cash in enough time to pay the school fees for the next year. Using all her available funds to clear Sam's debt had been a risk but Ma had told her for years, you get nothing if you risk nothing, and she knew better than most how to turn a penny.

Perhaps Ruby could stop worrying now. "That's good news Sam, we'll have to keep thinking of ways to approach other tradesmen though."

"Well, there's another idea I'm going to try, we've purchased a copy of a new book called Cookery Reformed and we're planning a regular feature using it. Ann will cook one of the recipes in the book and we'll then print details of said recipe on our pages, along with my comments on the taste of the dish."

He held up a copy of the book for her to see, "I hope that will interest women, housekeepers and housewives, to look in future editions and perhaps keep the recipes, perhaps build up a collection. I also intend to approach the tradesmen who can deliver the ingredients needed for each recipe, with a view to them advertising with us."

She nodded enthusiastically, she would have never thought of reading such a thing, but could see it was a sound idea.

"That was a suggestion from Ann and she's had another idea since. You know Mr Whitehouse of course, the chap who shares the land with us." Ruby nodded, she'd seen the old man shuffling about many times since Sam had been working on this place. "Well he's very keen on nature, remedies and cures that can be grown at home using herbs and such things. He's agreed to give Ann some of his recipes which we'll make up and then we can either tell readers how to grow and make them for themselves or they can buy some ready made from us here."

Sam was once more a man in control. He seemed excited and energetic again, he was more like the Sam she'd known years ago. He admitted that things were far easier now he knew Henry would not be dropping in to throw confusion into the mix, he was confident he could deal with whatever came his way.

Henry was a man who expected all his ideas to be taken up gratefully and Sam had found it very difficult at times to do the right thing for the paper without causing offence to Henry. Now he was his own man he was going to make this paper the finest in the land.

Ruby was excited by his enthusiasm. "I can see this is going to be a thriving concern by the time Richard is ready to leave school and join us."

"Long before that Ruby, trust me."

They spoke then about Richard and his success at Malvern. He'd moved up a grade and was proving to be quite an accomplished sportsman. He was working hard and his masters all said his work was good and his nature exemplary. He was flourishing being among boys his own age and a bright future lay ahead for him.

"When he's ready I shall teach him all I know here and he will take the paper forward. I know he'll do well Ruby, he's a fine young man."

As Ruby tried to thank Sam again for the way he'd helped steer Richard for her Sam held his hand up. "No need for thanks, I think as friends we come out about level, don't you?"

"Perhaps we do Sam, perhaps we do."

This day is published, price four shillings and sixpence and in one volume neatly bound in calf, Cookery Reformed or A Lady's Assistant, containing a select collection of the best and most approved recipes in cookery, pastry, preserving, candying, pickling etc, together with a distinct account of the nature of ailments and what are most suitable to every constitution.

(Copyright and courtesy of the Worcester News)

CHAPTER THIRTY FOUR

Hugh Daventor shook hands on a deal that was destined to take his business to far greater heights and he was looking forward to the look of approval he fully expected to see on Henry's face when he relayed the details to him. He was delighted to have pulled this off and was glorying in the knowledge that it was because of him that the family fortunes had taken another upward step.

Initially Tom's appearance had left him reeling, coming so soon on top of the death of William, but before long he had showed himself to be a good solid lad who would be a useful addition to the business in time.

Planning a future for Tom had completely preoccupied Henry which was definitely a good thing for Hugh as it gave him some much needed breathing space. He was having to work harder than ever before to impress his uncle just at the time when he'd thought he was home free. Anything that diverted Henry's attention was a welcome relief.

Henry listened with great satisfaction Hugh told him what he'd done. "Hugh my boy, I'm impressed. I can't imagine how on earth you managed to pull this off." Henry was happy that the business was growing so well, and he prided himself on being amongst the first men in town to appreciate the role that canals would play in the future, but there was no denying it was Hugh who had brought in their first important contract. He slid a bottle across the table toward Hugh who took this departure from the norm as a sign that Henry was very pleased indeed.

"There's been so much talk for such a long time, about items from the porcelain manufactory arriving at their final destination damaged, or even not arriving at all. You know it's been the subject of much debate with complaints that the toll roads are not being adequately maintained and so on."

Henry nodded, the roads in England were a disaster

whatever the time of year. During the rainy months they were mainly mud and treacherous potholes that during the dry times became baked into an impassable state of furrows and dips. This was the prime motivation behind Henry's own obsession with building canals. Anyone who'd travelled any distance soon discovered that England could produce everything she needed, the problem was always the same, how to transport those goods safely and quickly.

The talk in the coffee houses recently was of the growing popularity of the porcelain works, they were producing elegant, desirable but fragile pieces. Much of which was either broken or stolen on the terrible roads before it could reach its destination.

“I overheard a particular conversation about a consignment that had been ordered by the Spencer family. Every single piece had a picture of Althorp hand painted on it. It had taken months of work to produce and was a sight to behold. Everyone was highly pleased with it and of course as soon as visitors to Althorp see it, they'll want something similar. It's one of the most important commissions they've had."

"Got a good name already those fellows." Henry nodded, not sure what point Hugh was making.

"When the service was completed it was packed up in crates lined with straw, and then loaded onto two wagons." Hugh explained. "Halfway through the journey, the wagons fell foul of a track that had been destroyed in the floods and they got into such a tangle the wagon went over. The coachman was killed and half of the goods for delivery were smashed. By the time people got there to help out the other coach driver he'd been robbed.”

Henry nodded with understanding. “It's happening every day my boy. Disaster waits on every track.”

Hugh went on to say that he'd decided to join in the men's conversation at this point. He introduced himself and informed them that he was almost ready to launch his own fleet of canal boats and that he could guarantee safe and fast delivery. They weren't all convinced but they were losing so much to breakage on the roads that he could see they were willing to be persuaded.

They were simply not in a position to manage the deliveries themselves. The other thing that helped Hugh convince them the information that he already had his own canal on the other side of the Severn. He assured them he could move their goods as soon as they were completed. He assured them that he could store as much as they want in his warehouse and deliver to their customers when they wanted him to. The knew immediately that this would work very well for them, it would free up space in their premises allowing them to expand their production area because their made goods would be out of harms way.

"This our chance to show people what can be done. It also means they'll be paying us to cross the Severn twice, for storage and then for delivery. I also said that we would have one of our fleet inscribed with their name, for the benefit of future clients of theirs."

"It's a wonderful opportunity Hugh, well done. It's a grand start and we must build on it by telling others who we do this kind of work for. I don't think it will be very long before people in other fields see what a difference we can make to their business. It's a very impressive contract though I don't suppose on its own it will be worth much to us. I mean to say, how many families are there in the same league as the Spencer family?"

Hugh smiled, he'd been expecting Henry to attempt to prick his pride. "The Duke of Gloucester is awaiting a service, one that is to be decorated with hand painted pieces of fruit. The decorated porcelain from this part of the country is much sought after, so much so that the men told me that the King himself has ordered a service and has also recommended that a shop be opened, by them, in London."

"The King and the Duke of Gloucester, you say." He

was impressed. "And a shop in London? By god Hugh, if all this comes to pass then you will have exceeded my expectations. Well done, my boy. Well done."

Hugh felt satisfied. He'd pulled off a great deal and Henry was satisfied all he had to do now was work every hour that he could in order to keep his promise. Every time he managed to make Henry happy he found the constraints the old man put upon him ease a touch. If he could have more freedom he could turn this town upside down, he knew he could. Of course he ran everything now, in name, but once a week without fail, he still had to report in full to Henry. It was galling but there was no way round it. Henry could decide to close off the supply of funds in a moment if he so chose.

And now there was young Tom in the wings, Hugh would have to be very careful to include him in everything. Tom, who he'd not spent very much time with since they first met, was the best student the school had ever known, according to Henry and his stories. He could also play a fine tune on a piano, though what use a skill like that could be was beyond Henry but he'd die before admitting it. Henry felt that he'd been given a second chance with Tom and whereas his son William had been able to do nothing right, Tom could do no wrong.

It was a queer set up Hugh thought. Tom was, without a doubt, William's son but Henry only visited him at school and he rarely had him home for holidays. He said he didn't want to put too much strain on the boy when he was so young, it was better for him to continue to go back home to Jane regularly. In time he'd come to live with them, but not yet.

Hugh didn't remember Henry ever caring about who he caused strain for in years gone by, but perhaps he was growing soft with age. Although, when he stopped and thought about his own childhood Henry had never bothered about Hugh and William at all until he thought they were going off the rails. Then he came down on them very hard indeed, but causing upset never crossed the man's mind.

Just let young Tom put a foot wrong, Hugh thought, and Henry will bring him to heel as he did William. Damn the man. Hugh was not prepared to see everything he'd worked for be snatched away again. He knew he'd have to bide his time but get Tom on his side he must. The only way forward was to have young Tom in his pocket and then keep him there. He hadn't been mature enough to do that with William but it would be different this time.

Nowadays he tried not to think of William because that inevitably led to thoughts of Ruby and the power she now had over him, should she choose to use it. The old Ruby would never betray him but he was sometimes quite sick with fear when he faced up to the fact that the old Ruby was gone forever, the new Ruby was a very different person. She was the only one he'd ever known to stand up to Henry and get away with it, he was terrified to think of how dangerous she could be if she put her mind to it. It was best not to dwell on what might be, he told himself briskly. Deal with the here and now, Ruby had no reason to betray him.

Hugh knew to his own cost it was quite easy for a young man to fall out of favour with Henry. With any luck at all Tom would be the architect of his own downfall, Hugh could then leap in and save him, thereby earning eternal gratitude from Tom and Ruby, both of whom were more important than Henry in the long term.

The boy's schooling was almost over and he'd need to start work soon enough, they'd all get the measure of him then. The world of work was quite different to the classroom and he'd need the support of his Uncle Hugh then.

As the Leominster stage wagon was proceeding towards Worcester between Cotheridge and Broadwas, the driver, finding the waters greatly out and realising it was very dangerous to proceed on, thought proper to take the horses off and left the wagon in the road all night. However there was such an extraordinary rise in the waters that they flowed through the wagon and greatly damaged the whole loading.

(Copyright and courtesy of the Worcester News)

CHAPTER THIRTY FIVE

Exploring the alleys and side tracks of Worcester never ceased to give Ruby endless entertainment and food for thought. She loved searching out the old places Ma told her about before they were flattened to make way for the new, she marvelled at the increasing prosperity in the city which was bringing about incredible changes. The city seemed to grow every day and she felt her desire to play a bigger part in the development of it grow at the same incredible pace.

The newspaper and Madame Eloise were both thriving enterprises and they provided an air of respectability that she relished and a small, but steadily growing, profit.

But that wasn't enough for her, Ruby wanted to build something that was hers alone. There must be a place here somewhere for her to provide the citizens of Worcester with an object or a service they lacked. When she discovered what that was, then she would know what to build.

As she spent more and more time in the heart of the vibrant city she was beginning to appreciate that there were a great many wealthy people situated cheek by jowl alongside grinding poverty and absolute filth, yet neither seemed to notice, much less care about the other. In fact they supported one another. The rich despised the poor but needed them to their dirty work, the poor resented the rich but relied upon their patronage and good will.

The city was growing faster than many of the inhabitants realised and huge changes were taking place in the city almost daily, the boundaries were being moved ever outwards and new buildings were springing up everywhere to provide homes for those who had come into money or soon expected to.

Talk in the coffee houses and inns had been of a man called Jessop who had been given the task of estimating the cost of digging out the Severn where it was shallow and creating tow-paths for horses alongside. She'd heard the talk amongst the customers at Ma's, some claimed it was the daftest thing ever heard of while others though it the work of genius.

More recently people spoke of a fellow called Young was about to try the same thing. She assumed they didn't get the answer they wanted from Jessop so now she imagined they'd keep taking on a different man until they got the answer they wanted. Ma was right, men were fools and nothing changes.

All Ruby knew was that engineers and map makers and the like were visiting her place of work in vast numbers and swelling her coffers and those of the town's merchants, very nicely. Having experienced first hand the feeling of powerless desperation that went hand in hand with being poor and homeless, she was absolutely determined to take as much as she could from all the wealth that was flowing around the city and put it to her own good use.

She had her dreams, unusual though they may be. She never wanted to wear the finest silks, or to have a carriage outside her grand house and servants to attend her every need. She wanted enough money and power to enable her to live as she chose, in peace. She'd get that because she'd work and learn and do whatever she had to in order to make it happen and once it happened no-one would take it away from her.

She'd been more than grateful to work firstly for Ma and then alongside her and, the more she saw of other peoples poverty the more she appreciated just how lucky she had been in her life so far. She'd learned so much about people and their needs and desires since being with Ma and that education would not be wasted.

Until she'd needed Sam's help with Richards schooling she'd confined herself to Barbourne and the area around Ma's houses and she hadn't always understood, or cared, how much else there was going on in Worcester but the more she saw of her city the more certain she was that there was something big here for her, just waiting to be uncovered.

It was whilst walking the length and breadth of the town that she found her mind was at its most creative and it was for this reason, in addition to her never ending search for opportunities, that she took the walk with enthusiasm whatever the weather and no matter how tired she was. She was open to any and all possibilities.

She'd been very excited when she found out that the plot of land, and all the buildings on it, that they had let Sam move into belonged to Ma and therefore would be hers one day. She had got used to considering the area she still called the water fields her own but of course that was worthless and barren. The knowledge that she owned land at both ends of the city gave her a feeling of deep satisfaction. To be a landowner was everything, she'd heard Henry say so many times. Of course she no idea what could be done with the land but in time she'd learn.

She idly wondered what else Ma had hidden up her sleeve, but it was only an idle thought, she knew she was about to make a difference herself, she could feel it inside. She didn't want to be dependant, she would use all that Ma had given her to achieve something greater for herself.

Ruby could see so much potential here in this Worcester. What she wanted to do was build a business for herself and her son that would provide a worry free future financially, but more importantly, what she craved was respect, not the dutiful respect afforded a married woman, any silly chit who found a man could have that, oh no, she wanted the respect in her own right and she wouldn't stop until she got it.

Ruby wanted the deference that goes only to those who are rich and powerful. Those are the people who don't have to live within the rules, they make the rules. That's what she wanted for herself and her sons.

To have a feeling of pride in oneself, surely there could be no better feeling. She'd never experienced that personally but had witnessed it in Sam and Ann and more recently Ellie. They all took such pride in producing something good that was desired by others. They were proud to walk around the town knowing that they were making a contribution and that was feeling that she craved for herself. She was not ashamed of Ma or the work the girls did, but she was uncomfortably aware that she lived off them and their endeavours and somehow that knowledge was beginning play on her mind.

It was time she made a contribution of her own, while her body was strong and her mind sharp and this was the place and the time to do just that. Her association with Sam and the newspaper gave her a degree of respectability and knowing that Henry Daventor personally had very little business this side of the river any more gave her peace of mind. The only thing holding her up now was her own lack of imagination and she vowed to herself that she would find the very thing she was overlooking if it killed her.

She was not intending to interfere with the day to day running of the houses in Barbourne, now she'd made the changes she felt were desirable, moving the pregnant girls and newborn babies away, she was certain they'd continue to do as well as ever. Bella had done a grand job over the years running those little enterprises and would continue for many more, she was sure of that.

Financially they were all secure, Ma had a home for life, the girls had money to spend and Ruby had all her material needs provided for. She had many friends now, all from Barbourne and that was something to cherish and preserve. But there was a lot more scope here in Worcester, and she wanted more.

Her preferred walk ran parallel to the river but was on much higher ground. In between the buildings, both commercial and residential, it was possible to look down and see the river and the hive of industry that it was, but it was also possible to look the other way, upwards and see that this was the area that those citizens who had other interests enjoyed. The air was fresher and sweeter the further away from the river one went.

Here were the inns that catered to the better off, both residents and travellers. The May Pole and the Crown both offered waiting rooms for the London coach and good food could be had as well as the finest French brandy and Jamaican rum.

The coffee houses here were smart and prolific, there was something to suit those for change and those firmly against, there was a place for the tradesmen and yet another for the men of letters. The citizenry here wore fine clothes and their horses and carriages spoke of wealth and comfort.

Ruby knew that here in this town, at this time, there was nothing she couldn't do if she put her mind to it. Her only concern was that every thing she could think of was being provided. Surely there was nothing this city lacked.

She kept her eyes and ears open looking and listening in a quest to find her opportunity. She talked to her sister and her friends and gradually a plan took shape in her mind.

She was in the market for a house. A house of substance in a decent area. Not the smartest perhaps, but a place where good honest people worked and lived. She would install a cook and a maid and gradually bring in the girls that came to Ma's to have a baby but didn't want to be whores after the event. She knew from talking to her sister, that the women of the city were often in a state of despair, they needed good staff but had no means of training them themselves. People new to money had heard how society lived in London, with all their servants, maids and valets and the like and they wanted the same for themselves but they didn't know how to go about it.

This was where Ruby felt she could make a killing. She would have her lost girls trained up in the domestic arts. It would be a slow process but she knew she could make a success of it. All she needed was the right woman to be a housekeeper and she could nurture the venture along slowly and surely.

Satisfied that she'd found what it was the good people of Worcester would soon need she set out to ensure that she was in a position to provide for them in the shortest possible time. A good house and a good woman were the first two items on her list and then she would be ready to supply whatever kind of servant those with new money wanted to buy.

To be let and entered upon as soon as the present owner can possibly quit the same, a very commodious dwelling-house fit for a gentleman's family in New Street in the city of Worcester, now and for some years past in the possession of a Mr Thomas Chetle, together with all convenient out-offices, a large kitchen used for washing, baking and brewing, a very good laundry and corn-chamber over it, and two garrets, a very good stable with standings for three horses, a cider house and a good room over that, a large place for feeding poultry, properly fitted up for this purpose, and a coal-yard that will hold 35 tons of coal, a large rack for bottles, and pump, with several other useful conveniences; also a garden walled in and very well planted with the best fruit trees, and a kitchen garden well planted.

(Copyright and courtesy of the Worcester News)

CHAPTER THIRTY SIX

As a child in St John's the river Severn had always appeared to Ruby as a gently meandering strip of silver, glinting steadily in the sunlight and teeming with a variety of craft. It had seemed to hint at excitement and adventure when she was young.

The reality, when she came to know it better, was shockingly different. All along the river's edge was bustle, with warehouses and wharves, all packed with men and horses loading things on and off the boats that were jostling for space. The air was full with the sound of men shouting to each other, either instructions or curses. Wagons pushed past carts and porters and watermen cursed each other richly. Boats of all sizes squeezed past one another in their hurry to get unloaded and loaded and away, the chaos never stopped.

Occasionally the men had to pause for rest and food and there were any number of drinking dives within spitting distance purely there to cater for these same men. They could find whatever they needed here, food and drink and then either a bed, a woman or a fight, depending on their preference.

There were a couple of smarter looking inns but these were for the merchants and traders who demanded a better class of food and cleaner surroundings but needed to be close enough to keep a watch on what was going in and out of their warehouses. Everyone here was consumed with the need to protect what was his and get a little extra into the bargain if a way could be found.

Workshops were piled high with broken wagons and parts of boats all in various stages of repair. Many of the City's distilleries were situated here at the riverside, providing employment to those who wanted work, and gin for those that didn't. The walkways were never dry, being so close to the river and so heavily used, it was a permanent stinking quagmire. Walking was a treacherous and unpleasant activity to attempt for those unused to the surroundings.

Half starved dogs skittered around hoping for scraps to be dropped whilst cats stalked around taking what they wanted from the dogs and chasing off all newcomers.

A woman walking alone here was subject to all manner of attention, varying from the friendly advice to get back where she belonged to the more threatening promise of what would happen to her if she didn't.

Ruby had risked a walk here a couple of times because she was determined to know all about the town, and thanks to the training she'd had at Ma's she could give as good as she got and frequently did. Men shouting out offers of a variety of sex acts accompanied by either cash or violence were no longer something that worried her. She long since learned how to lower a man's temperature with a withering glance or a snort of derision and felt unafraid. However, once she'd seen all the riverside had to offer she knew her future lay up there, on the higher ground and she was happy to stick to the walkways in town.

We are informed that a day labourer in the parish of St Peter, Worcester, has died of the smallpox and leaves behind him six small children who now have that disorder. The smallest donation of the charitable and humane, left with Mr Wilkins, grocer, or at Hoopers Coffee House, will be expended with the greatest frugality by his disconsolate widow who is in the utmost distress, and being at a distance from her parish, destitute of every means of support.

(Copyright and courtesy of the Worcester News)

CHAPTER THIRTY SEVEN

In the four years since he had lost his son and discovered his grandson Henry had spent more and more time hidden away in his own home and now he was a virtual recluse. He was still very demanding but it was only visitors to the house bore the brunt of his cantankerousness.

He insisted that the estate workers and tenants came to the Great House with updates and information on what they were doing and to explain themselves in any way he saw fit. What often happened was that once Henry was informed of their arrival he'd make them wait, outside in the courtyard sometimes for hours and sometimes he'd insist they came back the following day. It fell to Chambers to conduct these meetings with Henry sitting in a darkened alcove, watching and listening.

This was a wicked waste of everyone's time as they all knew Hugh was the master and they did what he said, however he wanted Henry to feel a part of things and so they all participated in this charade as a sop to keep the old man feeling important.

Henry raged about the troubles in France and he was adamant that if proper control had been maintained on the working men no such thing could have occurred. Keeping on top of things, or at least feeling that he was kept him happy enough to leave Hugh alone to do what he had to do. He'd turned into a tyrant and a drunk and the bitterness that had always shadowed him had now taken over his personality completely. Hugh would sacrifice anyone else's time to buy his own freedom.

Most of the people who were forced to venture up to the house to answer to him, though mindful of the memory of him as he was and how he used to be, were grateful that although they had one extremely difficult day a month at least Henry was never likely to appear at their place of work and demand answers on a whim as in days gone by.

Henry had fallen so far into the bottle that on a daily

basis his sense of grievance and general discontent at having been short changed somehow gained the upper hand. He felt a constant bitterness over what he chose to think of as his forced marriage to Elizabeth, in order to have a son and please his father, he felt cheated that he'd lost them both and he was left with nothing to offer comfort or solace.

He still had rare visits from friends and distant family, who were often forced to listen as he ranted about how the last quarter century of his life had been a waste, building up something for a son who no longer lived. He had a grandson, true, but he fell far short of Henry's mark though pride wouldn't let him admit it when sober. These unfortunate visitors seldom returned.

Hugh himself was rarely to be found at the Great House, nothing seemed to please the old man these days and he'd found he enjoyed his life working with the men on the waterways much more than anything he'd ever done before. Once out working he could forget Henry and his drunken tyranny.

When Henry had turned him out years ago he'd build up the tannery and begun trading in gloves, then, as he'd grown more confident he'd had his own house built, to his own drawings and, when Henry had welcomed him back into the fold he'd gone along with everything except for moving back under Henry's roof. He liked having his own place and had flatly refused to give that up.

He also had a real affection for the tannery and his glove manufactory and, although his days were now fully occupied with the family business's, he retained control of his own enterprises and had a good man overseeing things for him. He remembered Henry's promise that he would own everything one day but in his heart he knew that Tom had a greater claim and imagined that ultimately Tom would be the owner. Henry was never quite ready to put things in writing and it gave Hugh some comfort to know he had created something of his own to fall back on.

Canal fever was sweeping across the land, the doubters had been silenced and canals were being navigated the length of England, and, because of Henry's foresight he was at the forefront of the movement. Daventors canal was the talk of Worcester and was attracting business and attention from all quarters.

The men Hugh now worked alongside treated him as one of their own and for the first time in his life he felt as though he actually belonged somewhere and was doing work he could be proud of.

He regularly travelled the route with the men to Droitwich and back to Worcester. He could then cross the Severn and travel along his own canal home. The main business on that route was salt, of course, but Hugh never missed a chance to take his gloves into new towns and villages. He managed to discover the secret of how Dents had got gloves into walnut shells and now as a matter of course he took some with him where ever he went.

The ladies he presented these novelties to were suitably grateful and generally insisted their husbands go on to do business with him. The workmanship his men prided themselves upon was second to none and Hugh was determined to spread the word far and wide. He got immense satisfaction from knowing that something he'd worked so hard to set up was now as important to the town as the porcelain factory. His gloves were by far the finest in England.

Nevertheless he was always ready to tell all who asked that his main business was the transportation of the goods made by others. It seemed that every day now people were being bitten by the canal bug and were prepared to give him a chance to show what he could do.

Business owners realised that soon they'd be free to sell in towns and cities they'd never even known of in the past. Working men and women expected to buy things that their parents had never dreamed of even seeing.

Each time he secured a new customer he made sure he

personally travelled with the first cargo to ensure that it was handled properly and delivered promptly. Finding at last a pride in a job well done had given Hugh a confidence and sense of worth that had made life for young Tom very much easier than it could have been.

At sixteen years old Tom was a quiet confident lad. He'd been happy as a child living with Jane, and he still enjoyed his visits with her in the school holidays but as he matured he had almost as much pleasure on the holidays he spent working alongside his Uncle Hugh on the canals.

School had been an ordeal for Tom in the early years but it had taught him how to get along with others, even the most difficult types, and that certainly stood him in good stead in later years as, although he'd never stopped being slightly afraid of Henry, he had an easy relationship with Hugh. Strangers would often assume they were father and son and both of them were content with that.

Tom's first love was sketching, if he could snatch a moment he was drawing something, a house, the cathedral, a scene on the river. At school he would draw caricatures of the masters and, as word got out he'd draw special requests for the boys. As a result of this talent the boys that had ridiculed him started to treat him with more respect, and many of them wanted to spend time with him. He had often received invitations to stay with this boy or that during holidays but he rarely took up those invitations preferring to spend his time with either Hugh or Jane.

This had been the initial cause for Henry's disappointment in Tom. Henry felt that the friends made at school were the stepping stones to a strong future in business, or even politics, and should be nurtured, then in time exploited. He'd expected Tom to make friends with the sons of men he himself could do business with.

Tom was firmly opposed to making the right sort of friends and wanted nothing more than to spend his time here, in the warehouse or on the boats with Hugh. The two had become close, much to their own surprise and that of all around them. They worked well together and had a sense of humour and fun in common.

The men on the boats and in the docks had all got used to him and most of them refused to call him Tom. They all swore his name should be Hugh Two and that's what they insisted they would call him. Where Henry had found Tom to be a bitter disappointment, Hugh had found a kindred spirit.

On Sunday morning, a young traveller was decoyed into an inn near Worcester by two persons who pretended to him that they were strangers to each other, but it is evident they had a premeditated design to plunder him, for, before he left the inn, they had managed to defraud him of about £40. We mention this to show how cautious every one ought to be in forming an acquaintance with entire strangers.

(Copyright and courtesy of the Worcester News)

CHAPTER THIRTY EIGHT

Although Tom usually enjoyed accompanying Hugh when he had meetings with potential customers he generally made his exit as they prepared to seal the deal with an afternoon of drinking and card playing. It was a crucial part of building a good relationship, Tom understood this, but at just sixteen he had yet to develop an appetite for that kind of thing, far preferring to be left alone with his sketch book.

The Cathedral grounds held a particular fascination for him and he especially enjoyed having time to sit at the foot of the old city wall and look across at the hive of activity on the river. Watching as men loaded and unloaded goods to go either upstream or downstream, many of them in the employ of his own family, brought alive the sense that these days if a man could dream, he could find another to make that dream a reality. These hard working men and all that activity were his world. There was always some activity to amuse or interest him and his fingers were often sketching away with almost effortless skill and speed. He drew what he saw, and his little sketches had, over the years, been a source of comfort to Jane. He had moved on, far away from his humble beginnings but he'd never neglected her. She had no wish to visit his world but she was so proud of the insight into his new life he furnished her with in the shape of these amusing sketches.

As Tom cast his eyes across the river he could see the church at the top of the hill and knew that just behind it, hidden from this view point, stood the Great House, dominating the whole of St John's.

It dawned on him as he sat enjoying the view that one day he would own it all, over there as far as the eye could see everything was his, or would be one day. That was a wonderful thought but he got more of a thrill from knowing that he was a part of the greatest change England had ever seen. The days of waiting for weeks upon weeks for the rains to stop and the tracks to harden before anything more than a man on a horse could be moved had gone for ever.

His grandfather and men like him had transformed the country for everyone. People who had never gone more than a mile or two from home and had rarely seen a thing that had not been produced locally were now able to enjoy products from around the country.

Traders could load a boat or a barge up with produce and take it a few hours away and sell to people who had never been able to enjoy such novelties in past times. The Midlands were no longer land locked, the canals had opened them up to the rest of the country.

News could be transmitted from one end of the country to the other in hours now, when it used to take weeks or even months to know what was going on in London, and he was a part of all that.

Tom had no doubt that working on the canals was what he was meant to do but he also knew Henry expected him to be a figurehead not a worker. He felt that an owner should keep himself above everyone else and as his direct kin, Tom should be this way. Tom did his best to appease Henry but only to keep him happy, in his heart he would never be that man.

Tom was woken from his daydreams by a man's voice, “Richard, what are you doing here, why aren't you at school?” He jumped to his feet and explained to the stranger that he had mistaken him for someone else.

Sam Thatcher smiled and apologised for disturbing him but as he looked directly into Tom's face his smile faded. "You looked familiar to me, you're so much like a young man I know."

Tom introduced himself and Sam told him that he had known Tom's grandfather Henry and had in fact been a tutor to his sons, William and Hugh, in years gone by. The two parted company and Tom made his way back to the river and soon got on with his work and thought no more of the man he'd just met.

The Lady who makes miniature profiles at the premises opposite the Bell Hotel in Broad Street, Worcester, leaves the city next Saturday morning. In the interim she will make the most striking likeness at two shillings and sixpence each. She returns her warmest acknowledgements for the very great encouragement she has been favoured with by the respectable inhabitants of this city.

(Copyright and courtesy of the Worcester News)

CHAPTER THIRTY NINE

Sam Thatcher was a prosperous and contented man, he'd recently gained yet another advertiser and was being widely complimented about the quality and frequency of the publication of the newspaper, all in all he was feeling very positive about the future. He and Ruby had just completed the monthly accounts and had agreed that things were looking very encouraging both for the paper and the country in general.

The King, who been suffering with poor health since the death of two infant sons, had recovered his health and it seemed as though the entire country had breathed a sigh of relief. There was connection between him and the ordinary people. He seemed to suffer the same things as they did. Poor health and dying children were things that ordinary people knew all about and that made them feel as though he really was one of them.

When it had been announced that he was coming to visit Worcester the whole city turned out to greet him and Queen Charlotte. He toured the porcelain factory and ordered a dinner service and the news of this great honour spread like wildfire. Once again the citizens of the faithful city shared in the feeling of pride at serving the monarch.

As Sam sat with Ruby talking over more mundane events he remembered the young man he'd met near the Cathedral and wanted to know whether Ruby knew of him. “He introduced himself to me as Tom Daventor. It was quite extraordinary, at first glance I thought he was Richard but once we'd spoken and I got a clearer look at him I knew it wasn't Richard, but, do you know, they could have been brothers."

Ruby shuffled some papers and appeared distracted.

"I assume he must be a son of Hugh but I didn't hear anything about a wedding and that surprises me. Such a high profile man being able to marry without anyone in the local newspaper knowing would be odd, very odd indeed.”

“Ah.” They sat in silence as Ruby put her thoughts in order. It had to come out sometime and perhaps now was as good a time as any.

“Sam, I have told you the truth, but not all of it, I held some details back, not to keep things from you but because that has been my habit. It's a habit of self protection and I hope when you hear the whole story you'll understand and forgive me.”

She told him then of all that had happened to her, aware that at some point in the story Ann had come in to listen. They sat in silence as she filled in the gaps of her story and when she finished all she could hear was the pounding of her heart. She knew they would find it difficult, struggling as they were to have their own family but she so wanted their respect.

Sam spoke at last. “Ruby, I need you to help me to understand this, are you really saying you had twin boys and you were prepared to *sell* them?” He looked at her as though she were a stranger, someone he could never know. "I just don't see how you could think of doing such a thing."

She felt her face grow hot with shame and her eyes pricked with tears. She wiped her eyes angrily and looked at Ann who had the same look of horror on her face as Sam did. In an instant the shame ebbed away from her as fast as it had come. She straightened her shoulders and took a deep breath.

"Giving poor children to wealthy families who will give them a better life is not a bad thing. Many girls who find themselves in trouble would starve if it weren't for that simple fact. Babies would die or be killed. You both know the lengths poor women are reduced to when they can't feed themselves never mind a child."

She stood up slowly and nodded to herself, she was right and they were wrong and if she could she'd make them see it. "These situations are not black or white Sam. I did what I needed to do and neither of my boys have come to any harm. In fact they have both come to a great deal of good. I'm sorry I didn't tell you the whole story, but I'm not sorry for what I did and I won't ever say I am. When I was fourteen years old, scared and alone, then I might have listened to your advice, but you weren't there to help me then were you, either of you?”

Ann, as usual tried to be the peacemaker, Ruby's hot temper and Sam's fixed beliefs often caused them to clash but she could generally bring them both to sense, but today her attempt was at best half hearted. Having suffered the loss of her second child before the age of two and been forced to the conclusion that she would never have a longed for child of her own, she had little appetite for women who willingly gave up what she so desperately wanted. Sam had more recriminations to make and Ann lacked the will to prevent him.

"Your boys are brothers yet through your actions they've never even met. They've missed out on growing up alongside one another and the comradeship that they could have shared through manhood. How wicked a decision that was Ruby."

Ruby's body vibrated with anger and frustration, why couldn't she make them understand. “What I did to my boys was not cruel, they don't know each other and they can't miss each other. I don't know what will happen when they learn about each other but I imagine they will cope with things the way Ellie and I coped when we were torn apart as children. We learned to get on with it and they will do the same. I did what I thought was best for them both. I don't claim to have all the answers and I have no idea what will happen to them in the future but I do know they've both had a far better start in life than I had.”

She had said all she could say and so she made her way to the door, sad, but unashamed.

“But you must see that you're misleading them both, that's going to reflect badly on you in time to come.” Sam said.

At this Ruby laughed long and hard. “I run a brothel, I sell babies and have offered protection to those you would see hanged, and you concern yourself with the way separating my boys will reflect on me. Good grief Sam we really don't live in the same world do we?”

He dropped his head and could not or would not look her in the eyes. She turned on her heel and left. She was devastated by the fact that Sam thought she'd done wrong and she was furious that he found it so easy to judge, never having experienced the things she'd suffered. Damn him. And damn everybody else who thought they knew how she should live her life.

To be sold at the Journal printing office in Worcester, at Mr John Bennett's near the county gaol in Hereford and by the men that carry this newspaper, a rich cordial which gives immediate ease in the most violent cholic and gripes, carrying it off by gently purging. It gives ease to any pain in the bowels proceeding from wind or cold. Price one shilling the bottle, sealed as in the margin with a dove and olive branch in its mouth, with directions for use.

(Copyright and courtesy of the Worcester News)

CHAPTER FORTY

Ruby angrily marched back through Worcester twice as fast as she had marched in earlier that day. Her temper made her oblivious to her surroundings however, by the time she reached the water fields her temper had calmed a little. She was out of breath and over warm and decided to rest. She resolved, there and then, to keep more distance between herself and her friends in future, she didn't like the way they made her feel about doing what she really believed was the right thing.

Their business relationship was good and that was all she needed from Sam and Ann, allowing a friendship to develop was mistake she wouldn't make in a hurry again. They were in no position to pass judgement on the choices she'd made as a child and she would hear no more of it.

As she came to that decision she relaxed and gradually felt her headache melt away. She breathed in the clean fresh air as she sat down and leaned against her favourite tree. The warm sun on her face and the gentle breeze all around was calming and soothing and she allowed her mind to drift.

She was woken from her dreaming by sound of voices and she jumped to her feet instantly, she knew how dangerous it was out here alone if you let your guard down and she had foolishly done that.

She made her way softly to where the voices had come from and she saw a young man and woman together. He had scooped up some spring water and was urging his companion to drink it. He looked up as he became aware that they were being watched, he was instantly defensive. "We're not doing any harm here, my wife likes the water, she's not been well and we were told that drinking it would do her good."

Ruby nodded her agreement and walked closer to them. "It's good clean water, I drink it myself, but who told you it would help your wife? I don't know you do I?"

“No, you don't know us." he held his hand out in greeting. "My name is Dennis, Dennis Jones and this is my wife Lillian.”

Ruby introduced herself to them and then sat down to join them. Seeing that she was not trying to move them on Dennis went on to explain to her that his brother was a clerk working with the doctors here in Worcester at the infirmary. Lillian had begun to suffer a cough that would not clear up one of the doctors agreed to see her in the infirmary. He told her all she needed fresh air and clean water and advised her to spend as much time as possible outside away from their damp living quarters.

Since then whenever they could they walked the length and breadth of Worcester. They had heard that there was a spring here they had decided to venture away from the city bounds and try to find it. Lillian's cough was showing improvements and they were both convinced that the fresh air was the reason.

Ruby assured them that she'd been coming to the spring and drinking the water for many years and had no health problems and neither did all the people she lived with. She explained to them her employer owned the land they were on but that she wouldn't mind them coming out to drink from the spring as often as they wished. They enjoyed a few pleasant moments together and all agreed to try meet again at the same time the following week.

Continuing her walk home Ruby found her normal good humour restored and she felt much better. She had made two new friends, she had work to do at home and she knew she should be thankful for all she had. There was another girl coming in to the house tonight and Ruby wanted to be ready for her, she'd no doubt be scared and she'd need Ruby's help. There was much work to be done and she was the one to do it.

All Ma was good for these days was meddling, if she ever did try to arrange something it generally caused problems further down the line for Ruby. One such problem was waiting for her when she reached home. She'd been expecting one pregnant girl, but there were two. Ma had agreed to help the daughter of an old friend out and then forgotten to tell anyone about the agreement.

Ma shrugged when Ruby told her what she'd done. "You'll sort it out girl, you always do."

Ruby threw herself back into her responsibilities instantly and put everything else out of her mind.

At the Assizes here in Worcester this week, Elisha Greenwood, John Martin, Nathaniel Whatson and William Whatson, all for petty larceny, were ordered to be whipped next Saturday (being fair day) in the Corn Market in this city.

(Copyright and courtesy of the Worcester News)

CHAPTER FORTY ONE

It was a couple of months before Ruby decided she must soon go back to Sidbury to meet with Sam and Ann again. She'd been overwhelmed with work until now but had no intention of letting their disagreement prevent her from paying proper attention to her newspaper.

It was her habit recently to read snippets out of the paper to Ma, whose eyesight was failing, in the evening and this night they were both sniggering at the barely veiled reports of the exploits of Emma Vernon who'd left her husband Henry Cecil and run off with a Reverend. Henry in turn had moved in with a village woman. "I told you years ago that marriage wouldn't do didn't I girl? God knows I never saw all this coming though."

Ruby nodded absently. She'd spotted a little notice in the paper offering a house and small garden to be let. If the advertisement was true it sounded exactly what she was looking for and, as the contact point was the newspaper office, she now had a sound business reason to pay a visit to Sam. Any residual awkwardness would be short lived.

She duly set off for Sidbury first thing the next morning feeling optimistic. If she could secure the house she'd seen advertised then she could move her plans for a training house for servants forward quickly. It was a dry bright day and Ruby made the journey in record time.

Finding no-one in the office she walked around the side of the building to the courtyard that led to Sam and Ann's little house, calling out as she went. As she entered the courtyard she heard a dreadful scream and within seconds saw Ann running from the house to the workshop in the other corner of the courtyard.

Following quickly behind Ruby saw Sam lying on the floor, now groaning quietly. He was deathly pale and barely conscious. One of his legs was bent underneath him at an awkward angle while the other had gone right through a rotten floorboard and was clearly stuck. As they got closer they could see his foot had gone through the board and impaled itself upon a wicked piece of twisted metal that had lain hidden underneath.

Ann, in panic tried to pull his leg free but Ruby pulled her away and sharply ordered her to stop for fear of causing more harm. It looked as though one of Sam's leg's had broken but the other was trapped and they would need help in getting him free.

Taking control Ruby dispatched Ann to search out Mr Whitehouse, the man that shared their grounds. He was an advocate of herbs and natural medicines, and there was a fair chance that he'd be here working with his precious concoctions somewhere. He might have a better idea than either of them of how to help Sam. If not at least it would be another person to help them make a bigger hole in order to free Sam.

When Ann had gone, Ruby lay flat on the ground and looked through the hole to see what she could of Sam's leg. She shuddered with horror at the mess she saw and turned away again very quickly as Sam groaned weakly, he then began to vomit copiously and she had no more time to think. She moved him slightly so that he was on his side and then held his hand talking to him calmly and willing Ann to hurry back with the old man.

At last Ann came back in and the man with her took over straight away. He was a much younger man than the one Ruby had met previously, this must be his grandson she realised.

The man held Sam's head and made him drink a cup of something that clearly tasted foul, Sam appeared unwilling to drink it but lacked the strength to pull away, and he made sure to pour every last drop down Sam's throat, all the time speaking to him reassuringly, and within a moment or two he was much quieter and almost slept.

Mr Whitehouse then told Ruby he was indeed the old man's grandson and introduced himself as Ben. He went on to explain to the two women that Sam's pain would be dulled for now and it was possible he might even sleep. It was essential that they use this time quickly to get him free and cleaned up properly. He would need them both to de exactly as he said.

Seeing that Ann was still shaken and in a state of considerable distress he directed his next comment quietly to Ruby, "I shall need your help here for I don't think she'll be up to it." He nodded a head in Ann's direction as he spoke.

Ruby agreed. "Tell me what you need me to do?"

Ann was sent into the house to prepare a bed for Sam as near to the entrance of their cottage as she could. She was also instructed to prepare copious quantities of hot water and have clean rags made available. Once she was out of hearing range he explained to Ruby what would happen next.

"We need to get his leg out of this hole first as steady as we can. We must straighten it, and the pain of that will likely wake him up again. He'll likely scream and thrash about for the pain will be cruel and that's when you'll need to hold him as still as you can. I must clean out the hole in his foot properly and then we'll strap him to a board. Are you ready for me to start?"

She nodded but he hadn't finished speaking. "Just understand this, once we start we must see it through. To stop halfway would cause him far too much pain, do you understand?"

"I'm ready."

The next hour or so was a torment for Sam and draining for Ruby, she gave thanks for the years of delivering babies and taking care of all other sorts of ailments people turned up at Ma's with. She'd developed a strong stomach and a steady hand and they stood her in good stead now.

Ben Whitehouse gave Ann a soporific to keep Sam asleep through the night and told Ruby she should be proud of herself. "If I ever need an assistant again I shall ask you to step in. Few women have a stomach as strong as yours."

For some reason this made her feel more proud than anything she achieved for a long time. She left them soon after, promising Ann she would be back first thing in the morning.

She'd forgotten all about the house she'd come to enquire after.

Mr Hull, surgeon of Evesham, informs the public that he inoculates according to the best and most approved methods which has already benefited 30,000 patients around the kingdom without one person being lost. Mr Hull has opened two very large and convenient houses near the Evesham turnpike, remarkable for their beautiful prospects and wholesomeness of air, where constant attention will be given and every accommodation made available. Those coming for inoculation will be expected to pay three guineas for which they will be suitably accommodated with tea, wine, washing and linen.

(Copyright and courtesy of the Worcester News)

CHAPTER FORTY TWO

There followed a difficult few weeks for Sam and Ann. Ruby did all she could to help as she found that Ann was unable to do much apart from talk to Sam. The paper was not being produced regularly and it was obvious that help was needed here if all was not to be lost. Sam was going to be bedridden for some time, that much was plain to see and Ann couldn't possibly nurse him and produce the paper at the same time.

Richard would be home from school any day for a holiday and Ruby knew that he'd be insisting on coming straight here to work and she'd have no grounds for argument this time.

It had always been agreed that he'd work here with Sam once his education was complete and he'd been begging to spend more time here with Sam for a couple of years now. The only thing that had prevented him was Sam and Ruby's united front that his education must be completed. She'd have to let him step in now and she knew he'd be delighted.

Sam's leg showed signs of healing but as his health returned so his temper deteriorated. His concern about his work increased and he was anxious and irritable. Knowing that Richard would be at his beck and call soon was a huge relief to him, but he was extremely frustrated at his own inability to move about as he had in the past.

He was reluctant to accept that in future he would only walk with the aid of a stick and then only for short periods. His frustration was taking its toll on Ann who was bearing the brunt of his anguish alone. She was working her fingers to the bone, caring for him, running the home and trying to print the paper with only Ruby to help whenever she could spare the time.

Without the paper there would be no money and nothing to fall back on. She was so worried about all that could go wrong that she was wearing herself out. Her slim body was now gaunt and in truth she looked more sick than Sam. There was nothing anyone could do to help right away but.

Richard would be with them in a couple of days. Until then she would cope.

On Saturday last, an inquest was held on view of the body of William Hunt, late of the Parish of Inkberrow, who hanged himself. This man it seems, was a kind of an idiot and, lately on the death of his mother, came into possession of a cottage. Some neighbours who knew his weakness persuaded him, out of "fun" as they term it, that he would soon be dispossessed of his dwelling unless he took to him a wife, whereupon he prevailed on a person to marry him. Soon after, the same indiscreet persons, though without the least foundation, began to insinuate things that caused him to be jealous of his wife, and which had such an effect on his mind as to occasion his destroying himself.

(Copyright and courtesy of the Worcester News)

CHAPTER FORTY THREE

Richard had just completed his second full year of working at the paper and he had loved every moment of it. Ever since he'd first come to live with Sam and Ann as a small boy the newspaper had fascinated him and Sam had done all he could to encourage him. Since those early years he'd considered their home to be his home and so moving in and taking over when Sam needed him had been a natural progression.

It made sense to him to be on hand at the paper day and night and Ruby certainly didn't want him to move back into Ma's; that had been good enough when he was a newborn with no awareness and no choice but would be quite wrong for him now.

At that time Sam had been confined to his bed for a large part of most days but he made up for that by having Richard run here, there and everywhere chasing a snippet Sam had heard a whisper of from one quarter or another. When Richard returned with what he hoped was the full story Sam then questioned him in great depth in an effort to show him how little of the story he had in fact uncovered. Richard soon learned to check and double check everything he heard. Being an assistant and confidant of Sam's had ensured that Richard matured into a thoughtful and intelligent young man.

He knew nowadays to look at what appeared on the surface to be the story but then to dig underneath and make sure he had uncovered the whole and never to assume he knew everything. He had also learned to simply sit and listen, silence was a valuable tool Sam had taught him, many people felt the need to fill one and there, often, lay the treasure.

Gradually Sam's health returned and although his leg plagued him from time to time he refused to give in to it. When the doctors had told him he might never walk again he had been badly afraid but determined to fight the prognosis with all his strength and now, two years on he determinedly walked up to the Cathedral and back almost every day, it had become a point of honour to him.

Richard found the stories he was covering absolutely fascinating, he was completely caught up in the passions and excitement of the times. There was talk across the country about the rights of the working man, all demanding fair pay and safer working conditions. Men were getting together and protesting about bad owners and greedy business men. The situation had become so serious the King had issued a proclamation warning against sedition.

Sam told Richard they were lucky these days that they could cover events like these in fair and reasoned manner, in Henry Daventors day Sam would not have been allowed to report such things without being forced to put the owners slant on his reporting.

Richard attended the meetings for change that were being held in inns and coffee shops across Worcester and beyond and he became a well liked figure as the men realised he reported the truth of what he saw and not what one side or the other wanted to see. The consensus was that he was worthy successor for Sam.

This is to acquaint all persons who have a desire to assure their houses from fire that the Royal Exchange Assurance Company have appointed Mr Bonham Caldwell, of Bewdley, to be their agent for Herefordshire, Shropshire and Worcestershire, or any part of the adjacent towns or counties.

(Copyright and courtesy of the Worcester News)

CHAPTER FORTY FOUR

Ruby found the house she wanted. The tall red brick house in the Foregate was now her pride and joy. The glossy black front door with brass furnishings was polished daily and the steps leading up to the door were swept and scrubbed and the windows gleamed. The black railings that marked the boundary were free of dust and pretty plants decorated the border.

Ruby had installed a cook, a thirty seven year old woman who had made the mistake of believing the lies a dashing butler had told her. She'd longed for love, a husband and a home of her own and she truly thought she'd found them at this late stage. When she discovered she'd been fooled it was too late, her reputation was gone, she lost her position and had nowhere to go.

Ruby rescued her and now her job was working with girls who'd made the same kind of mistake as her, teaching them skills that could take them into any house in Worcester.

Ruby had found her maids the same way. Her dream of training girls to go out and work was at last coming to fruition. She'd not yet placed anyone in a family home but she'd been prepared for it to take a year or two before people accepted the service she could provide and also for her to train the girls properly. The right kind of enquiries were starting to be made by housekeepers and ambitious wives and she was ready.

Producing a good tea and serving it properly when Richard visited to present Ruby with her monthly report was part of the training for the girls and they each took it in turns to serve. Some did better than others but it almost moved Ruby to tears to see how desperately hard they all tried. Every single one of them knew how close they had come to losing all hope of a decent future and most were determined to seize this chance with both hands.

There were, of course girls who would never be

suitable. Clara for example, she'd be taking Bella's place at some point in the future, that much was clear to everyone, she was born for it.

Then there was Sara, Ruby had caught her rifling through Ma's room looking for something to steal. Ruby didn't judge any girl for finding herself in trouble and doing what she had to, but a thief or a liar could have no place in the world Ruby was building for herself. She was very selective about who was offered a place here and she would not accept a girl if she had even the smallest doubt about her integrity or desire to work hard. Everything that happened in this house was a part of a reputation she was building and nothing would be allowed to spoil that.

One of the things that had most worried Ruby in the beginning was how to tell Bella and Mary that they couldn't come to visit her new house. She'd lain awake at nights trying to think how to explain without hurting her dearest friends but when she finally sat down to talk to them they made it easy for her.

"We know you don't want us to be turning up at the house Ruby, we 'ent daft girl. That's a part of your respectable life you're always talking about. Me and Mary know we don't fit in there, we don't want to. Don't worry, we'll never show you up."

Ruby was at pains to convince them that it was the reputation of the girls in the house she wanted to protect, not her own. She continued to live at Ma's and always would, she preferred that way of life. She enjoyed playing the lady every now and again but the house in the Forgate was a place of work not a home for her.

She had continued to work at Ma's and spend half a day a week with them. Bella could, and frequently did, still shock her and Mary with the tales of her night time adventures. Ruby in turn entertained them with tales of how tea should be served, and what a gentleman should wear when visiting a lady. How soon he could remove his gloves and hat, and why his jacket should never be removed.

“What a load of bleedin nonsense. I like my gentlemen to be undressed, then I know there won't be no surprises.” Bella declared. "I can handle any man, so long as he's naked."

Her friendship with Dennis and Lillian had continued to develop and she also tried to see them once a week, at the spring in good weather and in their little house in poor weather. They had become trusted confidante's and knew most of her secrets and had been ready to give her sensible advice when she'd worried she was trying to do too much.

Dennis was now a highly skilled painter at the Porcelain works and it was said that in some of the best houses in the land decorative porcelain vases could be found with his name on them. Lillian was a lace maker and their home was filled with exquisite examples of both their work. Ruby found them both a restful antidote to her more raucous times with Bella and Mary.

She saw Ellie whenever she could but that was infrequent as Ellie herself was extraordinarily popular and now had several girls working with her, Madame Eloise was all the rage in Worcester.

Ruby spent most of her time with Ma, the old lady was a shadow of her former self and Ruby wanted to do all she could to keep her as comfortable and as happy as she could.

Whereas some spiteful and malicious person hath reported that the wife of Thomas Malpas of the Red Lion Inn in Mealcheapen Street, Worcester, did carry or send, on Sunday last, instruments to Robert Pritchard, now a prisoner in our City Gaol, to break out, this is therefore to give notice that if any person or persons will discover the author of such report so that he may be brought before any Justice of the Peace for the city or county of Worcester shall have one guinea reward, paid by me. Thomas Malpas.

(Copyright and courtesy of the Worcester News)

CHAPTER FORTY FIVE

Hugh Daventor was putting a good face on things but he was a worried man. Despite the fact that he was working harder than he'd ever worked before and increasing his workforce threefold his accounts were terrifying. He had gained three new contracts, was drowning in work and yet he had made little profit. He was both exhausted and confused. He seemed to do nothing but race around the area he'd set aside for the movements of the crates of china he'd agreed to transport to London.

The storage area was too small, he could see that, he'd had several near misses and now lived in fear of having to pay for replacements. He could lose a years worth of money if that happened, which would be catastrophic as things stood. But the crates had to be moved to make way for other goods to be loaded and unloaded.

He'd initially been delighted that his plans to provide transportation for other business had proved far more popular than he'd expected but he knew he wasn't coping. He was beginning to think that perhaps this entire idea for a business was unsustainable.

When he wasn't physically working on the boats he was going over his orders and receipts. Why was there no money, what the hell had gone wrong and how could he change it before Henry found out?

Hugh had made commitments to several local merchants to transport their goods and if he let just one of them down the word would spread like the plague. He'd lost a load due to the weather last month, the Severn had been wild and he counted himself lucky to have lost the load but saved the barge and men, nevertheless it was a cost he could hardly bear to carry.

He had sufficient men, good men, working hard and depending on him to keep things running well and thereby providing for their families. And yet, all he seemed to do was move piles of other peoples stock from one place to another.

Every time something was moved the chance of damaging it increased and thus ate into his profits. He didn't know what to do, he'd got himself into a situation and he couldn't see a way out. He hadn't felt this alone and exposed in business ever before.

Thank God Tom would be home from school later that week, at least then he'd have another willing pair of hands at his disposal. At the very least that would allow him the opportunity to step back and try to see where he was going wrong. In the meantime he'd just have to keep going.

Tom could see at once how relieved his uncle was to have another young, strong worker available. Nothing was said but Tom observed that the chaos they were working in was slowing everyone down. He kept quiet and watched and worked alongside his uncle at any task he was given with a good humour and energy.

Hugh thought the boy was quieter than usual but as he didn't have the time to listen to chatter anyway that was probably a good thing. It was towards the end of his holiday that Tom made his move.

"You know Uncle Hugh things could be a lot easier for you I think, if I didn't have to go back to school. I've given this a lot of thought and I'd like to stay here and work with you."

Hugh stopped what he was doing, he had a mountain of work to do but he couldn't ignore Tom when he had this on his mind. He sat down reluctantly and looked at Tom, who was looking more and more like William every day.

"Tom, I know you'd rather stay here, and I'd love to have you if I'm honest, but you must finish your education properly. You have a great future ahead of you and you'll need all the knowledge you can get."

Tom nodded his head in agreement but Hugh knew it wasn't going to be as easy as that to get Tom back to school, he had a plan, that much was clear.

"I agree with you, and I've had a fine education. But I'm

fully prepared to join the world of work now, I don't need any more time studying or playing silly games. I know what I want to do with my life and I'm ready to start now."

"What do you intend to do with your life then, tell me?" Hugh smiled at him. Tom was still so young and so passionate about everything, it was almost like being back with William sometimes, he'd always had great dreams and plans and he'd never wanted to do what Henry expected of him. At least Tom was a little easier to sway, and he didn't mind working hard, something William would never do.

Tom pulled himself up straight and took a deep breath. "I want to become your manager, working here. For three weeks now I've worked alongside you and the other men and I know I could make this entire enterprise faster, safer and a lot less difficult. You're too close to the problem to see where it's going wrong. I need a bit more time to think things through but I can tell you now that we've moved those crates of china six times since I've been here. That's complete madness. Until the load is taken to London and unpacked we won't know what has been damaged, but we can be certain that some has and that we'll have to pay for the replacements."

Hugh nodded but had no chance to speak, Tom was becoming more and more excited as the words spilled out of him and he outlined how well he felt the two of them could work together.

Belatedly Hugh realized that Tom had a well thought out plan and had been waiting for right moment to strike. The torrent of words increased now. "I can see the answer to our problem and I'm ready to start working on the solution now. I'm not proposing to give up school to be a waterman. I want to make some big, but much needed organizational changes. Can I explain to you what I've got in mind? After all this is my future here, surely you'll listen to me?"

Hugh laughed, despite his own worries he loved seeing

the boy's passion. “Well, I admit I can't see a way forward. In fact I've half a mind to give this moving goods business up, it's taking all my time and I'm neglecting the tannery and the glove makers and I can't afford to do that for much longer. There are a couple of chaps in town improving things for the glovers, if I don't start paying a bit more attention to that I'll lose the whole thing. I've just had a load of hides supplied and they're damaged. I need to get a grip on things like that elsewhere so if you plan to talk yourself into a job this is the best time to do it. I'm listening.”

“Right.” Tom began. “The china shipments are where our big money comes from at the moment so that has to be executed properly. That's why we move it all so often, to get it out of harms way. To simplify this we need to make crates on wheels and we also need a building that can be made secure just for the china. The factories tell us what needs to go to the London or Birmingham showrooms, and then we go and pick up from them and move it from pillar to post until they tell us when and where to send it, right?”

Hugh nodded his agreement.

“We've plenty of spare land here to make a safe storage place, just for the china, we can keep all the stock they send us on hand in one place. It could then be brought here and not moved again until it goes on the boat to be delivered. If we had the products here already that would save several moves, thus reducing the chance of breakage.”

Hugh's spirits sank, he'd foolishly hoped for a miracle and should have known Tom couldn't provide one. “Tom, that would be impossible, we don't have that kind of space available!” He hated quashing the lad's enthusiasm but they had no time just now for daydreams.

Tom however was up and running. “Not now we don't. But it's the first thing we must do if we are to retain that business. The porcelain men will be looking around now for someone who can do what we do, but more efficiently.

There will soon be someone on their side of the river hoping to steal their business from us. The biggest thing going for us is that we have vast swathes of land here that simply isn't available in Worcester and we must utilize it Uncle Hugh. We need to think much bigger than we have been because what we have now is unworkable."

"Go on."

"We have a couple of choices as far as I can see." He told Hugh that they needed to build a line of storage sheds all along their canal. One for gloves, one for salt, one for porcelain, another one for who knows what may come up in the future. They were utterly dependant upon the porcelain business and if anything went awry with that they'd be sunk.

"We must offer them a better service, storage and transport. We need, in effect, to be their agents, but we must also develop other arms to our business. It is foolish to be so dependant on one customer. We must increase our other business's and become important to them all."

"But we can't do any more than we're currently doing. You don't perhaps appreciate that we're working twenty-four hours a day as it is. I can't do more." Hugh was becoming frustrated.

Tom pulled out a piece of paper that was covered in drawing and columns of figures. He proceeded to tell Hugh that the canal that Henry had built was not big enough, they need branches to be built off that existing canal, branches that were wider than the canal itself. Each branch would need a warehouse to be built on it. They also needed Hugh to stop working and get back out into the world talking up the business and bringing in new customers.

Hugh waited a moment or two before replying. He didn't want to hurt Tom, or prevent him coming up with ideas but this idea was ridiculous. "It all sound good, very good, but we don't have time to extend the buildings or these canal branches. We can't stop doing what we're doing to free up the space. We don't have the time Tom!"

"Uncle Hugh, if you don't make the time to do this properly you might as well stop now. I've looked at what is going on here and we both know you're not making any money, how much longer can you afford to let this situation continue?"

The question gave them both pause for thought. If all that Henry had built here failed the Daventor reputation would be destroyed, possibly even held up to ridicule, which might be the worst of the two.

Henry had heard from every quarter that he was a madman when he'd embarked on this scheme and yet he kept on regardless, certain they were wrong and he was right. Hugh and Tom were his heirs and it was their duty to put things right and to keep the enterprise going. Failure was unthinkable. As they were they might last another year, but if they were not making real money there was no point. Hugh conceded that things must change dramatically or it would all end. He still couldn't see how he could continue his business and make such sweeping changes.

"We must slow down our commitments now, we can manage to continue moving the porcelain but everything else must be put on hold. Every man we can spare has to be put onto the expansion and we should begin that immediately."

Hugh was appalled at the thought of losing so much trade and argued vehemently against such a radical plan but Tom could clearly see it was the only way to move on and he was prepared to fight for what he knew had to be done. Hugh had become so enmeshed in hard grinding work he'd lost sight of the big picture.

"Look Hugh, if we do this now, while we have a strong name and lots of business it will be taken as a sign that we are doing too well to do anything but expand. More people will believe in us and more business men will want to join us because they will see that any business that takes time out to improve and expand must be doing very well indeed."

Hugh conceded that he could see the sense in that but he said he wasn't so sure that people would be easily fooled. In truth he'd been almost convinced by Tom's argument but felt it essential to test how workable the plan would be, he wanted Tom to prove to both of them that he had thought of everything.

"It isn't a case of fooling anyone, we *are* trying to do too much. We're the only people providing this service at the moment which is why we're getting away with not doing it very well. We must improve now while we're ahead because you can be sure that someone else will be setting up in competition to us soon and they'll learn from our mistakes even if we don't."

Tom leaned back and gulped his drink. He'd given it his best shot, it was up to Hugh now and Hugh was no fool. He also had no time to play games."How old are you Tom?"

"Quite old enough, I think you told me once you'd finished school when you were eighteen, the age I am now."

Hugh nodded his head, Tom had convinced him and it would be marvellous to be able to share this burden with someone he could trust. "Yes, indeed. I'm not going to put you off. I'm going to suggest that as a way of marking your birthday we make you a very hard working partner in this messy, badly run, unprofitable and chaotic enterprise? When we make it profitable, which you assure me we can, then you'll take over here and I'll go back to what I do best."

They had a quick meal together and raised a glass to mark this great change and then they began to plot and plan in earnest.

Before night was done Hugh had confidence that they could pull it off and they would be successful. He had been too close to the problem and failed to see the situation clearly, Tom had put him back on track and he felt the immense pressure lift from his shoulders as dawn broke.

Last Tuesday, Sir Henry Harpur of Calke in Derbyshire, Bart., was elected representative in parliament for this city of Worcester, without opposition, in the room of the Rt Hon Samuel Lord Sandys, Baron of Ombersley. And the same afternoon, he set off for London in order to attend the business of parliament. The said gentleman was met, the preceding evening and ushered into this city by the corporation. A very great number of freemen and several gentlemen of the adjacent villages, all on horseback, attended with streamers, drums, etc., making a grand cavalcade through the streets.

(Copyright and courtesy of the Worcester News)

CHAPTER FORTY SIX

Ruby and Ellie were taking tea together, something they did as frequently as they could. It was ostensibly to discuss business, but also because, although they'd never quite regained their childhood intimacy, they were determined not to let anything in future come between them.

They'd grown up very differently there was no doubt about that. Ellie had developed a taste for finery and had never truly known hard work or seen any ugliness. She had grown used to smart clothes and good food and nowadays would settle for nothing less. Ruby, who had known nothing but hard work in the midst of all life's seediness had little time for Ellie's irritating finer sensibilities. Yet there was an unbreakable bond between the two, they loved each other dearly and were able to laugh at their differences now, where they had fallen out about them a few years earlier. Both of them were aware that without a doubt that they were on the same side and always would be and that gave them both a feeling of security neither of them had known since they'd left home all those years ago as young girls.

One thing they were agreed upon was the need for financial stability that would be theirs come what may and today they were working on the next step in improving this very situation.

Their recent decision was that Ellie and Hannah, her number one assistant would move into the house that Ruby had bought and was having girls trained in. The business of Madam Eloise would continue to be run from the original location but it was time now for Ellie to be a mistress of her own home.

Ellie had built up a very good reputation in the city and people trusted her judgement. When they heard where she was living it would give a seal of approval to the house. There was a need in Worcester for good quality, respectable lodgings for gentlewomen and Ruby intended to serve that need. Madame Eloise was widely used and very well respected in the town and the word would spread into all the right quarters.

Ruby wanted people to know that her house was of the finest quality and that her staff were the best trained girls, all of which was true. The story that was to be whispered about, in confidence you understand, was that the house was financed by a wealthy widow who, in her twilight years was giving girls from decent, but poor, families training for a better life.

Anyone looking for rooms, comfortable and fashionable naturally, need look no further. Here they could be assured of receiving the very best of attention and should a lady in town find herself in need of a servant then she need look no further.

It wouldn't serve for Ruby to be living there, her main work was still out at Ma's and that was where she preferred to be. She was shrewd enough to know that her past was not far enough behind her to be forgotten and she was quite happy to be an invisible force behind other people.

Besides which she had no desire to live life the proper way. The freedoms she enjoyed at Ma's were not something she was prepared to give up. When she'd had nothing she'd dreamed of living a fine lifestyle with all the trappings that went with such a life but now, she had all the money and comfort she needed and she could not bear to relinquish her personal freedom simply to be accepted by society.

She'd learned from Ellie that the fine ladies she'd so much envied had no freedom whatsoever. She'd stay where she was, living as she chose. Society didn't expect her to behave in any particular way because society didn't even know she was there and Ruby was at ease with that.

The sisters had just agreed that Ellie and Hannah would move in to the house early in the coming month and, once settled, would start a gentle whispering campaign in the right ears about the fine new lodging house they had discovered in Worcester.

They were interrupted as a message arrived from Ann asking if Ruby could call on her urgently. As this was the first time Ann had ever sent her a message Ruby knew something serious must have happened and so, as soon as she reasonably could, she left Ellie to it and made her way into Sidbury.

The best Bristol Soap is made and sold by Thomas Willoughby and John Pember, tallow chandlers in Worcester, where all dealers and shop keepers may be supplied per order at a reasonable rate, and the goods shall be as good as if the purchasers were present to see it boxed-up at our Soap House.

(Copyright and courtesy of the Worcester News)

CHAPTER FORTY SEVEN

As Ruby hastened from the centre of the city to the outskirts of Sidbury she reflected that it had been some considerable time since she'd visited the newspaper. Her presence was no longer required for business purposes as she received a regular, and thorough, report from Richard every month which satisfied her curiosity and a quarterly sum was paid to her in steadily increasing amounts which satisfied her business brain.

Since the time when Sam and Ann had seemed to judge her harshly for the choices she'd been forced to take as a child their friendship had cooled. When Sam's accident occurred she was more than happy to help them through those dark days in any way she could and she would also be forever grateful for the way they had helped her with Richards education and indeed the way they cherished him still, but their relationship now was almost completely a professional one and she lacked both the will and the time to try to re-capture what they'd shared in the past.

As she approached the newspaper office she saw no sign of life and Ruby felt a niggle of concern as she trod the familiar path around the building towards the small cottage the couple still shared. She called out as she walked but heard and saw no-one.

She knocked loudly on the door and, as still no one answered, she pushed the door open and made to go in. Almost immediately she recoiled in horror, the room was filled with a foul stench that had enveloped her before the doorway was fully open.

She let out a cry of distress to see Sam, back in the bed that had been set up when he'd first had his accident and she was horrified to discern that he was the source of the odour. Moving closer to him she could see he looked worse now than he had years ago when he was first injured. He lay there unmoving, his skin a waxy yellow, his eyes closed.

Gasping with horror her eyes were drawn to his leg as it lay uncovered, a livid red swelling surrounded the old wound and the centre had split open and now oozed a vile mix of pus and blood. Ann sat in a chair by his side and held his hand, barely registering Ruby's presence. Ruby saw at once how thin and tired she was.

She crossed the room and put her arms around Ann and held her close "Oh Ann, what's happened? I thought he was fully recovered?" she asked quietly.

"He wanted everyone to think that, but the truth is he's been having bad spells all along. It's been good and bad but the bad has been getting worse."

Sam had been adamant that his recurring illness be kept between the two of them. He knew what it meant and he knew Richard needed as much experience as could be crammed in before he would be fully ready to take the reins.

If the general populace knew Sam was unfit they may have lost confidence in the paper and all that he'd built up would be gone. He'd needed to do as much as he could to get Richard in a position to keep things going as soon as was reasonable. What would Ann live on if he let it all go?

"So how long has he been like this?" Ruby asked.

"It comes and goes. I put a poultice on it when it swells and that draws out the poison but the swelling comes back faster each time. He forbid me to tell you or Richard, but it's been happening all along. One of the doctors from the infirmary told me what to do and I've managed but I could do with a bit of help now though Ruby, that's why I had to send for you. I know you've got things of your own to deal with but I can't do this alone any more."

She explained that Richard was running the paper single handedly now, he knew Sam was unwell but had not been told how critical he was. He was used to being kept occupied night and day and had so far not noticed any changes to the normal routine.

Ruby was distraught to think that these dear people had

been suffering and trying to keep it to themselves, they hadn't asked her for help and she wondered if that was her own fault. She bit back a sob, not wanting to add to Ann's distress.

"Don't upset yourself Ruby, we wanted as much time as we could get on our own, we know this is the end." Ann looked sad but accepting.

They'd spent hours talking, in Sam's lucid moments, and together they'd faced the fact that he would not recover this time. Sam, ever her tutor and guide, had helped her to understand and accept that he'd die soon. They spent all the time they could together and had said all they needed to say.

"What are you saying?" Ruby protested. "It's not the end, Sam's a strong man, he just needs a bit of help. I'm going to ask Ben Whitehouse to come and have a look. He sorted it all out before and he'll know what to do now. I'll go and find him now while you sit here and rest a moment. I'll try to be back before he wakes and then I'll stay with you until Sam's on his feet again."

She strode out into the sunshine, greedily gulping the clean air, and headed for the workshop that Ben could usually be found in, pottering about until all hours and sure enough he was in there tending some plants. There was no mistaking the pleasure he felt as he saw who his visitor was.

She'd barely explained herself before he was striding past her towards the house and by the time she caught up with him he was helping Ann adjust Sam's position. He caught Ruby's eye and very slightly shook his head. She made her way over to Ann and put her arm around her. "Let's go and sit outside for a moment and leave Sam with Ben in private for a moment."

She gently led Ann out into the sunshine and the two old friends sat on an old tree stump and leaned in towards each other.

"Don't worry about us Ruby, I know he's going to die

and so does he. We've said all we needed to say to one another and we've made our peace. He wanted some time alone with me and he didn't want you worried, we both knew what was happening and we knew there was nothing you could have done. I'm just so tired that I felt I needed someone here with me, just for the next few days."

Ruby knew it was true. Ann was so accepting of the fact and she'd understood the look on Ben's face. She needed time to come to terms with it herself.

Sam had been her guide and her teacher as a child and then he'd gone on to be an even more important factor in her son's life, she owed him so much and couldn't bear to think he wouldn't be here, shining a light onto the darkness some in Worcester would prefer remained hidden forever.

Ruby put her arms around Ann again. "I should have been here, helped you, made things easier for you."

Ann shook her head vigorously. "That would have been the last thing he wanted. If I thought you could have helped him I'd have called on you, but not for me. I was doing what I had to do."

Ann had loved Sam since she'd first met him. She had been a poor village girl, born to serve until she died, Sam was an educated gentleman, a tutor. Meeting him had changed the course of her life. He'd taught her to think and he'd taught her to laugh. She'd been captivated by his cleverness, his kindness, everything about him. The realization that this wonderful man loved her entirely changed her life. Working alongside him at the newspaper had been an honour and a joy and she'd never regret a moment of it. Caring for him at the end of his life was a task for her alone.

Only now at the very end could she bear to accept help. They wrapped their arms around each other and Ruby held her while she cried. Ben came out to join them as Richard approached them.

"How is Uncle Sam, is he feeling no better?" Richard asked.

Looking at their grim faces he knew the answer. “Can't we take him to the infirmary, surely they could help?” he said, as Ann shook her head.

“We went when he started to feel the most recent pains, there was nothing to be done, they said. We knew then it was just a matter of time. We know what's going to happen and we've come to terms with it now.”

Richard turned away quickly, not wanting them to see his tears.

Ben nodded in agreement with Ann. “He's struggling with all his might, but the infection has taken hold and he's too tired to fight it for much longer and I would be lying if I said otherwise."

Ruby insisted on staying nearby and would accept no arguments, she would share Richards rooms for the time being and do everything in her power to ensure that Ann and Sam had nothing to do for the time left to them but be together.

Ann did try to demur but Ruby's mind was made up. "Ann, you're too thin and too tired. I'll cook and clean and I swear I'll leave the two of you alone together but you need to start eating properly from today and I'm going to see that you do."

Richard could continue his work as normal but an assistant or two must be found with all haste and that was something else Ruby intended to see to.

Ben nodded his approval. “I'll make up a lotion for you to bathe him with when the fever gets up and I shall want him to take this drink every time he wakes up. It's not going to do anything for him but ease the pain, but he'll be glad of that and I have nothing else. I won't be far away and you must call on me at any time, but be assured I shall look in on him every day.”

He patted Ann's arm awkwardly and turned to Ruby. “Can you step outside with me for a moment?”

When they were at a distance from the house Ruby stopped and said. “He's not going to wake up again, is he

Ben?"

"I hope not, for his sake. The pain would be unbearable, it's essential that you see she keeps him drinking the mixture I gave her, it's not going to do him any harm but it will dull all his senses for the next day or so and that's the kindest thing we can do for him now."

Ruby slapped her hand onto the wall in temper and frustration. "He seemed to recover so well, I don't understand."

Ben nodded. "He did recover from the broken bone very well, but you must remember how badly torn his foot was on that mess of old tangled metal. If the infection had got into the bone before it healed, then it would never get better and I suspect that's what happened. There's nothing to be done once an infection has set in. All we can do now is offer her our support. I hope young Richard is up to the job in front of him."

She smiled sadly. "If he's not up to it now then he never will be. I know Sam thinks he's capable and Ann has a great deal of time for him so we shall see. I should go back in now, they may need me."

"Yes, they will do I'm sure."

Two days later Sam gave up the fight.

A few days since was married at Ludlow, Mr Thomas Blainey, attorney at law, to Miss Moreley, both of that place, a young lady of a £20,000 fortune. To pass encomiums of praise on the above lady would be useless, as a truly virtuous and amiable mind like hers is better displayed by actions than described by the pen.

(Copyright and courtesy of the Worcester News)

CHAPTER FORTY EIGHT

As part of his preparation for his weekly duty visit to Henry, Hugh had picked up the paper to read the local news. He found it pleased Henry these days to have the news relayed to him, rather than to read the paper himself. It was important to know what was going on it town as he never knew which turn a conversation with Henry might take and it paid to be up to date.

He also wanted to read the report of his own recent marriage to Gweneth Sanders. He'd known her for many years and admired her greatly. He'd always hoped to marry her one day but his concerns over the transportation business had held him back from speaking for years.

Thanks to Tom, who had the confidence to show him what he'd been too blind to see the business was no longer the worry that it had been and so, as soon as her mother started to show signs of anxiety at his delay Hugh proposed, and in no time at all it was done. At thirty five years of age Hugh Daventor was joined in matrimony to twenty five year old Gweneth Sanders.

His bride duly moved into his house and began to turn it into the home she'd always dreamed of having and Hugh rapidly realized that his quiet, gentle bride had a backbone of steel and very expensive tastes. She was every inch as formidable as her mother.

Henry had been unable to attend their wedding - to the great relief of both Hugh and Tom - but Hugh knew he would want to see the report in the newspaper. Henry always felt it was important that the affairs of the family were conducted, and reported upon, respectfully. He was less and less involved with anyone on a day to day basis, nevertheless to be seen to be doing the right thing was still essential to him.

Once Hugh was satisfied that the report of the wedding was accurate and sufficiently deferential Hugh glanced through other news. He was saddened to read of the death of Sam and he sat for a time remembering the tutor who brought order and structure into what had been a chaotic childhood. This led in turn to memories of William, and then Ruby and Ellie. He sighed deeply alerting Tom. "Problem Uncle Hugh?"

"No, nothing to concern you, an old friend has died and I was just thinking back."

"Who was it?"

"A chap called Sam Thatcher, you won't have met him. He was our tutor here when we were boys. He tried hard to knock manners and education into us and we put up quite a struggle I can tell you. He was a decent chap though and the first civilising influence we had, he certainly experienced the worst of us. When he'd knocked us into as good a shape as possible he left and ended up working with Henry on the paper, then took it over completely when Henry lost interest. I thought many times to go and look him up, for old times sake but I've never made the time."

Hugh had been unsurprised when Henry had told him he was giving up the paper. It was at a time when Henry had given up on everything, but he realised he had never stopped to wonder how hard that might have hit Sam. In fact he'd rarely thought of Sam more than fleetingly at all.

A look of recognition lit Tom's face. "I think I did meet him once, in the Cathedral grounds. He mistook me for someone else but I remember now he said he knew our family. We never met him socially though, did we?"

Hugh smiled as he shook his head. "No we didn't, and that's no credit to me really. Too late now though. He worked hard for us and I should think he probably struggled to make a success of the newspaper when Henry pulled out. Sam felt very passionate about it I know, but there was never going to be enough money in it to hold your grandfathers interest for very long. He was rather left high and dry to be honest. I have no idea how he'd managed to keep going for so long. I imagine it will have to close now. Damn shame, that paper's been around since the sixteen hundreds.

"Did he have any family?"

Hugh nodded and smiled as he remembered Ann. She could have been little more than a child herself when he was a boy but she was the one who nurtured all four of them. She slept with them and helped them dress. She cared for them when they were sick and she protected them from Susan and her whip when they'd been naughty. When all else was hard and cold she was there, soft and warm. When Sam came along she helped him take their lessons. What a louse he was to have neglected those two good people, both of whom helped make his childhood bearable.

He realised Tom was still waiting for him to answer. "Yes, he was married to a girl called Ann, she had worked here for your grandparents at the same time Sam was here." He heard the church bell toll and leaped to his feet. "I must go, Henry wants to spend a little time with Gweneth so we're dining with him tonight." Tom grimaced in sympathy and Hugh grinned.

Henry had managed to put on a reasonable show of civility when first he met with Gweneth's parents but now the two had married he saw no reason to put himself out and any further. She was family now and she must get used to doing things his way. He was still the head of the family and he was going to make damn sure that Hugh and his new wife never forgot that fact.

The dinner was a difficult and uncomfortable experience. Hugh was distracted, thinking about Ann being left alone, whilst Henry was anxious to impress upon Gweneth the importance of his family and her duty. She, newly married and coming from a refined, though impoverished family was unused to being lectured to by a man who had drunk far too much. In fact as dinner progressed Henry could barely speak and eventually his head dropped forward and he slumped in his chair and began to snore, loudly.

Gweneth was badly upset by Henry's behaviour, she found it offensive and humiliating. Hugh agreed but had got used to Henry's behaviour and had ceased to notice it, however watching as his new wife was exposed to such rudeness was an uncomfortable reminder of how low Henry had sunk.

Hugh took some time to assure her that she would not be subjected to a dinner with Henry again for a very long time, if at all. Henry had wanted to mark the occasion of their marriage appropriately and would in all likelihood forget all about her from now on. She became even more angry when Hugh said that. The rudeness of the men in the family was appalling and she didn't hesitate to let him know her feelings. Hugh realized his error at once and had to work even harder to appease her.

Once she was somewhat pacified Hugh made sure Susan was keeping the place up as it should be, spoke quickly with Chambers, the man who still took care of a great portion of their land and made haste to remove Gweneth before her headache grew unbearable. By which time he was totally drained himself.

Early on Sunday morning last, several hundred persons, chiefly women and children, assembled in the neighbourhood of Pershore in order to intercept and pillage some vessels laden with corn and meal that were going down the river Avon. It was yet another result of the exorbitant price of provisions currently prevailing in this kingdom. However, notice of this assembly was sent to the commanding officer of the Dragoons quartered in Worcester and, in offering military aid to the authorities, a party of soldiers marched that day to Pershore. A justice of the peace was likewise applied to and he also attended at Pershore, causing the riot act to be read. As a consequence, the mob thought proper to disperse without committing any violence.

(Copyright and courtesy of the Worcester News)

CHAPTER FORTY NINE

Once Gweneth was at last peacefully sleeping, Hugh found time to sit beside a dying fire and reflect upon his childhood and the security that Sam and Ann had brought to his life.

The newly widowed Henry had left his adopted nephew Hugh aged three and his newborn son William in the somewhat negligent care of Susan, mother of Ruby and Ellie and taken himself off for months on end. He wanted nothing to do with his children, he didn't see children as any business of a man. He said he'd take them in hand once they were old enough to do as they were told, until then Susan knew best. She treated the four small children in exactly the same careless manner. So long as they were not under her feet they were left to their own devices. Ann was there of course, but she was helpless when faced with the four terrors single handedly.

It was when Hugh was eleven years of age that Henry returned unexpectedly and found all four children rolling around in the mud and fighting like feral cats that he realised he'd have to do something very quickly or his boys would be beyond helping.

Samuel Thatcher was employed and began to take the children, and Ann, in hand. His task was to prepare the boys for school but he saw no reason not to include the girls in this programme whenever they could be spared from helping their mother in her work.

Sam had his hands full, but he never lost his patience or his enthusiasm. Pretty soon a division began to appear between the children, William and Ellie found the classes difficult and never took to the studies very well.

Prior to Sam joining them Ruby and William had been as thick as thieves, often plotting together and if there was trouble to be had they'd find it, Hugh and Ellie would simply be pulled along in their wake.

Studying with Sam had pulled Hugh and Ruby closer,

they shared a desire to learn and the childhood affiliations began to shift. It came as a dreadful shock to her when she realized that the boys would be going away to school and that she would not. She ranted and raved and cried bitterly to no avail.

It was ironic that the very thing that pulled Hugh and Ruby together, a love of learning, was the thing that William came to resent the most about her. He couldn't stand the fact that a servant, as he learned to call her once he started school, sailed through things he couldn't master. He hated her cleverness and he deeply resented the fact that she craved education while he was left feeling hopeless and inadequate in his lessons.

Her strength served only to highlight his weakness and it was so tragic to consider how much harm William's bitterness had done to Ruby. Hugh decided that it was time he made up for his neglect, he would go to Sam's funeral the next day and pay his respects. He also decided that at some time in the near future seek out Ruby and try to make his peace with her.

For some time past a sharper has made it his business to inform several persons within a few miles of this city that parcels, carriage paid and directed to them, were lodged in the warehouses in Worcester of our London carriers, by which artifice he has obtained gratuities, besides being kindly treated for his false intelligence. We thought it necessary to take notice of this new species of imposition that all persons may be upon their guard for the future.

(Copyright and courtesy of the Worcester News)

CHAPTER FIFTY

The size of the crowd of mourners was a testament to Sam and a measure of the amount of good he had done in his life. People had travelled from far and wide, and were vocal, telling each other tales and sharing memories of Sam, and, as is often the case, the mood gradually lightened as the entire group appreciated all the good that Sam had done in his life.

His open mind and warm heart had made a difference to a surprising amount of people. It seemed that no one had ever gone to Sam for help and been turned away. Coming here today and sharing their stories of Sam was their way of thanking him, and it helped them all.

The throng was such that it was some time before Hugh was able to secure a few moments alone with Ann. She was sad, of course, but nonetheless proud and grateful that Hugh had found the time to come and pay his respects. They exchanged pleasantries and he apologised for his neglect of her and Sam. She smiled sadly and told him not to think of it any further.

He and Ann spoke of the old days and the problems he and the other children had given to Sam in the beginning, they laughed as they reminded each other of the pranks they had played on Sam and she looked happy, almost as though she was already coming to terms with his death. Hugh thought again how strong a person she was. She assured him that she and Sam had shared a wonderful life together and she wanted him to know that Sam had watched, with a great deal of satisfaction as he took the helm at Daventors with such skill.

Being aware that there were many others waiting to talk to Ann he called Tom over wanting to introduce them to one another, prior to taking their leave. She seemed a little disconcerted but he put that down to the sadness of the day.

It was Tom that alerted him to Ruby's presence. “Is that

another branch of our family Uncle Hugh? He looks so much like me we could be brothers, I must go and talk to him."

He had spotted Richard escorting Ruby as she moved through the crowd towards Ann. Hugh was now as disconcerted as Ann had been. "Who is he?" he asked her.

"That's Richard, Ruby's son."

"But that's extraordinary." He muttered to himself for a second and then realised that of course it wasn't extraordinary at all, Ruby herself was a twin, she might have had twins herself. He tried to puzzle out what she'd done and why.

Ann and Hugh stood together and watched as Tom approached Richard and Ruby with his hand stretched out in friendship. They shook hands and stood upright each staring into the face that was reflected back at them on a daily basis. Tom was heavier and better dressed, Richard wore his hair longer and had a more relaxed face. But as the two stood side by side to talk, the likeness was clear for all to see. They laughed and began to talk animatedly, trying to work out their history and discover how they were related. Richard turned to Ruby who was also watching.

"Aunt Ruby this is extraordinary, there must be a family connection surely. Isn't it amazing?"

Ruby glanced over at Ann who was looking at her with a half smile of sympathy on her face. Hugh was waiting to hear what she would say.

Ruby nodded and took a moment to gather her thoughts. "Of course you're related and it's time you both knew the facts of your complicated history. I'll tell you both the whole story tomorrow, if you wish, but today we're here for Sam, and Ann. I'll meet you both together and tell you how you're related in the morning."

They left her alone then, but of course they couldn't wait and they spent the next two hours together, happily comparing life stories and trying to untangle their backgrounds. They soon realized that as small boys they'd lived very closely to each other but, apart from that they couldn't discern their connection. So occupied with each other were they that neither of them noticed that they had become the focus of interest to most of the people in the room.

They were being watched avidly and many of the mourners were reluctant to leave without knowing exactly what was going on. As they whispered amongst one another, when Henry Daventors nephew turns up in public with a young man who is the exact double of the lad that works on the newspaper, there's bound to be talk.

Of course the likeness was obvious now, but no-one had ever seen much of either boy in the past and certainly never side by side. There had been talk about the Daventors for years, the most recent being that Hugh's bastard son was working on the canal for him. That rumour had been scotched by his recent marriage, old man Sanders would never have allowed the marriage if their was any substance to that rumour.

Whoever this boy was, it was clear he wasn't Hugh's son. Yet seeing the two boys together meant there was something afoot. What could the connection be? If there was a scandal they wanted to know about it. Sadly for them, common decency forced them to leave before their curiosity could be appeased.

On Monday, three impudent fellows, full of liquor and mischief, posted themselves on the margin of a pool by the side of the road between Droitwich and Bromsgrove and saluted all passers-by, whether on foot, horseback or in carriages, with mud etc. One Gentleman in particular who was on horseback, was dangerously hurt on the temple by a stone thrown at him. But two of these audacious chaps, whose names and places of abode have since been learnt, are likely to smart pretty severely for their ill chosen diversion, as prosecutions are going to be commenced against them, particularly by a Gentleman on foot, whom they grossly insulted, and upon his asking them the reason of it they cursed him and threatened further abuse if he did not immediately proceed forwards.

(Copyright and courtesy of the Worcester News)

CHAPTER FIFTY ONE

Circumstances dictated that it was in fact almost a week before Ruby was able to sit down with Tom and Richard and tell them her story. It was her choice to sit with them both together and go through the thing just once and it took that long for all three of them to be free at the same time.

They eventually met in the grounds of the Cathedral and Ruby asked them both to remain silent until she had told them the whole story, then she would attempt to answer all their questions.

Initially both were light hearted but they could sense that she was ill at ease and that calmed them down. When she described her rape and the circumstances of their birth she saw shock and sympathy on both their faces. As she recounted the details of her first few weeks at Ma's they were appalled and neither of them could see this as the piece of good fortune she now felt it to be and neither could appreciate the humour she tried to put on those days. Most of the circumstances were a shock to them both even though Richard had lived there with the girls, he'd left to live with Sam just as he was approaching the age when he might have begun to know and understand what was actually going on.

"So we're actually brothers?" Richard looked quite taken aback while Tom, who'd had a lot more surprising information to process was, momentarily, struck dumb.

Finally the stunned silence was broken again. "So you're my Mother?" They both said at almost the same time. There followed a stream of questions she tried to answer, accusations she had to refute and exclamations of wonder she became impatient with. Her maternal instinct, scant at the best of times eventually deserted her entirely.

"Will you please stop talking like a pair of village idiots, you've both had the benefit of expensive educations and have lived long enough to know that people's lives are often more complicated than they seem. I would remind you both that this story begins with a fourteen year old child who was raped and then thrown out of the only home she'd ever know. That was far more of a shock and disappointment to her then, than this is to you both now."

Ruby told them both to go back to their work and think about all she had told them, she encouraged Tom to talk to Hugh about the early years at the Great House and advised Richard that he would hear as much valuable information from Ann. Once they'd got a grasp on things she felt sure they would see that what she had done was in the best interests of all of them. If they didn't, well, that was something they'd have to come to terms with, as she had no doubts she'd done the right thing. With that ringing crisply in their ears, she left them to it.

On Thursday night, about seven o'clock, as Mary Perkes, the Clifton upon Teme carrier, was returning home from Worcester on horseback, she was attacked by two footpads, one of whom struck her a violent blow on the arm and breast, and then they seized the bridle, after which they robbed her of about two shillings and threepence, a wallet and two bags containing some tea, sugar, pepper, stockings and divers other things. Upon her crying out "Murder" they threatened to kill her. One of them had on a great coat with broad metal buttons and had a pale complexion.

(Copyright and courtesy of the Worcester News)

CHAPTER FIFTY TWO

Tom arrived home much later that day only to find Hugh waiting to hear all that happened with Ruby and Richard.

Tom was in a terrible state of mind, his mood swung from high to low in seconds. He told Hugh the story, jumping from point to point as he struggled between his own conflicting emotions. He was still reeling from the discovery that he actually had a living mother, he'd understood all his life that his was dead. He was delighted to find a twin that he'd never expected, and he was offended to realize that Henry and Hugh had kept the truth from him since the moment he'd arrived.

Hugh tried to explain that as soon as they'd known about Tom they wanted him, he was their family and they wanted to provide for him. They'd never mentioned Richard because they hadn't known he existed and Hugh was as stunned as Tom about that. Surely he could see that it was far kinder to let a small boy think his parents were both dead rather than that he was the product of a brutal attack.

"So he really did rape her? She said if I asked you, you would be able to tell me more."

Hugh had thought of nothing but his childhood all evening. How Ruby was like a thorn in William's side. Not at first of course, they loved each other as small children. Everything changed when he and William went away to school, that was when the children themselves realized there was a huge difference between them. They were the masters, Ruby and Ellie the servants.

He told Tom about their childhood and how they'd all grown up together.

"It sounds as though you were all good friends then." Tom was desperately trying to grasp how one true friend could do such a terrible thing to another.

Hugh nodded his agreement. "We thought we were all equals you see, we'd been brothers and sisters almost.

Everything changed once we all realized we were actually very different."

He revealed to Tom how Ruby was inconsolable when she understood that she would not be going to school with them. And how ashamed he'd felt to leave her behind. How during their first holidays at home she pestered them both to tell her what they'd been learning. Which was when the friendship between William and Ruby had broken down completely, Hugh had information from lessons he'd enjoyed that he could share with Ruby, he described the books he read and repeated the conversations he'd had. He even told her of the food they ate and the sports they played.

William was unable to share anything with her, he hadn't learned anything at school and she could tell. She was angry at the way he wasted what he had been given when she, who would have cherished every moment was prohibited from doing so. She longed to learn and couldn't, he hated it and was forced to. She teased and mocked him and he wanted to hurt her.

Tom was revolted. "So he raped her as punishment?"

"No, not quite like that. I think it may have started as a fight. We had always fought, all of us, proper fights with feet and teeth and fists, before we went to school and became a little civilised. I think that's how it probably started, rolling around fighting turned into something else."

The silence hung heavy in the room, Ruby and her pain was at the forefront of both their minds.

"I still don't know why Henry had to throw her out though, didn't he want us around?" Tom was trying to understand.

"It wasn't about you Tom, you didn't exist then. Henry knew that something had happened between them and she had to go. I'm sure that the idea of a child being born didn't cross his mind. He was simply trying to protect his son from an unsuitable liaison. William was a young man and not a very sensible one, he made a wicked mistake and Henry did what he thought best."

Tom, ever the realist asked. "So why didn't you do anything to help her, you said you were all friends?"

Hugh had been avoiding asking himself the same question for years. Why hadn't he helped Ruby? Henry was a difficult man and Hugh never quite felt secure, knowing he wasn't Henry's real son, knowing he was here because of Henry's generosity and could be sent away at any time crippled him inside. He'd been unable to stand up to Henry then, and he still couldn't now. It shamed him but it was true for all that.

"I was weak. A coward if you will. I let my fear of Henry stop me doing what I should have done. I'll help her now though, by telling you that I admire her. She has done something most people couldn't dream of doing. She's supported herself and given a future to both her sons. She's someone you will in time look up to, not down on."

This clarified something for Tom, he realized that he didn't look down on Ruby at all, in fact he admired her. He was actually looking down on Henry who had caused such chaos because of his own stupid ideas and selfishness. He felt badly let down because everything he'd been led to believe about his past was invented. That stupid story his Grandfather gave him when he came to live back here with them, his mother dying when he was a baby and his father being killed by robbers.

"Were you both laughing at me when you made up my history?"

Tom was distressed and it pained Hugh, he'd been a hero to Tom for years and to be looked at by him with something akin to dislike was heartbreaking. "Tom, we've never laughed at you. Finding out about you was the best thing that has happened to Henry since William died and you're like a son to me, you know that."

Tom sat deep in thought, he was working through the things Ruby had told him and putting them together with the story from Hugh.

"So Henry only wanted me when William died. I was to be a replacement for a dead son?"

Try as he might Hugh couldn't convince Tom that Henry wanted him for any reason other than to fill his dead son's shoes, which is of course precisely why he did want him. They talked for a long time but eventually Tom declared he wanted to be left alone to digest all that he'd learned.

Last Tuesday evening, as the housekeeper of Lady Pakington of Perdiswell, near Worcester, was returning home, she was attacked on the high road by a man and a woman who bid her deliver her money and on her giving them a few shillings, they left without searching her, whereby she saved some guineas she had in her pocket.

Soon after, the same fellow, being observed to go into a barn not far from Lady Packington's, some persons went up to him and upon asking what business he had there, he behaved in a very insolent manner and threatened to set fire to the barn if they molested him, upon which they thought it proper to secure him and take him into custody.

(Copyright and courtesy of the Worcester News)

CHAPTER FIFTY THREE

Ann glanced across the table at her friend and knew how lucky she was to have had such a strong supporter in her time of need. “I want to thank you for spending so much of your time with me over these past few days Ruby, it would have been overwhelming without you to lean on.”

Ruby tried to brush the thanks aside, she had helped because she wanted to, thanks were not needed or wanted.

“It can't go on any longer though Ruby." Ann said firmly. "I've got to get back to work and so have you. Sam would be furious to think of us like this, me sitting and weeping and you mopping up after me. I've got a newspaper to run and thanks to your help I now have an even bigger task ahead of me."

Ruby nodded apologetically. From the start she had known that Richard could use some help, he'd done so very well working single handed but he couldn't keep standards up and cope with such a vast workload for very long and so she had gone along to the parish charity home and told the matron what she needed.

It was a day or so later that Ruby met Jacob, a sturdy boy of around twelve years with flame red hair and fierce blue eyes. Ruby looked him up and down, he looked fit and strong so she asked him tell her about himself.

He looked at her defiantly and said, "I can't come with you without my brother." The matron stepped forward with a curse and boxed his ears before Ruby could intervene.

"You'll do as you're told and like it my lad." The woman hissed in his ear.

Jacob's eyes filled with tears and his face was desperate as he looked into Ruby's eyes. "I can't leave my brother, I promised Ma." He said simply.

This time Ruby got between him and the matron and asked to be allowed to meet Jacobs brother. Ruby managed to convince the woman to leave her alone with the two boys, Jacob and his small brother John. They'd lived with their Mother who'd been abandoned by her husband so long ago that Jacob had no memory of him.

She'd turned to the parish for help when desperation overtook her but she'd been suffering from hunger and fear for too long. She was feverish and weak and she'd died shortly after they were all admitted. "She told me I had to look out for the little un and I must." Jacob declared bravely.

If Jacob was twelve then John was probably eight, Ruby guessed. Jacob could read a few letters and he could add up in his head, his poor mother had done all she could to educate him. He was bright and brave and Ruby decided to take a chance.

She told Jacob she would take him and his brother, they would live with a friend of hers and would have to apply themselves to their lessons but they'd be given work, food and a safe place to live, if that was what they wanted. If they worked hard she could promise they would stay together.

She then stood, stiff and still as she received a rather smelly hug and a promise that they'd never let her down. No doubt educating the two boys would fill up Ann's life and they would be a help with the manual work from the start.

They weren't what Ruby had intended to bring back with her, she'd wanted an older lad, just one, who could read and write properly, but Jacob won her over with his initial refusal to leave his brother and she was sunk. Her mind raced with memories, herself and Ellie, Richard and Tom. It had been three days ago that she'd come back with the two little boys in tow and when she'd introduced them to Ann as her new apprentices Ann smiled for the first time since Sam died.

"They'll be a handful." Ruby said ruefully by way of apology.

"They'll be just what we need, go back to work Ruby.

I'm going to."

Ruby still felt hesitant, she carried still the guilty knowledge that she'd stayed away for so long that she'd not known Sam was ill and she didn't want to make another mistake like that.

Ann continued to speak, though she could see Ruby was thinking of her own things. "Sam admired you so much Ruby. He loved me, but he admired you. We have to carry on now and ensure that we are worthy of his love and respect. He taught us so much and we must put it all to good use. He'll be watching over me and I will not let him down. I know you think I'm weak and I must be protected, and I have been that way. But you see, I always let Sam take care of me because that was what gave him pleasure. I enjoyed it, but I didn't need it."

This made Ruby smile because she'd often thought Ann gave way to Sam because it made him feel better and having it confirmed be Ann now convinced her that their friendship was back as strong as ever.

"I thought I would always have to provide for myself and I was on the way to doing that before I met Sam. When you were only a baby I ran the first school in St Johns, alone. Elizabeth Daventor was the patron and she taught me how to do it, but I carried it on in her name. I had to decide who had a place and I had to plan the lessons and speak to fathers who kept their sons off to help with the family work. I dealt with the church when they wanted to tell me what to teach and what to avoid. Truly Ruby, I'm not as weak as you seem to think I am."

Ann was not given to long speeches and Ruby could sense things were changing within her, perhaps she was coming through the worst. "I'd almost forgotten about the school Ann, I was so young then, why did you stop doing it?"

"It lacked funds. It was all Elizabeth's idea so funding was never a problem, until she died giving birth to William, that changed everything. When that happened

Henry virtually disappeared for quite a few years, your mother had her hands full taking care of William so I had to help her with you two and Hugh, the school became neglected as more of my time was needed helping your mother with you four and the house."

Ruby still remembered those times, fighting with the boys and then cuddling with Ann. She sighed as Ann continued the story.

"Henry came back of course and decided the boys were to have a formal education and I was reduced to being an assistant. Had it not been Sam that took over it would have been a bitter pill for me to swallow. In the event it was the best thing in the world for me. Henry of course wouldn't allow the school to continue, as you know he doesn't agree with education for all, he's convinced it's a waste of resources and breeds discontent."

Ruby knew this all too well and wondered how a man with his ideas ever came to open a free school in the first place. Ann had the answer to that. Elizabeth, Henry's wife was a marvellous woman, she had energy and passion and she believed it was her responsibility to share what she had with those who had less and she worked day in and day out to learn what was needed to help folk help themselves.

She didn't have any time for handouts nor charity but she felt anyone who worked hard should be helped to prosper. When a school had opened in Hallow there was talk all over the district about it. Some folks envied those in Hallow and some ridiculed the whole idea. Elizabeth went all the way out there to meet the people and see how it worked. She came back began her mission to use Henry's money, and position to do the same thing for the children of St Johns.

Henry did as she asked because he adored her. It was Elizabeth that brought Ann and Susan into the home, she'd found them in the old hut huddled together with the newborn twins. She gave both women work and a home.

"I dread to think what would have become of us if she

hadn't. Susan was put in charge of the house, cooking and cleaning and I was to be her little maid. Elizabeth taught me everything, how to read, how to speak and dress properly. She was a wonderful woman and it was a happy time for me Ruby."

"So she saved us all."

Ann nodded her head. "Your poor mother, losing your father on the day she got you two was too much for her to come back from, but at least she was safe and secure. We thought we were in clover, and for a time we were. Poor Elizabeth though, she kept losing her babies and she got weaker and sadder. She had William, the only one that lived and it finished her off. It was her death that made Henry the man you know."

"I didn't know any of that."

"It was all before you were old enough to know what was happening. But I've gone way off track Ruby, I simply wanted to let you know that I'm perfectly capable of taking care of myself and steering the newspaper in the right direction. I must stand alone now and do something to make Sam and Elizabeth proud, and to let everyone else see that I'm capable of running a newspaper and working alongside men. And you my dear must strive to calm those two sons of yours, they are struggling to understand the circumstances of their birth. Perhaps you felt they didn't need you as babies but Ruby, they need you now."

It was time to get back to their lives and work.

On Monday last, an itinerant quack who calls himself George Walker was committed to our House of Correction at Worcester, being charged on the oath of Susannah Cole with being a cheat and an imposter, pretending in the art of physick and having actually imposed upon several persons thereby obtaining money by several false pretences.

(Copyright and courtesy of the Worcester News)

CHAPTER FIFTY FOUR

In the twelve years since Ruby had taken Ma's business in hand it had changed greatly.

The front approach to the house was kept clean and bright and the first room inside the house had been opened up from the vile warren it had been into a light and airy reception hall. It was in the rooms that led of this space that the various business's were conducted.

Yes, girls were still available, but that was no longer the sole attraction. There were regular card games held here and good food was cooked at all hours. Ruby had employed a cook who'd trained in London and the food now at Barbourne House was exceptional, and was drawing a crowd on its own merits.

A small library had been installed in what had been the nursery, coffee and newspapers were provided in here, along with the peace and quiet needed to digest them.

Ma had spent the last few years living quietly with Jane. She hadn't wanted to leave her home but she had known that repairs to the fabric of the buildings were long overdue and she hated seeing the things she built being ripped out and changed so she went, grumbling every step of the way.

Ruby visited her every week and kept her abreast of all that she was doing but they both knew Ma was less and less interested as time went on, and towards the end she faded fast. It was losing her sight that finished her, she'd struggled when she could no longer read but not being able to watch as people went about their business distressed her. She'd accepted her loss of mobility and the breathing difficulties, but without the words and the people there was no point in living.

Her funeral quickly turned into an unseemly and raucous affair, exactly as she would have wanted. Ruby knew many of the people who attended but even she was surprised to see a couple of very well set up gentlemen she never known to have come to the house in attendance. Ma had taken some of her secrets to the grave.

It appeared that Ma had made a considerable contribution to Worcester during her years here and Ruby was proud to be the one Ma had chosen to succeed her. It gave her a great deal of pleasure to know that so many people over the years had been helped by Ma and appreciated that help so much that they were prepared to fly in the face of popular opinion and come here today to publicly respect her.

It was long past her usual bedtime before Ruby was able to find a moment to sit alone and ponder over the events of the day and spare a moment to reflect on all she owed Ma. When she'd been at a point of absolute despair Ma managed to show her there was whole world she knew nothing about available to her. There were good people who loved and cared for each other at all levels and she had been welcomed in to join forces with them.

She pondered over the laughs they'd had when she was teaching Ma to read. All the scandalous nuggets that Ma got so much pleasure out of hearing about were even more of a thrill for her once she could read about them herself. They'd spent years together and Ruby would miss Ma for a long time to come. Tiredness overtook her and she dozed off in Ma's old chair.

A banging on her door shocked her awake. Not surprisingly it was Bella who interrupted her reverie with some news that couldn't wait a moment longer. "The thing is Ruby, I found this fellow and he wants marry me so I can't be doing this no more."

All signs of fatigue left her, courtesy of this startling piece of information. Bella looked different somehow and Ruby realized her friend was excited but also afraid. Ruby opened a bottle and made Bella to tell her all about it.

He was a widower and, after three years alone, one of his pals had taken him along to Bella's because they thought it was high time he re-joined the world. He'd gone into the room with Bella but made it plain to her that he wasn't interested in doing anything other than talk.

He was having a tough time with his pals so he'd gone along with their plans and he'd be grateful if Bella would go along with his. They sat and talked. Bella was grateful for a night off, her appetites had dimmed as the years had passed, so a few pleasurable hours were spent together chatting and playing cards.

She thought no more of it but he'd come back the next week and they did the same again. He told her all about his wife and how happy they'd been. How her death had completely knocked him back but how he was coming out of it now. He had been visiting Bella each week now for two months and she knew his life story and he knew hers. Last week he told Bella that he wanted to be with her but only if she would agree to marry him. He felt it would dishonour his first wife if he were to consider any other kind of relationship. He'd fallen in love with Bella and was ready to make a new start.

"Bella, how could you have kept him a secret from me?"

"I didn't really. I never dreamed he'd come up with the goods. If you'd asked me I'd have said that would be the last thing I'd want, but now he's spoken I can't think of anything I want more."

The two woman hugged each other and both had tears in their eyes. "What's his name?"

Matthew he's called. Matthew Deakin. He's older than me but that's a good thing. He can look after me for a year or two and then I'll look after him for the rest of his life. He may not know it but he's a miracle for me and he'll die happy, that I swear."

"What does he do, what will you live on?"

Matthew Deakin and his wife had kept a small lodging house towards Worcester. Just a simple place that catered for those with no money to waste on frills. Plain food and a freshly swept floor was what they offered. Since his wife had died he barely bothered to open up and now only gave a room to those he already knew, he'd lost his interest in life when he'd lost his mate.

Meeting Bella had changed all that. They planned to open up again, she'd learn as she went along. He had a patch of land where they could grow vegetables and he kept a few chickens, they wouldn't need much. Ruby was thrilled to hear Bella's news but couldn't hide the fact that she found the idea of Bella digging vegetables was quite ridiculous. "My God we've only planted Ma today and you've got her spinning in her grave already."

Bella had never lacked confidence in her own abilities and she laughingly assured Ruby she'd cope. The rest of their night was spent re living their early days and remembering the bawdiest moments they'd shared and they laughed until their faces hurt.

Last Sunday afternoon, as one Francis Williams, a tailor of St John's, Worcester, was walking out with his wife, some high words were exchanged between them when, in his passion, he had the rashness to cut his own throat in a very desperate manner, upon which, as soon as the wound was dressed, he was sent to our infirmary where he continues very ill. His wife it seems, was the unfortunate mother, by a former husband, of William Gosling who was hanged here a few years ago for the murder of his apprentice girl.

(Copyright and courtesy of the Worcester News)

CHAPTER FIFTY FIVE

Richard and Tom were accustomed to the idea of having a twin and had soon learned everything they needed to know about each other and their lives so far. They spent as much time as they possibly could together relishing the freedom that came from having a true friend from whom they had no secrets.

Their early lives had differed yet they were in agreement on many subjects. The discovery of a long lost brother had been such a joy that they soon forgave Ruby and Hugh for the lies they'd been told. They had each other now and that was compensation enough.

Tom considered Jane to be his mother and Richard had Ann to thank for most of his home comforts. Ruby was just Ruby, they liked her well enough but had been unable, or unwilling to develop a closer relationship with her. She carried on with her life and they with theirs.

They were only reminded of the distance between them when they heard of the death of Ma and both of them understood how difficult Ruby would be finding things. She had grumbled from time to time about Ma slowing her down when she wanted to make certain changes but there was never any doubt about the genuine affection she felt for the old lady.

They wondered if perhaps it was time for them to do something special for her. They decided to plan a day trip for her, somewhere she'd never been before and give her a lunch and spend a whole day with her. As they talked about where to take her they both became excited and more adventurous with their plans.

Ruby received an invitation in due course, a printed cream card arrived by messenger inviting her to spend the day with Mr Thomas Daventor and Mr Richard Morgan. The card stated that a carriage would collect her from her home on the morning of the 16th June. She was delighted, both with the card and the invitation and was ready an hour before the stated time.

Richard was in the carriage waiting to greet her and they talked easily as the carriage headed towards Worcester. He told her his view of the newspapers and made her laugh as he reported on the progress of Jacob and John, both educationally and in matters of personal cleanliness. They'd both been horrified at the instruction that they were to wash, from head to toe daily, but Ann insisted and they eventually came round.

They were now both strapping lads, Jacob seemed suited to talking to people, he had a relaxed and confident manner that had endeared him to many of the local tradesmen. John was quieter and more studious, he spent most of his time working as a clerk under the beady eyes of Ann. They were both cheeky and boisterous at home but adored Ann and she, in turn blossomed in their company.

The conversation flowed easily and both mother and son were startled to find they'd travelled through Worcester and reached the outskirts without an awkward moment. Tom was waiting for them here he jumped up into the carriage without delay and the threesome headed excitedly towards Malvern.

The spa towns were thriving since the King, who had been so ill a few years ago he had made for Cheltenham Spa, he had duly recovered and as a result many people were now convinced of the healing powers of spa waters and as a result spa towns were the height of fashion.

Ruby was enchanted by Malvern Spa.

The smart people and their sumptuous clothes were a sight to see. Some walked about carrying pretty parasols as protection from the sun and many more clipped along slowly in open sided carriages.

Everything around was fashionable and designed to be shown off. The ornately decorated carriages and coaches were either open topped or had glass panels on the sides. The visiting ladies paid great sums of money to look as wonderful as they did and it was vital that as many people as possible saw, and envied, them.

The spa itself was a revelation. Having heard stories of the health properties of Malvern water Ruby expected to find something a little like the infirmary but she found only rolling hills and fresh air with little wells set up here and there surrounded by seats to enable the drinker to enjoy the surroundings. The spring water was an odd tasting drink that didn't make her feel inclined to go back for more but she could see from the prosperity all around her that many people found huge benefits of one sort or another here.

There was a bathing area that a group of women were taking advantage of though Ruby though it looked most unappealing. The one thing above all else that resonated with her was that the entire town it seemed was brimming with prosperous folk walking and talking and generally having a good time.

She fell silent as the morning wore on, content to observe the fashionable people, preening and vying to be seen. All spending ever more ridiculous amounts of money on ever more pointless trinkets. At lunch Ruby was subdued and her sons wondered if she was tired or bored but she denied this emphatically and told them laughingly that this day out was the best she'd had for as long as she could remember.

She really was having the time of her life, but she told them she would be happy to sit here in the pump room, surrounded as she was by ladies and elderly gentlemen, if they would like to go and explore without her for a while she'd be quite safe. They agreed with alacrity and soon she was alone to enjoy her musings without fear of offending them.

Her mind was racing with ideas, there was lesson here for her, this is what Worcester lacked. It was time to remember Ma's golden rule. “Keep your mouth shut, watch and listen.”

Richard had visited Malvern Wells as a schoolboy and

in later years Dr Wall had been quite vocal about the health benefits of the pure water and, as a result, the place had become an important destination for some very fashionable and wealthy people. But it was all a revelation to Ruby.

When the boys returned after an hour or so she was happy to see them and continue the tour, she was tireless in her determination to see everything the town had to offer. They visited both main wells and several of the subsidiaries and as she walked she noted everything and committed it all to memory.

Their carriage ride home was filled with laughter. The boys had given Ruby inspiration. She was energised and anxious to get home and begin making plans, but, in the meantime, she wanted to let these two sons of her understand how much she'd enjoyed their day together and how grateful she was that they had thought of it.

They parted on very happy terms and made a loose promise to try to have a day together sometime in the not too distant future.

The annual venison feast will be held at the Crown in Great Malvern on August 18. Dinner will be upon the table precisely at two o'clock, those attending to pay one shilling and six pence.

(Copyright and courtesy of the Worcester News)

CHAPTER FIFTY SIX

It was on a hot, sunny day in August that Ruby and Mary linked arms and smiled through their tears as their friend and confidant, Bella, became Mrs Matthew Deakin. The bride and groom stepped proudly out, hand in hand, as all their friends cheered.

Bella was radiant, she wore a soft grey dress that had been lovingly trimmed with pale blue silk rosebuds by Ruby and Mary. The three friends had spent many nights together, Mary and Ruby sewing as Bella entertained them relaying tales of old. The bride and the dress were glorious.

As was the custom the guests had each tied a piece of coloured ribbon to the marriage wagon and the riot of fluttering colour that greeted them as they walked across the churchyard was a testament to how well regarded they both were. Tradition demanded that they would now climb aboard the wagon together and they would ride through all the local villages in this way everyone would know that they had been married before God and in the presence of witnesses.

Bella stepped jauntily onto the wagon and smiled and waved at all her friends but when her eyes met those of Ruby and Mary her smile wavered and a shadow of regret passed momentarily across her face. They both waved and cheered as loudly as the others but all three realised that their times together were over. A respectable married woman wouldn't be leaving her husband alone to go gallivanting with her old friends.

The gaily decorated pony and trap set off and once they were clear of Barbourne Matthew handed Bella a cloth to wipe her eyes. She smiled her tearful thanks to him and he patted her hand gently.

We hear from Bewdley that during an elegant entertainment made there by the Society of Freemasons of that place, the necessitous situation of the poor came under consideration, whom they bountifully relieved by distributing money and bread without distinction in these times of exorbitant prices for provisions. This is an example well worthy of imitation.

(Copyright and courtesy of the Worcester News)

CHAPTER FIFTY SEVEN

Ruby paced her small set of rooms in some anxiety. For the first time in her life she had nothing to do and she didn't like the feeling at all. She was not accustomed to leisure and found she had no desire for it. She had a full life, but there was something she wanted to do and she resented having to wait in idleness until the time was right.

Since the trip to Malvern Ruby and her sons had got into the habit of meeting together once a month for a meal, sometimes they would talk about business but more often they discussed their hopes for the future. The day in Malvern had set the groundwork in place for the three of them to build a workable relationship with each other.

Ruby had been eased into the role of big sister, and they were all comfortable with that. She chided them when she thought they were acting like children, and they were constantly trying to introduce her to suitable men, telling her it was time she married and settled down, she was now almost forty after all and far too old to be living such a rackety lifestyle.

She would scoff at that and remind them that she was barely thirty-seven and regardless of age marriage was not on the cards for her. She intended to remain a single woman, thereby having enough time to poke her nose into their secrets and cause them both trouble.

They were, at twenty-three years old both constantly meeting and falling in love with girls and then falling out again in a matter of days and she enjoyed being a witness to the natural way in which they teased one-another out of the depths of despair. They were established in their own careers now and free time was a luxury they had a little more of and they were enjoying the fruits of their labours.

As was she, her training house was stable, it had a good reputation and kept itself going, mainly thanks to Madam Eloise and Hannah. The returns were healthy and she knew she could ask for no more. The newspaper was on a very firm footing with Richard now the acknowledged head and Ann running the office, both ably assisted by Jacob and John. There was no work in that quarter for Ruby to do.

The house at Barbourne, still known locally as Ma Jebb's place kept on doing what it did best. There had been a few minor hiccups when Bella first left them but nowadays Clara ran things smoothly and again Ruby was surplus to requirements. She was bored for the first time in her life and she resolved to alter that situation immediately.

"You can't go to London alone. You're quite safe walking around alone as you do here, but it's not the same there." Ann said, sensible as ever.

"Oh, when were you last in London Ann?"

"Ruby!"

She explained that the idea of a trip to London was one that had been teasing her for several years and it was only now that she felt she had the time to be away for a week, or even two. The weather at this time of the year was changeable and such a trip was out of the question but she intended to go in the spring and thought that by telling both Richard and Tom now what she planned they might be able to make themselves available as her escorts.

They both agreed promptly. Tom could arrange to visit the grand shops and merchants in the capital and tell them of his canal transport links while Richard could fill pages of newspaper with reports of the sights he'd find in London.

Their trip would be a mix of business and pleasure and both were full of ideas of what they might see and do. They both happily assumed that Ann and Hugh respectively would cover their work for them while they took a week away.

Ruby smiled quietly to herself, neither son had hesitated to agree to come along and neither had asked her why she wanted to go to London. They were still so young and full of themselves, they imagined the whole world would spin around them forever.

This is to give notice to all gentlemen and others that there hath been a false report, raised by some ill designing people, that I am going to leave my business and house, the Wheatsheaf Inn at the Corn Market, Worcester. This is to assure all my friends that it was not, nor is not, my design to discontinue the business, but on the contrary, gentlemen etc., may still depend on civil usage from their very humble servant, John Cookes.

(Copyright and courtesy of the Worcester News)

CHAPTER FIFTY EIGHT

After six months of planning and anticipation they were finally here, London lay before them. Ruby had been prepared to be amazed, having listened to Ma and her stories for years and then latterly being forced to endure her cook constantly telling her how poor Worcester was in comparison with London, but the reality of the place was just fantastic. It even smelled different.

All around her was energy and excitement. More people than she'd ever seen in one place were here and all in a hurry to get somewhere else. As these people moved about they shouted instructions and curses at each other in what she knew to be English, but was not spoken the way she'd ever heard before.

Overloaded carts and filthy wagons rubbed alongside gleaming polished carriages, whilst horses and men bustled about oblivious to each other. Skinny dogs and ragged children scampered about fighting over anything that fell off the brim full barrows and wagons.

There were women selling everything from bunches of lavender to a midwife's services, or even themselves, and being far more brazen about it than the girls Ruby was used to. Some people were falling over drunk and others just walked on by unseeing and uncaring.

The buildings here were all so much closer together than those in Worcester, they threw shadows over much of the walkways and these shadows were hiding who knew what. The streets were filthy, running with all the rubbish man, horse and dog had no use for. And, because of the proximity of buildings and the heat from the general populace the stink was incredible.

But the life and energy hummed and Ruby was smitten. Nothing could dim her excitement or that of Tom and Richard. This was truly an adventure and, once they'd caught their breath they linked arms and marched joyfully into the fray.

They'd been told of a decent lodging house which they sought out first. It was a clean and sizeable house and the landlord Seth Porter along with his daughter Liz, greeted them cheerfully enough. He left them with Liz to be shown their rooms while he hastened out to the kitchen to arrange some refreshments for them.

They were given three rooms at the top of the building, one sitting room and two bedrooms all of which had shining windows and fresh bedding. There was no dust on the floors and the rugs appeared freshly beaten. Ruby nodded in satisfaction, both Ann and Mary had been full of the tales of the terrible filth Londoners were used to living with and she was relieved to find that at least in this instance they were in error.

Having freshened up as quickly as they were able they made their way downstairs to the tiny parlour that had been set aside for them, all looking forward to the promised refreshments. Liz was ready and waiting with steaming platters of meats and roasted vegetables for them which they enjoyed along with good strong bread. There was wine and coffee and some delicious pastries waiting on the side table for them and with each mouthful they felt the stress and strain of their journey melt away.

Ruby asked Liz to sit with them and tell them how to get the most out of their visit and she kept them entertained with her tales of the pleasure gardens that were the talk of London and said whatever else they did these were not to be missed. She was able to help Tom with directions to the shops he needed to visit and urged Ruby to be sure to go with him as she would be sure to see some sights around those parts. There were shops selling silver and gold trinkets alongside the porcelain shops and Ruby would love to see the quality out on parade, Liz was sure.

She seemed to sense that she had no need to stand on ceremony with these visitors and, before very much time had elapsed, they were telling her about themselves and where they had come from as she happily finished eating their pastries.

Vauxhall Gardens were to be their first destination. From the moment she had heard about it Ruby was enchanted and anxious to visit and experience it for herself. The idea of a pleasure garden, open and available to everyone, that was dedicated purely to the pursuit of entertainment was a novel idea but one she could fully embrace, it was all part of her plan.

In Malvern the town was dedicated to better health, and from that had come society bringing fashion and entertainment along with it. Could London really have anything better than that? Her mind had been painting pictures for her and now they were here and she could see and experience it all for herself.

Every class of Londoner was here, some were serving and more were being served. There were entertainers the like of which she'd never seen, not even on the best of days on Pitchcroft. There were men and women in sparkling costumes suspended above their heads and spinning in ways that made it seem impossible that they wouldn't collide.

Fire eaters walked amongst the crowds thrilling them with their bravery while tumblers dressed in red costumes called out directions to the various attractions and entertainments.

Here and there were stages lit by lights suspended from wires where groups of players performed a play, around a corner another group gathered and sang opera. Over there was a man telling stories in a voice quite low, people stood and listened until he'd finished and then the surprise at what they'd heard made them laugh until they cried. So daring.

It was all far too much to take in on one visit, and far superior to anything she'd seen in Malvern or anywhere else. She vowed she'd be back here, again and again. This energy, this drama, surely a little of this was what every life should hold. Why should only Londoners have it?

It seemed to her as though there must be many hundreds of people here at one point, and then, just around a corner, all was peaceful and pleasant. It was so cleverly designed, with paths that meandered through groups of plants or around painted screens. Every path led to some new delight, nothing was wasted and nowhere was dull, ugly or uninteresting.

The air was fresh and sweet and every now and again snatches of music reached out and tempted them to walk just a little further. Tonight there was to be a display of music and fireworks to end the evening and of course they had to stay and sample everything. The musical fireworks were a dramatic and thrilling end to a perfect day.

We hear from Malvern Wells that there is the greatest expectation of a very full season. Persons of nobility and distinction have already arrived at Mr Carey's at the Great House. A publick breakfast and ball is to be held at the Great House on Monday next after the races at Worcester.

(Copyright and courtesy of the Worcester News0

CHAPTER FIFTY NINE

At breakfast the following morning Ruby told Liz Porter how much they'd enjoyed their day out. "I'd no idea London was so lovely. Thank you for telling us where to go, I shall never forget it."

Liz laughed at Ruby's words. "It's a treat I grant you, but don't you run away with the idea that all London's like it cos it's not. Vauxhall keeps itself nice 'cos it earns money being nice, if it didn't it'd turn ugly as fast as you like. Enjoy your breakfast now, Miss." And away she went.

Ruby confessed to the boys that she was feeling tired after the rigours of the previous day, they had walked, or at least been on their feet for at least twelve hours on top of two days of travel and today she wanted to take it easy. They confined themselves to strolling around the shops near their lodgings and again they saw things that were more grand and much more costly than the things available at home.

By lunchtime however Richard and Tom were thoroughly bored and Ruby sent them off to whatever it was they wanted to do, she would spend the afternoon resting and working on a plan she had. They left her with almost indecent haste, not bothering to ask her what her plans were, but she was not sorry to see them go. Her mind worked better when she was alone.

The two young men walked briskly away from the lodging house and headed towards a place they had heard about from the landlord where, for a small entrance fee, they then proceeded to find out how easy it was to become sickeningly drunk while listening to music and watching the most beautiful girls in the world dancing very slowly and eventually taking off all of their clothes.

Ruby didn't miss them, she was completely absorbed in her new idea. As she paced back and forth, talking quietly to herself and occasionally scribbling something, or crossing through a previous scribble she was perfectly content. So much so that when hunger finally forced her to stop and think of food she was staggered to find she'd worked through the night and it was almost morning.

She rapidly washed and changed and left her room and in search of breakfast. Entering the small dining room Seth informed her that Tom and Richard had returned to the inn less than an hour earlier and that neither was in a position to be of any use to her for a good portion of the day. However his daughter would be more than willing to act as a guide if that would suit Ruby.

It did. Ruby had already taken a great liking to Liz, she was a short, broad young woman who admitted she had long been resigned to the fact that most men were looking for something she didn't have and she was old enough now to find the whole idea of a man telling her what she could or could not do ridiculous. "I know I'm no beauty Ruby, but I also know that one day I shall own my old Dad's inn and I reckon they'll be queuing up to get near me then and I shall take my time while I pick the best. I shall have my day, don't you doubt it."

Ruby linked arms with her new friend and they set off for a day of sight seeing, all the while telling each other what they hoped for in life one day. They took a boat ride out as far as Chelsea and Liz pointed out Ranelagh to Ruby, explaining that for her first visit it there it would be best to go as night was falling. The attraction was open during the day but was undoubtedly at its best after dark. "It'll take your breath away." Liz declared confidently.

With Liz as her guide Ruby sampled the joys of dipping her toes in the Thames while eating oysters and thick brown bread all washed down with ale. As the sun went down they reluctantly made their way back to the inn as Liz had work to do. She desperately wanted to visit Ranelagh with Ruby later but, having had most of the day out with her she knew she couldn't leave her father alone all night as well. Nevertheless they agreed to spend a few hours together the following morning.

Ruby was highly amused to find both boys indignant that she had been out all day without leaving them a message. Before they could get too self righteous she reminded them both that they were all adults and free to go out and over indulge to the point of sickness or see the sights as they choose.

Ruby told them that she was taking them out again that evening but this time they had a motive and a clear objective. They were to bring with them the papers they would find in her room and she also instructed them to bring a supply of drawing materials and to be ready to leave in an hour.

They reluctantly made the preparations that Ruby had ordered and they attempted to put a good face on things but in truth they both were still feeling sorry for themselves, much of the sickness had passed but the headache remained for them both. They both secretly hoped for something quiet and gentle this evening as the thought of trudging around another pleasure garden all night was almost too much for either of them to bear. The very idea of food, drink, or music was abhorrent but they knew she'd never let them live it down if they admitted as much to her.

She'd refused to explain anything to them as they made their way to the point where she had taken a ride to Chelsea earlier. The bracing air off the Thames had cleared their heads and lifted their spirits and they were now much more in the mood to have another evening of fun.

They warily followed Ruby down some treacherous steps onto a small jetty where they saw a veritable flotilla awaited them. She climbed aboard one of the larger craft and they somewhat gingerly followed her, sinking gratefully onto the bench seat she had secured.

When Ruby had made this journey this morning with Liz there had been few people around, now however there were throngs of people jostling for a place on board, all dressed in their evening finery. The men wore tall, shiny black hats and carried silver topped canes while the women were draped in rich velvets and glittered with jewels. They perfumed the air as they wafted past Ruby and she was once again reminded of the tales Ma used to delight her with.

Before they knew it they were off. From the water night-time London was at her best and out here it was possible to almost forget the filth and smell and just marvel at the grandeur of the place and the beauty of the buildings. They chattered excitedly between themselves, pointing things out to each other. All signs of tiredness and overindulgence forgotten, they were all in the mood for a good time. As they approached Ranelagh it was easy to identify who were the out of towners and who were the locals. The gasps of amazement and delight from the visitors were an amusing contrast to the studiedly casual air of those who'd seen it all before.

Ruby was not ashamed to be of those who gasped in delight. A thousand lanterns were alight, suspended, and swaying gently, from trees signalling their destination. It *was* magical and it *did* take their breath away, exactly as Liz had promised. Music wafted to them across the water as did the tempting smell of food. The boat pulled to the shore along-side half a dozen similar craft and the crowd surged forward as one and onto the path. Once the initial push was over it was easy to see there were paths leading in various directions some better lit than other. It was possible to walked for hours and not see the same thing twice it seemed.

Ruby spent a very long time marvelling at the clever use of lights and painted boards that were scattered amongst the trees and plants. But now she wanted to see past the magic and discover how it was done. Eventually she selected a seating area and told the boys what she wanted them to do. Tom was to sketch one thing after another as she pointed out the items that were of particular interest to her, some decorative and some informative. Richard was to be sure to make notes of colours and other details of whatever his brother was sketching.

They were bemused but soon gave up asking questions and resigned themselves to doing as she asked. She promised them plenty of sitting about and as much food as they wanted later so they joined in cheerfully enough.

Some time later they found themselves at the Rotunda. This was an enormous canopy supported by a single central column which housed a great fire. This ingenious structure meant that the smart people could enjoy Ranelagh whatever the weather. In here it was warm and dry yet allowed views of the outside and admitted all the fresh air that a person might need.

Liz had told Ruby to be sure not to leave until she'd seen the Rotunda and she could understand why. The fantastic structure was bigger than most of the buildings in Worcester and she was intrigued to see how much shelter it provided with what seemed to be little support. There was ample room for both musicians and dancers. A grandstand could be erected to seat more people and the whole thing was lit by the most fanciful lamps suspended from the wonderful domed roof. Ruby had found her dream.

The orchestra struck up and supper was served, cucumber sandwiches and sliced ham was delivered on huge silver platters to the wealthy party-goers who had their own boxes. These clever little devices allowed those desiring privacy to see but not be seen if they so choose. Liz had told Ruby what was reputed to go in these secluded spots.

The lower orders, Ruby and her boys included, dined off mutton and onions served with chunks of bread and were grateful for it. "What use is a cucumber sandwich to anyone?" Tom snorted with derision as he tucked in with relish.

When the musicians paused Ruby told them what she was thinking. “I want to build something like this in

Worcester on the land between us and the town. Nothing has ever been done on it because no one has ever thought of what it would be useful for. I don't see any reason why I couldn't do something like this there, do you?"

They both looked at her in amazement as she proceeded to tell them how she might start her project, and why. Her eyes shone and her cheeks reddened as she was taken up with her own excitement, she jumped up and paced about using her arms to help demonstrate the grandness of her plan.

It was some moments before she realised they were not quite caught up in the magical web she wove, on the contrary, they looked at each other, a little nervously and exchanged a few words.

They were in complete agreement with each other, Ruby never, ever seemed to understand that there were some things she could not do and perhaps now was the time for one of them to point this out to her. She was only a woman and getting on in years and they were both responsible for her after all.

On Friday, Mr Saunders, the so-much celebrated Equilibrist on the Wire, and his Company of Performers from Sadlers Wells, who have gained such high applause at Hereford, Leominster and Ludlow, arrived in this city and intend to display their wonderful and unparalleled performances on the slack wire and tight rope, ground and lofty tumbling, and entertainments of singing and dancing and balancing.

(Copyright and courtesy of the Worcester News)

CHAPTER SIXTY

What had begun as a pleasant conversation about a wonderful plan degenerated into a criticism of Ruby and her lifestyle in general and, once back at the inn she wasted no time heading for her bed.

How dare they presume to tell her how she should conduct herself. No-one had ever got away with that and no-one ever would. She turned her mind away from the boys and back to her dreams. She could do it and by God she would do it. She fell asleep with a smile on her lips.

The following morning at breakfast the boys were ready and waiting for her, both feeling a bit ashamed at themselves, they had laughed at Ruby's great idea, not realizing how serious she was and they had spoiled her excitement. Perhaps they should have been a little more tactful, but she was in danger of making a show of herself and what they had said was no more than the truth.

They filled their plates in polite silence and then sat trying to assess her mood as she ate. She looked happy and relaxed and ate with her usual good appetite. As the meal drew to a close she looked at her companions and smilingly told them that she'd decided to stay on in London, for reasons of business, but they were to leave for Worcester as originally planned. After a stunned silence came a barrage of protests, she must travel home with them, she was not safe alone in London, they felt responsible for her.

Ruby brushed their concerns aside, she'd be staying here with Liz, she told them, and had arranged for that good woman to be freed from her daily work to act as a companion and guide for Ruby and there was little more to be said. She wanted them gone and as soon as possible. They may feel they were responsible for her but she'd found the novelty of the company of such immature young boys was one that had worn thin. She needed to get on and they were holding her back. It was time, she said with some aplomb, for them to go back to the pleasant homes and safe positions she had worked to achieve for them

She took no further part in their discussion and they realized they had no choice. The coach was duly loaded and away they went.

We have the pleasure of assuring the public that the account in the London papers of the death of the Right Honourable Lord Sandys is entirely false, and his Lordship is in good health at his seat in Ombersley Court in this county. The late report of Lord Sandys death took rise from a piece of fun (as some call it). A person, booted and spurred and all over dust, came into a Coffee House in the neighbourhood of Covent Garden and it soon gained ground.

(Copyright and courtesy of the Worcester News)

CHAPTER SIXTY ONE

Once her sons were gone Ruby proceeded to view a London she might have missed, courtesy of Liz. She saw the Thames heaving and churning with craft and thought it similar to the Severn, though bigger and nosier. She visited areas the boys would have been horrified to have seen and she attended a show that would have sent Madame Eloise to her bed for days. She loved the Drury Lane theatres and marvelled at the art and daring of the infamous Dora Jordan

The differences between this life and the country life were what fascinated her, here anything could be had and it seemed no-one cared too much. She'd previously thought Worcester had everything to offer and only now did she realize how wrong she'd been. Here much more was available and she longed to take some of it back to Worcester

This was her fourth day without the boys and Liz was taking her to see the foundling hospital. By this time the two women knew much of each others histories and Liz was fascinated with Ruby's stories of Ma and how her business had worked.

Ruby's concern nowadays was the babies, and her inability to sell them. She'd tried and she had honoured one or two promises left over from Ma's reign but it was a hard business. When a girl was happy to let her baby go and a decent couple were in need Ruby saw no harm in it, but how to know if a couple were decent? And what to do if a girl couldn't bear to be parted from her baby?

These were issues Ma had quashed instantly as of no importance and though Ruby was cut from similar cloth, it was not the same.

There had to be a better way and she needed to find it. She currently had ten babies in the cottages and some of them were about to start walking. They were coming in faster than they were going out and a crisis was looming.

Thomas Coram was a sea captain who had returned to London after some years away, he'd been sickened to see, all over London, babies that were literally being left to starve or even be killed by despairing mothers. Young children were being forced into thievery and prostitution simply to survive and he resolved to do something about it. He decided to build a home for these destitute children and then feed and educate them. All of them.

He began with the help of the musician Handel and Hogarth the artist, and now the government had agreed a sum of money was to be provided every year to help the work continue. Babies were taken into their care and sent out to wet nurses until they were five years old. Older children lived in the hospital and were educated and fed well. They enjoyed all had the benefits of fresh air and cleanliness and in time would be apprenticed out to a trade. It was said that no child was ever turned away from the foundling hospital whatever the circumstances.

Ruby was fascinated by the story and wanted to see for herself what one man with a vision could create. She knew from her time with Ma that there were babies being born every minute of the day to women who didn't want or couldn't cope with them and that couldn't be happening just in Worcester. She'd seen women jailed for trying to leave a baby where someone else might find it and she'd known one girl who had been hanged for smothering a newborn. She herself knew only to well the feeling of desperation that followed the knowledge that a baby was on the way and there was no way on earth it could be stopped.

She also knew there were people desperate to have a child of their own and were not able to. She'd learned how to match up the two for profit but was fast losing her taste for that trade. Perhaps Captain Coram was doing things properly and maybe she could learn a better way from him.

The building at Lamb's Conduit Field was a remarkable place. Directly facing the gate, though at some distances was a vast central hall with an imposing set of doors. At each end of the hall two massive wings had been built, one for boys and one for girls. In the centre was a small grassed area where the children could walk and play. The whole thing was surrounded by a brick wall with a few gateways allowing outsiders to see in to the grounds.

Ruby and Liz were granted permission to meet and talked to one of the nurses and to walk around the grounds but were not admitted into the house. Nevertheless Ruby had more than enough to think about. It was time for her to go home to Worcester and she knew what she was going to do when she got there.

Yesterday at Worcester Quarter Sessions, one Benjamin Mason, being found guilty of cutting the hair off the tails of some oxen and cows belonging to Mr Payne of Wick near this city, was sentenced to be publicly whipped at St John's on Wednesday next.

(Copyright and courtesy of the Worcester News)

CHAPTER SIXTY TWO

Seth was waiting anxiously when they arrived back the inn. "There's a gentleman to see you in the parlour Ruby, been here for hours he has. He's had a bite to eat but he's got something on his mind, he's that agitated."

Ruby went into the parlour with Liz just behind her. She stopped dead in her tracks when she saw Ben Whitehouse in there waiting for her and looking as out-of-place and uncomfortable in a London parlour as it was possible to imagine. He was shuffling from one foot to the other and twisting his shabby old hat in his hands.

Liz realized quickly that he was a friend and meant Ruby no harm so she told them both to sit while she roused the kitchen to get them some supper. She would serve them herself so that they could speak in privacy, she said, as she left them alone together.

Much to Ruby's concern Ben launched upon a prepared speech. He declared his love for Ruby and said that he wanted to protect and care for her and begged her to please put him out of his misery and marry him. He'd been out of his mind with worry about her, alone here and he'd come as quickly as he and Ann could arrange things.

Ruby fussed about with the drinks Liz had delivered as she thought about how to handle this unexpected complication. Of course she was fond, more than fond of Ben, but he was so far off track here that she knew she must get him back on the right path quickly. Eventually she told him how dear he was to her but, and here she trod very gently, she knew of no one in less need of care and protection than herself, furthermore it would be an unkindness on her behalf to agree to such a ridiculous plan.

"Truly Ben, I would lead you a terrible life, there is so much I want to do and so many rules I intend to break, I need you to be my friend and loyal adviser, not my husband. If you were out of your mind with worry about me this week, you would be even more so every day of your life if I agreed to your plan. No my dear, it simply won't do."

He sat silently, a little embarrassed at his haste in coming to London to rescue someone who had no desire to be rescued. He muttered an apology but she smiled and brushed it away. "Ben, my dear friend, I'm delighted that you're here and that you'll see me safely back to Worcester. I hope we'll always be friends, good friends, but for a wife you're thinking of the wrong woman. Ann is the wife for you, I'm amazed that neither of you have seen it. She's perfect."

Seth found a room for Ben, as far away from Ruby's as he possibly could. The following morning tickets were secured for the Worcester coach and Ruby and Liz made their tearful goodbye's.

In such forced intimacy their residual awkwardness had to be faced and overcome. Since their first meeting all those years ago they had become firm friends with a great deal of respect for one another and this stood them in good stead now, by the time they reached Worcester they were talking comfortably.

So much so that when Ruby repeated her statement that Ben should be talking to Ann, the more she thought about it the more she knew it was exactly the right thing for them both. "She's been alone for a long time now Ben."

He nodded his agreement. "It's been a few years."

"Don't leave it too much longer Ben, I know I'm right and I think you know it too."

He thanked her for telling him so gently what he'd been too blind to see and they parted company happily, both with a mission that would occupy them fully for the near future.

Notice is hereby given to masons, bricklayers, carpenters, plumbers, tilers and plasterers that a meeting will be held at the Rein Deer Inn, Mealcheapen Street, Worcester, on Monday next at ten o'clock and proposals for the rebuilding of the parish church of St Martin in this city will then be delivered to such workmen as shall be inclined to undertake the same. Signed Anthony Keck, Surveyor.

(Copyright and courtesy of the Worcester News)

CHAPTER SIXTY THREE

"What the bleeding hell is a pleasure garden?" Mary asked with a snort of derision. Before Ruby had a chance to reply Bella answered for her.

"It's what girls in our line of work, before we went respectable, used to let men have a little taste of, for as much money as we could get off em."

This rendered the other two speechless for a while, then into gales of laughter. Ruby pulled herself together first, "Well, they call it a pleasure garden in London and that's what I shall call it here. But listen to me, I want to know what you think of the idea, not the name. I want to create a place where people can come to get away from the stink of the city and breathe fresh, clean air. "

"But that's all around all of us already," Bella objected. "A body can take any track away from town and within minutes there's not a soul to be seen. Bloody frightening it is too."

Ruby agreed with her. "That's it exactly, there are all manner of dangers out there. But people need fresh air and sunshine in safety, we can provide that on Ma's land."

"I've never heard anything so daft in all my life. Who, in their right mind is going to come tramping all the way out here to get covered in mud. You must be having us on." Bella shook her head and Ruby allowed the talk moved on to how Bella was learning to like being a respectable married woman.

She hadn't learned how to cook anything yet, she said with a wink, but she certainly knew how to make Matthew that happy he'd cook for her.

We hear that Mr Turner, who has gained great applause from audiences in this city, will continue his lectures on electricity till the 31st and will then travel to exhibit the same at Birmingham and Lichfield.

(Copyright and courtesy of the Worcester News)

CHAPTER SIXTY FOUR

The next time Ruby found herself alone with Mary she mentioned the subject again. And now she was pondering Mary's response. It was the longest speech she'd ever heard Mary make.

"It sounded lovely, the way you described it and I know you reckon there's plenty of rich folks as will pay to walk somewhere like that, but you see I don't care about rich folks my love. They get it all given to them anyhow. What about girls like we used to be? I know you wouldn't want me to pay but that's not what I mean. I mean all the girls like me and you what got no money nor time, all them poor little skivvy's and laundry girls. Little girls what helps their dads do a man's work. They can't find enough money for food or fire some times, how do you think they can find money to spend on fresh air. And there's a lot more of that sort than there is of the rich sort and they need the fresh air and sunshine a bit more I reckon. What good is it going to do them? None at all I don't reckon. So, if that's what you want to do I wish you luck, but I can't get excited about anything that makes life even better for the rich and does nothing at all for them with no money."

Ruby was undaunted, it was a fine idea and any opposition must be considered and dealt with, but, her pleasure garden would be built and Bella and Mary would come round to it sooner or later and so would the rest of Worcester.

She'd told Ellie what was in her mind and she'd thought the idea terrifying, risking their income on a hare brained scheme when they had enough security now to live their lives in comfort. She was of the same mind as Tom and Richard, not understanding why Ruby wouldn't simply get a husband and settle down. Nonetheless she knew Ruby well enough to know if she said she could do a thing there was no point in anyone else telling her she couldn't.

She went out to the spring with John a few days later to

get the water and, bracing herself for more opposition she told him what she had in mind. They were standing together at what she imagined would be the entrance to her pleasure gardens from the Worcester side. Ruby pointed out all that could be seen of the city from where they stood, then she walked and talked as he followed and listened without questions.

"The first thing I must do, I think, is draw a plan marking where we need screens and also where we need to ensure that the view is left open. I can then think about what the view will consist of. I've got endless choices, I can build walls or plant trees, this is something that could live forever. I don't need to do anything in a rush."

John nodded his head slowly, then he poured himself a drink. Finally he offered his opinion. "I reckon the first thing you must do is talk to the men who'll be doing the work for you, let them help you with the plan, else you'll be trying to move stuff what can't be moved and digging up things that'd be better staying. You need someone who'll show you how to work with what you've got now."

She took this as encouragement. "So you don't think I've lost my senses then?"

He drank deeply and then winked at her. "Course I do. But I've thought that about you before and you always confound me, I do know you're the best thing that ever came to us at Ma's and if this dream of yours can be done you'll be the one to do it. Ma always said you was something special and if she trusted you, that's good enough for me."

"Thank you John." She had tears in her eyes.

"Aye well, hurry up with that water now, we've been gone too long and some of us has work to be doing." She nodded at that. John was an old man now, too old for heavy work but so against charity or pity that Ruby knew he'd be in her employ until the day he died. If he couldn't work he couldn't survive and she wouldn't let that happen

Her mind raced with ideas now she was back on her

land. She pictured exactly what she wanted to build but she knew John was right, she needed to talk to the men who were going to help her build her pleasure garden before her ideas ran away with her. Her inclination was always to rush in and start before she was ready, this was too big and too important. Ruby needed expert help before she made too many more plans.

She'd also known Mary was right when she talked about poor people needing something. The one thing Ruby decided there and then to change was, from now on she would talk to all her friends about her plans before she began. Her pleasure gardens were going to be bigger than any of them could imagine, she knew that, but she also knew if they were to be as wonderful as she hoped then she would need to listen to many other people's advice and opinions.

The wife of a publican near Evesham, having for some time been disordered in her senses and at last become raving, it was thought necessary to send her to a mad house, to which she was conveyed in a post-chaise on Sunday last, but she had not been there many hours before she found means to hang herself up in her apartment, and died in the swing before she was discovered.

(Copyright and courtesy of the Worcester News)

CHAPTER SIXTY FIVE

When Tom had arrived back in St John's after his London adventure he was not surprised to discover that Hugh was incredibly anxious that he'd stayed in London for so long. His uncle had hinted that work had built up while he'd been away and he was barely keeping up with things alone.

For a time Tom kept his mouth shut and got straight on with his work but he could tell that everything had been running perfectly well without him. Something else was worrying Hugh, that much was obvious, but it wasn't his ability to keep up with the work. Tom soon got into the swing of his old routine and the men he worked alongside let him know how happy they were to have him back. He'd get on with his work and wait for Hugh to approach him and tell him what was really on his mind, that would happen when Hugh was ready and not before.

It didn't take very long. As Tom was having a break with the men he saw Hugh walking purposely toward him, the men he'd been working with saw the same thing and casually drifted away. "Well I reckon you've brought some news back with you from your time away." Hugh spoke abruptly. "Are you thinking of going back over to Worcester to live?"

Tom saw what he was getting at right away. "I'm certainly not! This is my home and my business, it's where I want to be."

Hugh nodded, unconvinced.

"I like getting to know her and seeing her every now and again. She's my mother after all, surely you can understand that?"

"Put like that, yes I do. But dammit to hell boy, this place has doubled in size because of you and I've worked the men like dogs to keep it all going. Your responsibility is here and you can't be carrying on like that any more, swanning of when the fancy takes you. You've got to swear to me it's all out of your system. I've put all I had into this on the understanding that you'd be by my side building it all up. Are you staying here or not, tell me straight."

"I'm staying here Hugh!"

"Right then. I hope you pulled off a deal with Josiah when you saw him?"

"I did. He's going to be using us now to move his goods but he also came up with a few suggestions for a different type of business on the canals."

"Well, now is not the time to talk about new ideas. We need to concentrate on clawing back all the money this latest scheme of yours has cost. I'm serious Tom, the work is pouring in and Henry will never know how close we came to disaster if we can just keep going."

Tom had been taken aback to realize that Hugh had thought he might want to go and live with Ruby, it was the last thing he'd want to do. She was his mother but he thought of her as a slightly rackety sister, or an embarrassing cousin. He dreaded to think what scheme she might get caught up in next but if anyone hurt her he'd want to kill them.

Hugh appeared mollified. "Go on then, tell me how you all spent your time in London. You liked it?"

"Yes I did, Hugh. I enjoyed being with her as well, we're similar in some ways, she's always looking at things and asking questions. She's clever and funny and just like a man really."

"Huh?"

"I mean that she just gets on with whatever she wants to do with no thought for what's right or proper. The plans she has are amazing, she never stops plotting and she expects everyone to fall in with her. If they don't she just carries on alone."

"Just don't forget that your future is here, with us. Most of it was your idea you know. We built this up for you."

"Hugh please stop this. Ruby has plans to build in

Worcester and if I can I will help her but I won't be working with her, she'd drive me mad. This is what I want to do, here with you. This is where I belong and I'm going nowhere."

They went to see Henry together a few days later. He was drunk and angry but even he couldn't be sure what he was angry about, they let him have his say and then they sat and told him about the business and the new work Tom had secured during his time in London meeting Josiah.

Henry calmed down and there was a few moments of peace before the stupor overtook him and he began to doze.

Hugh helped him to his bed and they left with a sigh of relief that the storm, for now, was over. "Does he even know about Richard, do you suppose?"

"No." Hugh shook his head. "He's tired and confused, telling him about Richard now would be cruel and serve no purpose. Ruby has made sure you both have an independent future, so leave well alone. Henry doesn't need to be worried any more, you can see that for yourself."

On Saturday night, some villains found means to get into the garden at the new plantation in the artichoke field belonging to Mr Millington where they cut and carried away a large number of fine cabbages and did other damage.

(Copyright and courtesy of the Worcester News)

CHAPTER SIXTY SIX

Ruby strode across her land describing to Ann and Ben how she hoped to change this wild space and make it into a place people would want to visit. Her passion was infectious and before long they were making proposals of their own.

She'd invited them to join her and, as they sat near the spring enjoying the food she'd prepared Ben pointed out the rich variety of plants and herbs that were growing wild all around them and what their benefits and uses were.

As they enjoyed the rugged surroundings in the warmth it was easy to imagine that Ruby's plan was feasible but as they grasped the scale of her ambition they feared the plan would surely be fraught with problems. The initial works could be done using local labour but to build what Ruby had dreamed of would require skilled workmen and quality materials. All of which were available, but at a cost.

She described the glories of Vauxhall and Ranelagh to them and tried to demonstrate how she saw those marvels translated here on this unloved patch of land. It seemed she'd thought of everything and once she stopped speaking neither of them had any doubt at all that there would be a pleasure garden in Worcester and she would build it however difficult it proved to be. She let them see Tom's sketches and pointed out what she would do differently.

"If you're certain that this must be done then do it I say. Enthusiasm and energy are the most important keys to getting something done and you've certainly got those." Ben said at last.

Ruby nodded enthusiastically and continued. "I think if even Doctor Wall and his assistants are advising sick people to get the fresh air and drink the spring water it must be a good thing. I would like to let all the people know that walking in the fresh air is a good thing for all. You only have to look at me and Bella. We walked miles through that area whenever we need to get to and from Worcester. We're both strong and fit with colour in our faces. Now look at the merchants and people we see walking around in Worcester. They might be richer than us but they are soft and pale, sickly looking. No one has the energy that we do and I think it is because they eat and drink too richly and walk too little."

Satisfied that she could count on these two at least for support she wrote out a notice to be placed in the newspaper, to inform people of the plans and to attract suitable workers. Anyone interested was advised to contact Benjamin Whitehouse at the Talbot Inn where he would present the draft idea to those he considered suitable.

Ruby was happy to have Ben's support as a go-between for herself and the workers. Many men wouldn't be able to take orders from a woman and those that did would possibly be resentful and difficult. She'd be happy to let everyone think that Ben was working alone, she knew it was her work being done and that was good enough.

Yesterday, Ann Taylor, a servant girl, was whipped at the cart's tail through some of the principal street of Worcester for stealing some wearing apparel, the property of her mistress, the wife of Mr Kingsbury, stay-maker of this city.

(Copyright and courtesy of the Worcester News)

CHAPTER SIXTY SEVEN

Three weeks later Ruby was once again striding across her wild land with Ben, but now she was describing her dreams to one Francis Williams. Francis was an engineer who'd been working on the canal that would soon link Worcester to Birmingham, the very canal that bordered Ruby's land. He was familiar with the terrain and fascinated by her project.

He'd met, and fallen in love, with a Worcester girl and had decided that his future would be here in Worcester with her. He was looking for work but, as a highly skilled man he'd been doubtful that there would be anything suitable for him in Worcester once the canal works moved further on.

He'd been resting at the Talbot when Ben was explaining the plans to the interested workmen who come along in answer to the notice in the newspaper. When the men had gone he approached Ben and told him of his background. Ben knew immediately that this was the kind of man Ruby needed to help her lay the right foundations for her project.

As the sun came out through the clouds and the day warmed, so Ruby's excitement rose. She showed the two men the sketches that she had prepared and saw them both pay close attention to her every word. Neither showed any expression and they remained silent until she sat them down and asked them. “What do you think Mr Williams? Will you help me build it?”

“I say you've got bigger ideas than any man I've ever worked for, you've also got a bit more go in you than most of em. I've visited Vauxhall and I can see what you could do here. Yes, I can build what you want here, if you can pay for it. I'll tell you now though this is work that's going to take a long time to be done, if it's to be done right. I shall be proud to work alongside you and I'll thank you to call me Francis from now on.”

"There is a great deal that I can help you with," Ben said. "Starting from nothing as we are we can create perfect spots for all sorts of plants, even the ones that are hard to grow. It will take time though, some things need years and years to come to fruition but there is much we can do now. I'll be proud to help you."

She thanked her two partners and they drank a cup of spring water to celebrate. Then the arguments began.

“We'll need to clear large spaces and level off the land as much as we can, I think I shall want to start on the flat area here and work outwards. Those trees over there will have to go.”said Francis

Ben stood up quickly and began protesting. “Oh no they won't, we can't get rid of trees like that, those berries are useful for people with breathing problems and it will take years to grow a tree of that quality from nothing.” Ben paced about in agitation. “No trees or plants are to be moved until I say so. Anything that does a man good must stay and you must work around them.” He planted his feet squarely and put his hands on his hips and prepared for a fight. Nothing riled him more than trees being dug up for no good reason.

Francis snorted and nodded at him. “Do you have any reason why I can't start moving rocks and rubbish or do they do serve some purpose I'm not aware of. ?”

Ruby stood back and smiled with relief. She'd found the men who would help her to make her dream a reality. Nothing would stop her now.

The workmen employed in cutting the Worcester and Birmingham Canal have been recently digging near that part of our old City Wall which was situated near Sidbury Gate. They have in consequence met with many coins etc, and a few days since they dug up a sword which, from the appearance of the hilt, belonged to some person of distinction, and had in all probability remained there ever since the Battle of Worcester in 1651. The idea of this sword having belonged to the Duke of Hamilton, commander of the Royalist forces, grounded upon the supposition that the Duke was buried in the parlour of the Commandery, is erroneous as far as regards the place of that nobleman's interment. He was buried near the altar in Worcester Cathedral.

(Copyright and courtesy of the Worcester News)

CHAPTER SIXTY EIGHT

Tom relished the feeling of being completely in charge. Hugh spent more and more time these days on his other interests and people were now doing things entirely Tom's way.

He'd had some tough times at first with one or two of the older ones who'd remembered him as a boy, but generally he was respected and winning them over. A great part of this was the success that they were all experiencing due to his leadership. There was a living to be made by all of them and they were grateful.

Right now Tom was overseeing the movement of some crates of gloves that were due to be transported later that day to Hugh who was waiting for them in Birmingham, where he'd been for the past few days. He was meeting a distributor who was going to be taking delivery of this particular shipment of gloves, he'd promised to take charge of the sale and delivery provided Hugh could guarantee quality and production. Having a salesman was a novel idea to Hugh but he felt that it made sense, if this man worked out, why, he could have a man or several men out selling for him.

Hugh was due to arrive back in Worcester later tonight and had arranged to meet Tom in Barbourne where they were both planning to join the private tour of the pleasure gardens that Ruby had arranged for her friends.

It was fiercely hot day Tom was confined to the stifling wooden shack where he and Hugh did the planning and paperwork for their business. This was tedious work and he'd be much happier working outside with the men on the boats but he couldn't be doing that so much now he was older and the business was bigger, as Hugh repeatedly told him, he had a position to maintain. It was important the men respected him as the boss and for that he had to keep his distance.

When he heard a clamouring in the courtyard he

decided to keep on with what he was doing and see if one of the men could sort out whatever problem it was. The fast moving footsteps that pounded up the wooden steps to his door told him they couldn't.

"Mister Tom there's a fire at the Great House! We're all needed up there to help."

He followed the crowd of men all heading up in the direction of the Great House, before long his young legs overtook the older men and as he was halfway up the rise he saw the plume of black smoke dominating the skyline and feared they were already too late.

Still he rushed on though to be greeted by a terrible sight. The entire house was ablaze it seemed, the entire structure was circled by a line of people from the village, all passing buckets and bowls of water along to the ones nearest who were making a brave, though futile, attempt to douse the flames. Every vessel that could be found was being filled with water and thrown.

The heat was fierce and the noise deafening as Tom frantically searched the crowd for his grandfather. There was no sign of him and so Tom moved forward instinctively. All at once a crack could be heard above the roar of the fire and clamour of the men, they turned as one and saw the roof of the house drop down. "Get back, you young fool, get back." A voice bellowed out just seconds before the side wall began to lean outwards.

People trampled over each other in their rush to get away from the scene they had only just rushed towards. Bits of flaming wood and fabric was tossed all around and there was crashing sound and clouds of dust thickened the scorched air. A few moments of shocking silence then the screaming began.

On Saturday last, a terrible fire happened at Clifton upon Teme. It was occasioned by some children taking a fire-stick in order to startle two colts that were in a barn belonging to Thomas Louden.

The flames soon communicated with the straw and burnt with such violence that in a short time the fire consumed the barn and the two colts, together with a bay of peas, another of oats and a stable; two cow houses, two barns, a stable and dwelling house belonging to James Squire; and a dwelling house belonging to James West. Two roofs of thatch were stripped to prevent the further communication of the flames, otherwise the whole village must have consequently been consumed.

(Copyright and courtesy of the Worcester News)

CHAPTER SIXTY NINE

The funerals were very public affairs. Fire was a part of everyday life, there was talk most days of a house gone up or a barn and people were used to it. But for it to happen to Daventor and to have lost three souls, that was a shocking thing.

There were countless mourners as Henry had been a well known man who had once wielded great power and influence in the city. Most of the mourners however grieved more for his grandson, that handsome lad Tom who'd dashed into the burning building in an attempt to save his old grandfather. Foolish, no doubt, but very brave.

Then of course there was Susan Morgan, or Taylor as was. What a tragic life that woman had led. Her husband had been hanged about the same time as her babies had been born and she'd never known a day's happiness since. What a terrible end, going off to where ever she's going alongside Henry Daventor.

Now that Henry was safely dead and buried those that had only a little knowledge of the man could let their imagination and speculation run riot without fear of him hearing about it and punishing the rumour mongers. The most gripping topic of speculation was, as it had been before, the question of the parentage of the dead grandson. Hugh had proved to be a decent man with a quality wife, so surely he was not the father. Her family would never had allowed the marriage if that had been the case.

William, Henry's son had died young, but not too young for fatherhood? Henry had never re-married, one of them must be the father. As to the mother, she had to be a woman from the lower orders. There was a very obvious connection with the young man who ran the newspaper and no one had ever got to the bottom of that. The two boys had been seen together in public for the first time at Sam Thatchers funeral and then rarely apart since so a relationship of some sort was obvious to all. Ann Yeates,

Thatchers widow, had practically brought up William and Hugh and she'd lived at the Great House when they were just boys so was she the mother? And if so had poor Sam Thatcher known? Surely not?

But in order to burn bright, a fire needs fuel and the fire of gossip was destined to die out, sooner rather than later, because those who really knew who was who, and what was important were absolutely agreed that it was time the past, and all its ghosts, was put behind them.

No one would say anything.

On Tuesday evening, Mr Harris, glover of Worcester, was attacked within half-a-mile of Pershore by three footpads who knocked him off his horse and then robbed him of three guineas and some silver.

(Copyright and courtesy of the Worcester News)

CHAPTER SEVENTY

The pleasure garden viewing party, due to take place on the day of the fire, actually took place six months later, in November, on an icy cold, but mercifully dry afternoon.

Ruby had invited the small group of her most trusted friends, those she'd first shared her dream with to come and be the first people to walk around her gardens. She'd been at pains to let them know the work was nowhere near to completion but the skeleton was there and she wanted them to be the first to see it.

Up until Tom had lost his life in the fire Ruby had worked non stop with Francis for almost two years, and her passion had been the talk of the town, those who knew what she was up to were laughed down when they tried to share their knowledge.

The newspaper had from time to time carried a notice offering work for one craftsman or another and this would invariably wake up the gossips again but generally speaking Ruby was written of as a mad woman, probably a witch, and better ignored.

Since the tragedy though, Ruby had not been seen around the works. She ensured Francis continued to be supplied with funds but, where once she'd been insistent on overseeing every little detail, he'd been left to make his own mind up for six months now, with only Ben to refer to.

It was a sombre group that gathered for the walk. Most of them had lost someone they loved, or loved someone who had in turn had lost someone they loved and their complex relationship actually brought them all some comfort. The way their lives were all intertwined meant they were all comfortable with each other. These were all good friends.

Inevitably the talk at first was of those they'd lost. Henry, Tom and Susan, but gradually the extraordinary surroundings they found themselves in seduced them all.

Most of the trees were bare and there were no flowering plants to speak of but in a way this made the whole thing easier to understand. The walks, and where they led, could clearly be seen. The seating areas, that would in the height of summer offer privacy for people, were now completely exposed.

The view across the racing ground to the river beyond was unimpeded as was the sight of the new canal, still being worked on, on the other side of Ruby's land. The impression was one of being on a lush island, separated somehow from the cares of their regular lives.

Ruby had greatly admired the rotunda at Ranelagh but Francis and Ben together had managed to convince her that to attempt to replicate it here would be impractical. They understood what she wanted to achieve and had between them, during her absence, come up with what they thought was a better alternative.

A vast area around the source of the spring had been levelled off and paved. A well was sunk and the entire area was surrounded by fanciful little shelters, all of them large enough to provide cover for thirty or so people but all with two open sides affording a view of the central area and one looking directly behind. The pillars supporting the roofs of these shelters were decorated with tiles all painted with birds and little animals.

There were a series of huge screens available to shield the side that was suffering the most from wind or rain and these screen were decorated with summer scenes of flowers, trees and streams and were so well executed they almost gave off an impression of warmth and sunlight. These great screens could be wheeled about to be where they were needed and then outside when they were not.

The source of the spring had been cleared and was now a tiled area, again circled with seating areas and there were also several outlets now for the water to be drawn off either as a drink, or to go directly into the deep sunken areas for people to bathe in. Around this bathing area was a thick wooden walkway which would enable the bathers to socialise with those who were sitting or walking around the spa area. A circle of newly planted trees could be seen and in years to come these would offer privacy and shelter from the sun.

This last was as much a surprise to Ruby as it was to the others but she was delighted with it. She'd been prepared for surprises, realizing that the work had to continue with or without her and things simply had to be decided in her absence. Ruby looked at Ben and raised her eyebrows. He shrugged and explained that he and Francis had done a little research of their own and seen something very like this being used in Leamington, a place Ruby herself was unaware of. "Thank you Ben. I'd lost my appetite for this project somehow, but you and Francis have done a wonderful job, I'm so very grateful."

He took her hands in both of his. "Ruby, you've managed to cope with all that life has thrown at you and still I feel the strength in you. I know you'll get through this latest terrible blow and in the meantime we, your friends, will do all we can to help make your dream a reality. We don't want you to be grateful, my dear, we need you to get back to your old, contrary self." They laughed together and the tension eased, she'd be back with them soon.

As Ben and Ruby were talking her other friends walked around together. Now and again there was a laugh or a voice could be heard chatting. Ann was with Ellie and Lillian, they'd managed to get a moment together to compare opinions on Ruby and how she was doing. "She insists that everything continue as normal and I must say she is looking better than she was." Ellie said. "She hasn't been eating properly but she's regained her appetite for work. When she visited the house this week she was as tough as ever on the girls. There's no room for any of her standards to drop."

Ann nodded her agreement. "I think you're right, she's

getting better. She won't talk about Tom at all, but that will change in time I expect. She'll have to get back out here more now though, Ben says there's very little that can be done without her here to give direction."

"Speaking of Ben, when do you intend to tell her your plans?"

"Whenever it feels right, I'm sure she'll be pleased for us, it's just perhaps a bit soon for her. We'll marry as soon as she knows but we'll both be happy to wait until we think she's ready to hear."

Richard and Hugh walked together a little awkwardly behind Ruby and Ben. Their only real connection had been Tom, they'd both loved him and being together now was reminding them both of what they had lost and neither was in a position to help the other so the conversation was clumsy and painful.

Since losing Tom they'd both thrown themselves totally into work and in Richard's case it had been a saviour, he genuinely loved the newspaper and working with Ann was still a joy. He had fallen in love again and this time it seemed as though it was of a more lasting kind. He'd known Elizabeth, Betty, for almost two years and he was ready to settle down with her.

Hugh was not finding his work quite as rewarding, he needed managers now, to try to fill Tom's shoes and that was breaking his heart, but the news that he was to have a third child of his own was making a difference to him though. He had two wonderful sons and this time was hoping for a little girl. As their conversation halted yet again they made their way, by mutual agreement over to where Ruby was standing with Ben and joined them in time to hear Ruby say. "Ben that's wonderful news, I knew you should be together." She looked around to where she'd last seen Ann but her eyes fell on Richard. "Ben has asked Ann to marry him. Did you know?"

Richard smiled and nodded. Ann and Ellie heard the others calling them and the atmosphere lightened even more. Ann and Ben held hands and the others showered them with good wishes and cries of congratulations. They were so clearly right for each other it made everyone feel cheered to share their happiness.

Ann had been through some dark times of her own and to see her now glowing with happiness couldn't fail to cheer her friends. She had worried that people might ridicule a woman of her age getting married but here, amongst these people she felt secure enough to show her joy in finding Ben. She was amongst friends.

The afternoon light was going and it had turned bitingly cold, so by common consent they made their way over to the inn where Ruby had met Mary for the first time all those years ago.

Mary was still there but Bill had left her years earlier. He'd apparently been married in his youth and had decided to move back to Stourport and let his wife start looking after him again. She was a hard woman but a better cook than Mary and his belly was the most demanding part of his body these days.

Mary had been happy to see the back of him, he'd been a protector when she'd needed one but he was getting old and as he aged his temper soured and he grew ever more miserable, she'd had the best of him, his wife was welcome to what was left.

When he went she'd got in touch with Bella and suggested she and Matthew sell their little place and come in with her, they could run the place together and they'd all benefit from sharing a workload. They'd worked together now for over a year and had a good reputation for providing clean beds and good hot food.

Some of which was ready and waiting for Ruby and her friends as they hurried in out of the cold. Mary and Bella served them, giving great entertainment to the usual serving girls. Bella was far to big to be rushing about fast as she wanted to but she did all she could to help keep the small group laughing and drinking.

In recent months Ruby had been struggling but she wanted to move on and this was the perfect opportunity for her friends to see that she did. As Mary filled Ruby's glass she bent down and whispered in her ear. “Shove over and drink up my love, and enjoy what you've got now. Look around at all these folk, just here for you, they all love you, you know.”

Ruby had tears in her eyes and she wiped them away crossly. “I know. You don't have to worry about me any more, I know I've got more to be happy about than most. It's just been, oh you understand...” Mary kissed her cheek, drained her glass and went back into the kitchen.

“When is this pleasure garden of your opening then Ruby?” Bella called across the table. “Is it safe to ask?”

Ruby raised her glass and smiled as brightly as she could. “I think we have a wedding to arrange first." Loud cheers interrupted for a few moments as Ben and Ann were toasted. "I'll be talking to Francis and Ben tomorrow but if it can be done I want it open in the spring.

“If she wants it open in the spring it'll be open in the spring, you can bet on that.” Richard said quietly to Hugh.

Thomas Vaughan from London, glass-grinder, now living next to the wheelwright's house without Sidbury Gate, Worcester, maketh and selleth all sorts of looking-glasses, hanging-glasses, chimney-glasses, swinging-glasses, dressing-glasses, coach-glasses and glasses for snuff boxes, coats of arms engraved on guilt or glass. He likewise serves peddlers with all sorts of small-glasses by wholesale and retail at reasonable rates.

(Copyright and courtesy of the Worcester News)

CHAPTER SEVENTY ONE

When talk of the pleasure garden first surfaced, few in Worcester had a good word to say about the idea. It was deemed at best fanciful and at worst some kind of trickery to cause harm to someone or other. The general opinion was it was either the height of stupidity or the lowest kind of evil and decent people would have nothing to do with it.

What no-one could deny was that the city had felt the benefits from the day work started. All the men working on the garden, from the engineers down to the labourers, needed a place to sleep, food to eat and clothes to wear, all of which meant an increase in trade from the moment the work started and the tide of workers spending in the city had continued to increase for almost three years. That was a lot of money with which to sweeten the sourest tongue and the chatter was far more tolerant as the months passed.

Ruby had befriended a small group of players at the Pitchcroft fair in the previous summer and asked them to provide entertainment in the afternoons in her gardens when they opened. However when she realized that they had no work through the winter months and traditionally went their separate ways, re-convening in the spring, she made a change of plan.

Ruby employed them to stroll, on dry days, around the city and surrounding villages and play music at the markets until they had a crowd and then tempt people with tales of the wonders to be enjoyed when the gardens finally opened. They passed out handbills decorated with all the delights that would be laid out for them to enjoy.

The players were so grateful for the work that they became almost poetic in describing the gardens and its delights. People were promised plays and recitals throughout the afternoons and then in the evenings there would be music and dancing with food fit for angels.

Ruby had asked Madam Eloise and her team to talk to all their fashionable ladies about the elegant new pleasure garden and the safety and overall suitability of such a place for the ladies of the town to see and be seen in.

Richard had been talking of little else at the Guildhall balls he was now a regular at, and when he attended the race days on Pitchcroft everyone had to hear again about the marvels they would see if they would only give it a chance.

Hugh proudly informed everyone he met that he'd been in on it since it's inception, was a personal friend of the anonymous backer who wanted to add to the quality of life for his neighbours, and he was immensely proud of it. So much so that he'd had a boat specially decorated with scenes from the gardens and this very boat would travel the canals picking up passengers and delivering them to the gardens safely and in some style.

For her part Ruby had taken a full page in the newspaper announcing the opening and assuring the readers that they would find entertainment and excitement to rival the best that London could offer. All that she could think of had been done to ensure that word had spread far and wide.

What she had not advertised was that she'd had a hundred metal coins cast, all giving the bearer free entry. These she asked Bella, Mary, Dennis and Lillian to distribute to decent, poor people they knew from the city. The coins were to be redeemed on admittance and they would then be re-distributed to other deserving citizens of Worcester.

Sansome Springs was to be for everyone.

We hear that last Monday evening, a man, well dressed with boots on, a watch and some gold and silver in his pockets, was found drowned in a brook near Pershore. It is supposed he was returning from Evesham Fair, somewhat in liquor, and that while his horse was drinking at the brook he unfortunately fell off.

(Copyright and courtesy of the Worcester News)

CHAPTER SEVENTY TWO

The first day people came trickling in soon after two o clock. The musicians were already in place and playing pretty music, within an hour the trickle became a flood and in no time the seats were filled and the walks were thronged with visitors. All around could be heard the cries of people greeting friends and having fun.

Carriages arrived non-stop and Ruby smiled to hear excited voices as those from further afield arrived buzzing with anticipation and all feeling rather daring. They all knew this place was referred to by local people as the harlot's garden and everyone wanted to be in on the secret. Who was the harlot and why had she built them a garden?

One or two brave souls sampled the spring water and within moments there was a lively crowd all jostling for a space at the decorated founts. The archery butts proved popular as did the bowling.

At four o clock the acrobats came out to tumble and roll about on the walkways and in between the visitors, delighting them all.

In due course, the hundreds of lanterns Ruby had ordered to be suspended from the trees were lit, to exclamations of delight and, then cries of wonder as, when the crowd looked up at the lanterns they saw dozens of girls and boys in sparkling tunics dancing above the tree tops.

Some were on swings that soared overhead and others were suspended on wires and appeared to dance in the air. While the attention of the majority was on this spectacle the musicians changed over and a troupe of dancers were in place and ready to begin the evening entertainment. They would dance while the visitors ate the food that was ready to be served.

The food, all prepared by Mary, Bella and their girls was served from the central area. Roasted meats, and thick bread was available for those that wanted it, but also the thinnest imaginable sliced ham and cucumber.

Diners could eat in style in the covered area while watching the dancers or they could take their platters and find a spot that suited their particular needs.

Over in the beautifully crafted Greek temple at the other side of the lake Richard, along with Hugh and Ben were ready and waiting for anyone who wanted to play cards and lacked a partner. This attraction was incredible popular and a regular card school was started that very night.

Ruby strolled around listening to snippets of chatter, people had walked where they wanted and enjoyed the activities that appealed to them and now they wanted to simply sit and be entertained. The orchestra struck up and the first singer stepped out onto the stage to great applause.

Ruby knew she'd got a success on her hands. She'd have meetings over the coming day with all her trusted advisers and they'd all discus what worked, what failed and how they could improve things for the following week. Her intention was that the gardens would be open six days a week for those that wanted the benefit of the spring water, either for drinking or bathing. The sport and the walks would also be open every day but the entertainers and the dinners would only be available on Friday and Saturday.

Depending on the reaction of the visitor, and the time of the year, any or all of this could and would be adjusted. Whatever needed to be done to make her gardens a top class attraction would be implemented.

She may not have a Hogarth or a Handel to turn to but the children in her nursery would enjoy all the benefits those little mites at the Foundling Hospital enjoyed.

The Harlot's Garden would see to that.

Also by Nikki Dee

Losing Hope

In 2011 a young woman is rescued from a burning building in Portsmouth. She has clearly suffered many beatings over a sustained period of time, is pregnant and malnourished.

When at last her identity is established, the entire city is horrified to learn that she is Hope Gidson. Hope was the little girl who disappeared fifteen years ago from her family home, aged just five.

However, Hope is in no position to help provide answers. She knows only what she was told by her captors and she trusts no-one.

It's the police who have to painstakingly unravel the strands of the many different stories they hear, before they can have a complete picture of where Hope has been, why, and with whom.

As more is revealed about the events leading up to the disappearance, it becomes clear that the secrets and scandals of a group of teenagers in the 1980's will now come back to haunt some very respectable local people. But the truth must be uncovered in full if Hope and her mother are ever to re-build their shattered relationship.

About the Author

Nikki Dee believes she was born knowing how to read, and once started simply didn't stop. She reads for pleasure, education, inspiration and occasionally to garner gossip from the gutter.

Nikki's fondest memory is of the day her father gave her her own library ticket and, along with it, the freedom to read what she wanted.

She began with the Famous Five and swore if she ever had a dog he would be called Timmy. Nikki moved onto Mallory Towers and developed an abiding love for midnight feasts, which, regrettably continues to this day.

Eventually she was drawn to the works of Jaqueline Susann and Grace Metalious though she prefers not to reveal all she learned at their knees. She then spiced things up with large portions of Agatha Christie and John Creasey.

By some miracle Charles Dickens crossed her path, he opened her eyes, and her mind. She went on to develop a deep appreciation for him, the Brontes and Thackeray.

In between reading and writing Nikki mis-spent her youth mired in Sales Management until one day common sense prevailed.

She gave it all up, opened a small book shop and devoted herself to writing (and reading).

Printed in Great Britain
by Amazon.co.uk, Ltd.,
Marston Gate.